The Jane Castle Manuscript

The
Jane Castle
Manuscript

A NOVEL BY
Philip L. Greene

MADE IN USA

DELACORTE PRESS / NEW YORK

*All the characters in this book are fictitious;
and any resemblance to actual persons
living or dead is purely coincidental.*

To my wife

Prologue

WHEN I FIRST came to New York from my hometown in Connecticut I was twenty-six years old and I had exhausted the possibilities of that life. The girls my age were all married with families. A friend of mine who lived in New York said to me, "Come, there is a life here for you." Any single girl of my age with a college education understands the meaning of such an action, to stuff your belongings into a suitcase and leave the comfortable familiar streets to ride into undiscovered country. I was aware that the big city can break your heart with its coldness and indifference, but small towns like Waterbury can do the same thing and be much more cruel about it. But I didn't have the foggiest notion about the roughness of the terrain. It is ten years later now, and what have I learned? What has the long postgraduate education of Jane Castle been like? What does it really mean to live in the big city, a girl, some friends yes, but essentially alone?

One thing you learn in New York is how to eat rotisserie chicken. All over the city you see these butcher shops and markets and delicatessens, and near the window in a glass-fronted oven there are chickens turning on a spit slowly, all day, with some kind of electric coil roasting them. You go into a store and you tell the man you want one of the smaller ones and he opens the door, his white butcher coat not so

1

crisp now, a little bloodied if it's late in the day, and he takes out a spit with two chickens on it and you point to one and he slides it off, then on to the scale, wraps it, slips it into a paper bag, asks you if you want something else and you say a pound of potato salad, because if you ask for a small portion that they put into those individual cups he'll know you're eating alone, so you buy a pound brightly, nothing else right now, and you walk out, the heat from the package warm against your hand, your stomach growling with hunger, and maybe the butcher will throw you a "come again" because it brightens his day to flirt a little with the *maedlach*, and then you walk home, open the bag, cut off a leg, put the rest in the refrigerator for cold chicken tomorrow with the roasted rotisserie skin nice and chewy, dump some potato salad on the plate, get the newspaper, prop it up in front of you, and you eat. You go at the chicken like there is no tomorrow. Every once in a while you pause, startled at the sound of your crunching teeth, but you discover that it's the sound of pleasure and you eat on, chicken grease on your fingers, maybe staining the newspaper. In the big city you learn how to eat rotisserie chicken. I mean I didn't know that at twenty-six.

I have learned other things, but mainly I have learned to survive, which is something of an accomplishment. What gets you is the aloneness. I want to separate that from loneliness, which means being left out of the big swim. Aloneness means life without love, without the shareable experience. Eating rotisserie chicken alone does not represent loneliness. Hot food from a restaurant is always a treat, a kind of self-indulgence. It's much easier to accept the feeling of loneliness than the feeling of aloneness. When you're lonely, there are those dull patches of feeling mixed with a little despair, which you can adjust to. It is the condition of old maids, even young ones. I think it is a more superficial emotion, not really touching the deeper self. But aloneness. It is not the one in the many, it is the one without the one. It is that simple. The alone person has the carrot, takes a bite, and then has it snatched away. When you have a man and you move through the relationship, you begin to taste the possibilities of a life with meaning, and then it goes bad, like sour milk. One day it's perfectly good, and the next morning it has that funny taste. That is the taste of aloneness.

I live on the upper east side in an apartment that I was lucky to get at rent-controlled prices. I have a small terrace and I plant things there. On Sunday mornings I have rolls and coffee with the *Times*. Sometimes when I have a man staying with me we have a morning bop, sleep a little, and I make bacon and eggs. I always set a good table. Any man with eyes in his head knows he is getting a good woman. Basically, I was made for marriage. I feel happy in my peignoir, taking care of my man, serving him his hot this, his hot that. When I came to the city I saw men around me, a harvest of men. I said to myself, "Jane, a good-looking woman like you, pick yourself a fresh apple from the tree and set up light housekeeping." So I bit some apples and there were worms in them. Being twenty-six had nothing to do with anything. I was Eve before the big bite. Miss Know-Nothing you wouldn't believe.

But I knew enough at least to come prepared for the big show. I had a job lined up with a group doing industrial shows for the big car companies. I wasn't going to be caught like those corn-silk blondes from Ohio with the neat, correct faces and the little handfuls of breast, who come ready to launch into the world on a Remington typewriter, and end up catching the man in the J. C. Penney suit, unless they end up dead in a fifth-floor walkup because they said hiya to the wrong guy. I have a set of values not like the values of the smartypants Jewish girls from West Hartford, who are not so different from the girls from Ohio. What they do is shut off the current. Whatever you want to call them, ball busters or cock teasers or emasculating women, they are cut from a mold. Maybe for five minutes of their lives they get hot pants, but how long does it last? Before you know it they are off on their trips to the city, making their way to Georg Jensen's for this, that, and the other thing. They come in with the hard mouths, with Tiffany ice jangling from their arms. Where is love? Out the window from the beginning. That is why I have waited. I have had my opportunities. I may be a hopeless romantic but I want a man who has excitement in his bones, so we can love each other and fuck a lot.

I see myself as on a holy quest, or maybe you can call it a pilgrimage, a ten-year journey in search of truth. Who wants to live the stupid life of lies, the women who are dead at the center of their being, but who give you the how-do-you-do smile of superiority. As anybody knows, there are a lot of way stations to the cross, so to speak. To put it plainly, I have been in many a bed, the list is long and muddy with failure. I have know Tom and Dick and Harry and Bob and Bruce and Joe, lots of Johns to sum it up, and for the most part nice guys, decent men, selfish, vain, and sadistic at times, but just as often vulnerable, tender, and human. One thing is, they all want to get their rocks off, but as I see it, men need it like going to the bathroom, and especially the married men, who unfortunately make up a good part of the list. They need it good, because what can they be getting at home? His wife is too tired from shlepping the shopping bag from Altman's. I have given these men, all of them, a no dues feeling. They owe me nothing and they are grateful.

There is one thing I will not do. I will not succumb to the black alligator pocketbook and the expensive Saks-Fifth-Avenue-but-boring-looking tweed suit and the lovely looking face that is very hard around the mouth and very wrinkled around the eyes, and doesn't smile much. I will not give into that. I will kill myself first. As much as I have ranted and railed about suicide, this is the one thing I will not do to save myself. The image that is the antidote to that is large-bosomed, jovial Aunt Janie at fifty or forty-five, which is another image abhorrent to me, terribly abhorrent. So that if I must face the alone alternative I must devise a whole new self-image that does not exist in this world the way I feel.

I will not do the Henri Bendel scene. I won't go that route. I go to Kenneth, but I'm not like anybody at Kenneth, like no one there. I think that's a form of suicide, what those girls do. Throwing all their money into the fifty-dollar shoes and traveling. I've never been to Europe, I've never conserved the energy to save the three hundred dollars it takes to go to Europe, because somewhere in my mind I say to myself, when I go to Europe I'm going to Europe better than anybody else. I'll go either with a guy who has all kinds of loot, or I'll go with a guy who has none, and there will be a house and love and fucking and everything. Or I'll go on my own hook for six months. But I'm not going for three weeks because it's the thing to do. Never in a million years. I would rather piss away the three hundred bucks on cabs in New York. Honestly, the real honesty is that I don't want to do this thing alone. I want to share it with someone. These people who make the alligator bag scene, they are not afraid of it. To me it would be worse than *The Time of the Cuckoo*, worse than *Summertime*. To go to Europe alone and see all those beautiful things and the swans and the water, and not share it on a spontaneous level. Because now that I've got this new self-esteem, to go to Europe for three weeks and jump in and out of bed with any guy who looks cross-eyed at me is not for me any more. I couldn't do it. Whereas if I were in Europe for six months I could have a three-week relationship with this guy, a month relationship with that guy.

I want to know, when do I get mine. You have an image of a late Sunday afternoon in March, with the wind rattling against the window and the sky like lead, the papers lying all over the bed, and you rush out in desperation to whatever is playing at the Loew's, some stupid Doris Day movie, and you sit with the crummy candy bar as your only friend; how many Sundays in the dream palace can there be? And you rush home again to get out of the cold and the lousy phone rings, and who is it but Jack or Bill, bored, and wants an evening in the sack. No, no, you shout to yourself, but the search is for love, right, and the little snatches of pleasure are fake substitutes, but you have no choice. Come over, come over, and you put his hot hard cock in your mouth and grab a little ecstasy.

And then you face the terrible fact that with all the moaning and rolling and jumping and bed-rocking there is no payoff. There is a warm spot on the bed next to you and a wet patch of sex on the sheet to remind you something has happened, but what has really happened. "Janie," I say to myself, "fucked again." And I laugh at my joke. It is very hard to laugh out loud to yourself in a bedroom knowing that your lover is off, whistling his tune down the street, not knowing in his blind innocence that I trade a fuck for tenderness. Oh, they give you tenderness, five, ten minutes by the watch, and don't you think the eye isn't on the watch. "Stay a little." You sneak it out, not too pleading, just a little cool, protecting yourself. "I'd love to, baby, but if I don't get back. . . ." And there you are again, Sunday midnight, the good feeling already draining away, your thighs aching from the pressure, it might as well be a leg cramp from playing tennis, and you shove the pillow to the warm spot and if you're tired or lucky enough to fall asleep, troubled sleep, nobody there to jostle you out of it, comfort you, maybe give you another bang in the middle of the night. So maybe you wake yourself, go to the fridge, and eat the rest of the cold chicken and stare at the idiot tube, Yvonne de Carlo and John Payne in some kind of shit.

And I cry. I eat the chicken and cry. It's the oldest story in the world, I know, which makes it all the more legitimate.

It is very difficult to battle the self-pity, for one reason I think I earn it, for another it makes me feel good. But it's two maybe three in the morning, and the handy old Seconal is there. I take a couple and crawl back into bed. How often have I been tempted to take more than two. It is very hard to describe the feeling of despair, the hopelessness that settles in the stomach. But the funny thing is, despair is the wrong feeling for suicide. Despair says, there is no way out, no light at the end of the tunnel, and that you are looking for the light. You want out. Despair means I desire, a craving to live. The real danger is depression, a very different sort of feeling. Depression is beyond despair, beyond hopelessness, beyond feeling. That must have been what my mother felt when she took her overdose. As I look back at it now, she was frequently in a state of depression. I thought she was having another one of her sick headaches. And who could tell what it was about, my father's vulgarity, my mother's aging, my ugliness as a kid, the failure of beautiful Marilyn Cooper to make a great match and have a beautiful life? I grew up in that atmosphere, and when I think of reaching for that extra pill or two, I say no, I'm going to show her I can do it.

I talked this over with my doctor and we agreed that even though my parents are dead I'm still trying to succeed for them. It is very hard to grow up in a house which hammers at you, "You're a failure, you're a failure." Either you succumb to that or you fight it, and my rationale is, fight against the failure of their lives. I'm not religious, there was nothing like that in my house, but I know somewhere they are waiting and watching and listening, Sam and Marilyn, and I have an obligation to them. I feel I have to justify their lives. I came into this world a mistake, but the lesson I've learned in the theater is the lesson of tragedy. Out of the mistakes of a life you do not quit, you force a confrontation and pray for the denouement, the final reconciliation which squares your accounts with the world. I see it this way because the life of Sam and Marilyn Castle was a tragic mistake.

I'm convinced my mother married my father on the re-
bound. She was in love with a gentile boy and my grandfather broke it up. She was twenty-three. Everybody in Waterbury was getting married and she was afraid of being left
behind. She married my father because it was the thing to
do. My grandparents didn't mind because of this other guy,
the gentile. In her generation in the twenties life in Connecticut for a single Jewish girl was different from what I went
through. The Jews were in the Naugatuck valley, Ansonia,
Derby, Seymour, Naugatuck. Also New Haven. Hartford was
already a long way off. My mother was a beautiful Jewess, and
she was always invited to the very fancy balls. She considered
herself quite grand, stunning clothes, nothing but the best.
There was money. My grandfather's insurance business was
doing handsomely. He was going up in the world. My grandmother, being the snob she was, always lived up to the hilt.
The clothes were always beautiful, everything custom-made,
everything matched. They were a very correct family, trying
to make it in a small society. My mother was something like
Hedda Gabler in a provincial Norwegian town. She was a
big catch, this lady.

My father was born in New York. His parents were Dutch
Jews. He had one brother who was a ne'er-do-well, a weak
guy, a bright guy. His name was Al. He was a joyous guy, had
a sense of humor. I remember Uncle Al. He was like the
uncle in the plays who brings in the gifts and the mother
says, "It's too expensive, you can't buy that." Uncle Al married a woman who was in love with my father. Rose and my
father were going together and Uncle Al stole her away from
him with his charm. Much later, when they had moved to
California, Al divorced Rose and married a very young swinging chick and died of a heart attack, in the saddle probably.
My father was poor. He was always ashamed of his family.
He was ashamed of all his relatives in front of my mother
because they were poor too. When his father died he went

to live in New Haven. He was brought up in the house of Aunt Sarah, a Jewish matriarch beyond belief. He was ashamed of Aunt Sarah, too.

My father was a high school dropout. He was a very good dancer and very glib and very funny. He was a swinger with the ladies. He used to go to dances as a kid, a different dance every night of the week. He wanted to be in show biz. He worked around the Shubert Theater in New Haven as a stage-hand. After a while he went to New York and got a job as a chorus boy in a Broadway show with Eddie Cantor. He was long, skinny, and did a funny thing with his legs moving all over, like Ray Bolger. He was very excited about the job, so he ran down to the poolroom to tell his friends. It was in a basement. He was coming out and he didn't see the railing and he cracked his head on the steps. He woke up five days later in a hospital. He missed the rehearsals and never got into the show. So he came back to New Haven and started selling shoes.

He had occasion to go to Waterbury to trim windows in the shoe stores. He used to win prizes for window trim from the National Shoe Association. He met a girl by the name of Claire, who happened to be my mother's best friend. He and his best friend, Ed, doubled with Claire and my mother, and they drove up to Bear Mountain one Sunday. My mother drove a car with a rumble seat. My father didn't know how to drive. The girls knew how, they were upper class. By the time they got to Bear Mountain Claire and Bob were prac-tically engaged.

My father courted my mother for a year. He went through the normal middle-class procedures. She was a big catch. But the wedding pictures of Sam and Marilyn Castle are not happy. She had great eyes. They showed everything. She was unhappy on her wedding day. Where are all the dreams? Down the drain. They started their married life at 249 Syca-more Street. Every Jew in Waterbury lived on Sycamore

Street. The furniture here was what my grandfather bought for my mother. I was born at 249 Sycamore. Up until childbirth she was pretty healthy. From my birth on she was not a healthy woman. My mother was a sick woman and that was the image. After I was born, she didn't get out of bed for a whole year. When she was pregnant with me nobody diagnosed the pregnancy for months. They thought it was a tumor. She had a bad pregnancy, and a bad time delivering me. Then she did not get out of bed for a year. She started to smoke heavily at that time, chain-smoking. She had a maid. I don't know why she didn't get out of bed, how psychological it was, how trapped she might have felt.

After that first year we moved to Elm Street where we lived until I was six. That was the first place my mother tried to commit suicide. She stuck her head in the oven and turned on the gas. It was over a stupid thing like a fur coat that my grandmother said she couldn't have. They were tied economically to my grandparents. My mother always lived above her income. She had to have a mink coat when they couldn't afford a mink coat. She was selfish and demanding. She knew what the good life was and she wanted it in the worst way. She was a good shopper, tuned to a bargain. She knew where to get something custom-made so that it looked more expensive than it really was. It was terribly important to her what other people thought.

During those years, and even later in between illnesses, my mother worked with my grandfather in the business. My father of course stopped selling shoes and went in with my grandfather. So from the time I can remember my parents were always off to work. We had moved when I was six to a big house on Sycamore several blocks up from 249. Through my whole childhood the pattern was pretty much the same. My father and I would get up and drink orange juice standing up. That was all. We were not a breakfast family. My mother never got up for breakfast. She would come down to the office later. My father took me to school in the car. Then I walked home for lunch. It took me twelve minutes to walk home. I made my own lunch, practiced the piano for a half hour. I made the beds and ran back to school. After school I came home and put the meat loaf in. I dusted. I was about nine years old, a regular Goldilocks. If I didn't dust well I heard about it. I was the maid. And I was totally unaware of what was being done to me. I was so proud of myself for being able to do all these things. I did what I was told. I was terrified to disobey. I'm sure I was trying desperately hard to please them so they wouldn't be mad at me. They were mad at me for even being, so they acted it out in a zillion ways. If I hung up my coat instead of leaving it on a chair, I would forget to turn out the hall light, and if I turned out the hall light and I hung up my coat I forgot to buy the bread. They would never let anything go by. I remember I once had a beautiful velvet dress. It was my sixth birthday. I wet my pants, all over the velvet dress. I was always wetting my pants. My father was always screaming at me, "Why didn't you come home the minute you had to go." I still have weak kidneys.

They told me: "You've got to be self-sufficient. You are not too pretty, but you've got a good personality." They said this to my face. My mother was always trying to make me look nice. I was very skinny and I looked like my father. Everybody knew it. The first crack out of everybody's mouth when they met me was, "Ooh, you look just like your father." I would say something about my big nose like Daddy's and they would say, "Oh, but you have a nice personality." My mother would go to great lengths to buy things to make me look less skinny. She would take me to Ohrbach's in New York twice a year to outfit me. Her way of dealing with the skinniness was to do something about it. "If your arms are skinny we will get you puffed sleeves." I didn't like the puffed-sleeve dresses and the pink lace. I always thought I looked ugly. She yelled at me because I hated everything.

She would say: "You don't have any imagination. When it fits it will look nice. So just shut up your mouth and it's going to be all right." She was trying to teach me how to look better and what to look for. She was trying to bring me up. She felt that if she could impress some of these things on me they would stay with me, and they have. She had the same reputation I have for setting a nice table. My mother was the one who gave me the good values, no question about that.

She wasn't able to show much affection. If anybody was affectionate it was my father. He mixed gruffness with affection. He was cuddly. He was starting to get fat and I liked the fat. I remember the first time I saw his penis. I used to crawl into bed on Sunday mornings, and he used to cover up. I had a flash at the covers and I saw him. Why should he cover himself up? But he did. My mother was always covered up. She was always dressed, everything covered up. She used to wrap her sanitary napkins in a newspaper. I never even got a glimpse of their intimate life. They rarely showed any affection toward each other. They had twin beds, almost from the beginning. She was sick. I always had to be considerate of mommy. I had to walk on eggshells when she was ill. Today when somebody says twin bed I go into shock. I wouldn't have a twin bed if my life depended on it.

The happiest times were when an event was going to take place, something being planned. There would be a production, a sense of camaraderie. Saturday night was a big night for them. My father was a natty dresser, white on white shirts with the shirt collar high on his neck against a dark suit. He would dance me around in a fast peabody. I could smell the talcum on his face. My mother's role was basically to look beautiful. The beautiful Marilyn Castle. Everybody told her how gorgeous she looked, including my father. He liked women with style. He never really touched her because I don't think she liked to be touched. My mother was very conscious of her figure. She knew she was good-looking but she didn't quite believe it. They would get ready to go to a wedding, and she would be dressed to the hilt, and I would be squealing all over, "Ma, you look great," and she would put her hand nervously to her hair and throw out a sad, frightened little inside look. She was a regular Camille. But most of the time it was like a concentration camp. I would want to go someplace on a Sunday. "I want to go someplace. I want to go someplace." "Don't bother us about someplace to go," and the next thing they would be fighting. They kicked me out of the house when they had a fight. I sat on the front steps of the house on Sycamore Street and I could hear them in the den yelling at each other, about money most of the time.

My father started to play the horses. He was a *tummler*. He had to make himself into a big shot, have a lot of money, swing with the boys. He was a weak man. If you know who you are you don't need that. He was into the bookies for a lot of money. He borrowed some money from a friend of his who was on the fringes of the Mafia. They wanted the money back when the time came. They sent the boys up from New York to get it. My father ran away. He disappeared. He left my mother, he left me, and he ran. He was gone for several days. My mother went to New York and she systematically tracked him down. My grandfather bailed him out to the tune of several thousand dollars, and they never let him forget it. He was a little boy who had been chastised.

My mother worked until after the war, except when she was sick. Somewhere along the line I was told she couldn't have any more children. She had a kidney disease, the kidney enlarging itself. They took her as a patient at Yale. She was one of the first patients who had ever lived with this ailment. They replaced the diseased kidney, put in rubber tubing. She had influenza in the big 1917 epidemic, but she was pretty healthy up until childbirth. Evidently the childbirth did something to the kidney. She had me and she was a sick woman after that.

When she first got sick she started to play solitaire, and she never gave it up. She used to sit in a chair and play solitaire for five and six hours on end. She had a breakfast tray which she kept by the side of her table. She would turn it upside down and play on it. When television first came out they would watch television and she would play solitaire. She also read a lot, novels mostly, best sellers she would rent from Womrath's downtown. She did a lot of things like that by herself, read, play solitaire.

My mother died in bed reading. My Aunt Claire said my mother did not commit suicide and I believe her. She was on pills. She probably took more by mistake. The way my father found her sounds a little spooky. She left a note for my father saying she was tired and she was going to lie down. She was going through her change. On top of the kidney operation she had had a gastrectomy for a huge ulcer. So when it came time to have a hysterectomy she wouldn't go. She almost died from the gastrectomy. She didn't have the desire to live. My mother was tired of being sick all her life. My father went through the motions of showing concern. I don't know how much he cared for her by that time. He was already seeing this Bernice from the office, had been for years.

When I think about my mother and father having sex I get a hands-off feeling. I'm not supposed to think about that. They had a bad sex relationship, I'm sure of that. She didn't want any part of it. She didn't like him much. She didn't respect him. He didn't respect himself. And they both suffered from the same thing and neither one could help each other. For twenty-five years they floundered around. She was forty-eight when she died. I miss that lady. I miss her now more than ever. When I look in the *New York Times* on a Sunday and I see all these girls getting married, the daughter of this one and the daughter of that one, I understand the concept of the mother taking care of the kid until she is ready to leave the nest. I was always trained to be superself-sufficient, but I know that as I was growing up, if given half the chance this lady would have taken care of me. We would have been good for each other because I would have learned how to take from her. It was starting to happen when she died. We were having a reconciliation. I was beginning to understand. I was twenty-four years old but I wasn't a grown woman. And then she died. She died in bed reading. I don't know the name of the book.

Part I

Chapter 1

JOHN AMES came over this morning to get laid. When I opened the door to let him in he kissed me, ran his hand under my robe, and headed for the bed. What I like about John is his no-nonsense attitude. What does he care about a rumpled bed, dirty laundry lying around, the place a total wreck? John allows me to be totally human. I don't even mind not clipping the hair around my chin. I mean if a man sees you that way what chance do you have. How many romances have been wrecked by a stray chin hair? With Richard Doyle I would die if he saw me this way. For Richard the bed is made, the laundry stuffed away, the chin waxed, the body powdered and cologned, breezy fragrances sprayed in the smelly places. I put on the sheer chiffon thing, have my favorite whatever ready on the stereo. There is a code of behavior—cocktails, a little tit, shall we go to the bedroom, unpin me and I'll unzip you. John Ames doesn't care about houses and cleaning and pleasantries. I am grateful to him because he has liberated me. The only flower he brings me is a blossoming prick, the only gift the gift of sensuality. I've always believed in the guy who brings you the box with the pink ribbon. You unwrap the package, take out the gift, and you don't say, how lovely, thank you. You say instead, what can I do to make him think well of me. I proceed to unwrap my package for him. He never refuses the gift. I've constructed my whole life around the idea that the woman offers herself as a gift of love.

I have had a lot of takers. I have lost count of the number of men I have had here on Ninety-third Street. I have had Thursday cocktails men, Friday evening dinner men, Saturday night men, Sunday brunch men, midweek lunchtime men. I have served Bloody Marys and screwdrivers and martinis and twenty-five-year-old Scotch on the rocks. I have fed them artichoke hearts and smoked oysters and dips and thingies of this and that. I have chickened them and beefed them and fished them. They have come stoned and sober, big ones with little things, little ones with big things, fat and skinny, bald and hairy, young and old, lawyers and bartenders, the introverts, the extroverts, the sadists, the masochists, anal types, oral types, the dandies and the delinquents, with smiling faces and stormy scowls, beseeching, petulant, demanding, cajoling, whining, singing, raving, all with their blood at the boiling point, all searching for magic release, to discharge their aching passion on my crumpled sheets. There is this thing I have got, like Marilyn Monroe. I should be able to bottle it and hawk it, Jane Castle's Love Potion.

But John Ames introduced me to a new concept. On the surface John isn't any different from lots of men I have slept with. He is married, in his late thirties, two kids, produces a little, writes a little, a restless man in a restless business, nothing really serious at home, just hungry for the other woman, the way most of them are. I always had to be a little bit in love with every guy I went to bed with. I don't need that any more. John Ames is perfect for helping me let go. There is absolutely no emotion between us. We sort of like each other, but not too much. He is an animal in the good sense of the word. Anything erotic, he wants to do. What could be more interesting than starting out on a Monday morning, the beginning of the work week, with the city humming with back-to-work activity, people filled with nervous purpose, cramming down the crullers and swilling the coffee, racing for the subway and bus and cab, hurrying to their cubicles, desks, phones, typewriters, memos, and conferences, snapping out of their weekend indolence and crabbiness to the fresh pursuit of the absurd—what could be sexier than a roll in the hay at eight-thirty of that same morning with an adultering hubby?

I have spent my life hoping to be loved, thinking that sex was the door to love. I don't need to be in love any more. I'm finally getting real pleasure from sex. If I had my way I would fuck my way through the western world for about six months. Period. And the only thing that frightens me away from becoming a whore is that all the guys I know say, "Oh no, you don't want to do that," because there is something horrible about it that I don't know. So O.K., I can't be a whore, so they will bring Scotch. I can be sort of a semipro. Scotch, this, that, a little money here and there, some clothes. Is that bad? This is a new thing I never knew existed. I have to experiment with it. It is a state of mind that you have to accept. I have never even accepted it as an alternative, not wanting to be married, not wanting to have any permanent relationship. This is the great lesson of John Ames. I am learning to turn the tables, to use people for what I can get out of them sexually. I am learning to be selfish, self-centered in a new way—that is a liberation. I don't want to act out some dumb martyr role. I don't want to run to my friends and cry and carry on about how I am being used and abused. I know where I'm going and what I'm doing. I'm fucking every time I get a chance and the rest of the time I clean up my house and enjoy being alone.

John has promised me a threesome. He knows a belly dancer, she calls herself La Fatima, but actually she is a dark-skinned Jewish chick from Brooklyn. We talked it over this morning after we finished. The one nice thing about John is that he does not fuck and run, not like Jerry Kay, who has given me years of hit-and-run tactics. John lay naked on the bed, his dick limp between his legs, with an ashtray on his stomach, and we shared puffs on a cigarette. John only talks shop. He is always on duty.

"La Fatima will dig you. She likes to turn on with somebody who hasn't made it with a girl."

I watched the ashtray move up and down on his belly. He has light brown, downy chest hair which drifts to a point just above his belly button and stops. He is beginning to bald at the crown and he has talked, not jokingly, about hair transplant. I used to kid him about his Samson complex until he made me understand his feeling that loss of hair meant loss of virility. John taught me to see the importance of hair in sex. He freed me of my inhibitions.

"Does she like to work on a girl?"

"She goes both ways. She likes the whole scene."

"Can I do it to her?"

"You can do anything you want. It's open house."

"I want a shot at her."

"You want to lick her cunt."

"That's what I want."

"To lick cunt. You like to suck cock and lick cunt, right."

"John Ames, you never stop."

"That's what it's all about, baby."

John loves to fantasize. We lay next to each other, skin brushing, and we talked about what we would do if there was another guy and what we would do if there was another guy and another girl. He is so cool about it, so marvelously detached from my needs. I'm a love machine, we are all love machines. Yes, he says, in a foursome you have the advantage of watching the other three, so it's best for the guy who is big on looking. A foursome is a voyeur's paradise. But in a threesome you can watch two women and still have the advantage of being the only man. John has never tried two men

and a girl, which would be good especially if he could find
a gay guy to take the trip. He has also had a guy alone. A
friend of mine, David Astor, once said that John Ames is always trying to prove his masculinity. It is, "Hello, my name
is John Ames and I have two kids." He is kind of a weak guy.
He is Scotch but he is a typical kind of Irish-Scotchman.
Over in Ireland he would have ended up drinking, maybe
he would be a poet and maybe some lady would take care of
him. He does his job. He is a hack writer. His big job is
fucking well.

I tried a tongue down that small river of hair leading to
the ashtray. I wanted to see if junior rose. John looked at me.
"You have such gorgeous blue eyes," he said, and he meant
it. There is a softness, a kind of caring, but it takes funny
forms. Last week he showed up with a bottle of Grand
Marnier. He didn't even know I liked Grand Marnier. He
brought that over and poured it over my breasts and licked
it off. Then I poured some on his penis and licked it off.
It was love play. I went past the ashtray with the cigarette
still burning. It rose and fell like a raft at sea. I took a drag
and blew the smoke into the forest below.

"Fire, fire," John shouted.

I looked up at him, my hair drifting in a canopy over my
face. "I'll put it out." I was down there in familiar country.
This land is my land. John was quiet, hands folded behind
his head, head propped on the pillow, chin pressed down on
the chest, out of the way so that he could get a good look.
John Ames is a student of sex. Sometimes he is clinical.
"Sensory stimuli are enhanced by overlapping sensory func-
tions. If I can see what I feel, I feel more." So I watched him
watch me. When he goes down on me he makes me watch
him. He likes to have a tongue in my cunt and an eye on my
eye. I played. Down there I was sure of myself. I was powerful. I feel very strong about taste in clothes or interior
design. I know what is right. It is very sweet to identify that

power, know where it is, where it comes from. Stage things too, not drama criticism, I mean theatricality. I'm good, I know my stuff. That is the way I feel when I suck a man's penis. I suppose I can bite it off and that may be the real source of power. I can get Freudian too. My mouth is a substitute cunthole, and whatever threatens me down below doesn't in the mouth. I mean he can't choke me to death, can he? Anyway, Jerry Kay brought me up in sex, and the cardinal rule is Satisfy the man. That's what it's all about.

Some people say that technique is everything. True, but when I blow a guy I believe in what I'm doing. If you don't have the right attitude, forget it. My attitude is that I love it. When I'm down there I concentrate on the job. I'm out to satisfy myself. I communicate satisfaction. Anybody can tease with tongue and mouth; that's no trick. John Ames likes it when I work him up from the soft position. You get that reluctant dragon up from his sleep and feel it grow hard and insistent in your mouth. John is especially appreciative because he likes to talk, to coax me on. It's like the guy at the airport tower talking down an airplane. "There, that's good. Can you give me some tongue on the balls? Good. Now you're going. Come on now, baby." I hear the music of his passion and I'm a concert musician playing on the sweet, fierce instrument. "Here I come," he said, his hands moving around on my head, moving me up and down. And then the spurt of semen, hot, sticky, salty, lovely music of my power. I felt love. For a moment I felt exaltation. There is triumph, achievement, a delicious sense of accomplishment. I swallowed it. I like the taste. That's what I mean about attitude. If you're going to be squeamish about the taste of come, you might as well stop sucking cock. They are calling it fellatio now, and cunnilingus, giving the act some kind of propriety. I've always accepted it. From the first time I did it with Jerry Kay, I had a feeling of pride in an act of mutual satisfaction. It's a very moral thing, really. Two people sharing

ll be many years until I cultivate the icy Manhattan
n me." I giggle and curl my loafers around the legs
chair. He walks around the room, hands thrust deep
rench coat pockets, collar turned up.

e you the lady of the house?" This time it is the
y lisp of Bogart, who is very big as Sam Spade, and
tly the rage as Bergman's lover in *Casablanca*. I gig-
ain and clasp my hands over my bony knees. I forget
hing. I am Bergman and my lover has come. On the
of my mind I see my face, alabaster skin, soft eyes,
mouth. I risk a reply, his kind.

hink you have come to the right place." I am appealing,
rious. He stands indolently in front of me, a Bogie five
k shadow on his face. He sticks a cigarette, unlit, be-
his lips.

came here for the waters." He drags the last word out,
sleepy, menacing way.

m thrilled. I know the lines. My year with the Civic
ter is being acted out on the stage of life. I have heard
cue. "But there are no waters in Casablanca." I am
de Rains, villain collaborator, nasal, unctuous, threaten-

walks to the piano, sits down at the bench, turns
nd, lights his cigarette. He is smoking in a forbidden
. He puffs, inhales, shoots out a cloud through mouth
nostrils. "Then I was misinformed."

runs a few chords on the piano. I see a school ring on
nger. A senior, unless . . . it is a college ring. He nods to
nd I heed his call to join him at the bench. I walk over,
bby-soxer, correct pleated plaid skirt, a yellow sweater
my just emerging breasts. (My father and grandfather
d on the corner of Grand Street and see me coming by.
y whisper I was getting tits.) I had just started getting
period, a sophomore in high school. I sit at the bench
t to the total stranger, my Bogie, my world turning over

a feeling, very close, wildly intense. I'll never be convinced
that that can be a bad thing.

John started to get dressed. I lay on the bed trying to remember to be good. I'm supposed to be in my new turned-off
attitude.

"There's an Actors' Benefit downtown tonight."

John had put on his shirt and socks. The hair on his legs
was fuzzy, soft, like the stomach hair. He ran his thumb and
forefinger down the crease of his pants. I thought of all the
men who have straightened their pants in this room, in this
life.

"I have two tickets."

He stepped into the pants, zipped and buckled, combed his
hair, flecked off a strand from the comb. "Have a good time."
John is very good at keeping the dry manner. In the world
of John Ames things are always as they are. And then here it
comes, Old Faithful, the geyser of feeling rising from the
deep unknown region. The lessons have not quite been
learned.

"I'm inviting you. Don't give me a smarty-pants answer."

"I'm busy tonight."

I heard it. I was a grown woman. Don't violate the contract,
Janie girl. He is a stud. You are a stud. The morning at the
palace of love is over. Time to go to work.

"Call me."

"I'll call you."

He left and I surveyed the scene of the debauch. I was a
tough turned-off chick, the new image. Live to fuck has replaced fuck to live. I've arrived at a *modus vivendi*. Who
would I want to marry anyway? I love Richard Doyle, but
who can trust an Irish alcoholic? And the years I've given to
David Astor, trying to make a man out of him. Will he ever
give up his faggy life? And my Jerry Kay. He is an old shoe,
and a married one. Besides, if there is anything worse than
an Irish drinker, it is a Jewish drinker. And Bernie. Two

years of living with a man who sleeps before and after sex. And in ten years he will be sixty. Randy, my spade, is out. He is engaged. I would marry him in a shot, have a chocolate baby, and make the mixed scene. Just Randy and me and baby makes three. And the rest of the list, Neil and Leo and Ernie Weston and Paul Rabin and Mark and Hank and Lenny Faber, my internist from Jersey. They all came to this house for something.

I poured juice, made a cup of instant, dressed and left. The house was a mess. Who cared. Clean up tonight if I was up to it. I could have a girl come in, give her five hours, pay her whatever they are getting now, and have a clean place to come home to. Maybe she could wear a little white starched apron and cap over the black dress, Rosalind Russell's maid, or Irene Dunne's in a thirties comedy. "Miz Castle will be right with you. Won't you have a seat?" That kind of shit. A new life. What can marriage do for me? What has it done for anyone? I'm tired of love. I want to go to St. Croix in the winter. One of those guys will take me. Fly me to the moon, the islands, the whatever. I've turned it off, for good. I took the subway downtown and got to my building at ten. The janitor doubling as elevator man greeted me.

"Good morning, Miz Castle, going up?"

I am fifteen. I am standing in the recreation room of the Jewish Center. It is two days after another disastrous social from which I had fled in tears as a result of another rejection, my luckless scrawny body a hateful bundle under my mother's carefully purchased pale green empire dress with a little pink rose and little puff sleeves, all the way from Lord and Taylor's in New York, a dress designed to "discover my personality," another one of my mother's scheming euphemisms that she hoarded and doled out with a passion and talent born of her barely disguised contempt. I sit at the piano aimlessly punching out some tune, the end product of one of my father's designs for salvage, six weeks of lessons with some

creep who taught me how to play could be the life of the party since come right out with it, but I helpe "Nobody likes me." And tap danci very well, but that was too show biz. empty room, a May sun sliding thro dow, and I try the waltz clog, the o routine my daddy had taught me did the waltz clog together it was all tlemen, the dance team of Sam and J Tap-tap-tap-tap-tap. "The daughter." was nine. What could he have been? Janie, move into it." This in a crooke Jimmie Gleason manner. He had a big file he looked like a fat hawk with bug a two, all around the town. Sam and looked like my father. Fishface the rumor my father started himself, kid making the face, blowing up the cheeks humor they both practiced on me, mast down. "On the sidewalks of New York."

I am early for the Youth Canteen Europe is over and we will meet to plan I have a reason for my own celebratio on the heels of my last defeat with a b from Bristol, with my choking screams guished, desperate face, we decide on have a sweet sixteen party with a new nos personality. I sit on a folding chair near my nose and my future. The door opens He is wearing a trench coat, belt pulle waist. He has black, wavy hair. He's ha panic to seize me before the inevitable r into the Sam Castle banter, the shrill thru I have long been schooled in.

"Iz dis vere dey entertain for ze prison

It w
"pard
of the
in his
"Ar
gravel
curren
gle ag
everyt
screer
tende
"I
myste
o'cloc
tween
"I
in th
I
Thea
the
Clau
ing.
H
arou
plac
and
H
his
me
a b
ove
star
Th
my
nex

in the space of fifteen minutes. I wonder how I can live this way, a victim of every fragile, fugitive emotion. He plays the intro without a word, and we move like fluid motion into the chorus: "You must remember this, a kiss is just a kiss, a sigh is just a sigh."

At home I ask my father who is Jerry Kay. "That's Benny Kay's son. Benny Kay is a crook, got a finger in every cheap deal in town." Benny Kay is a shady real-estate operator with some side business in jukeboxes and he is tied up with some of the garbage people. My father lights a cigar, a big one, a Jewish Winston Churchill. Big cigars for big-faced people. He tells me to keep away from Jerry Kay. They are beneath us. Benny Kay is a goniff, a slob who wears dirty shirts. He has a girl friend he keeps who cleans him up. I see my father's eyes go hard, glinting with superiority and indignation. He is a year away from the beginning of his affair with Bernice in the office, twelve years away from marrying her after my mother's death.

"But he likes me. And when I get my nose fixed. . . ."

"When you get your nose fixed, you will get better than Jerry Kay. How long have you known him? Where did you meet him?" He is starting to boil.

"At the Jewish Center."

"What the hell is Benny Kay's kid doing at the Jewish Center?"

"He was looking for somebody."

"And he saw you coming."

"What would he want from me?"

I feel my skinniness next to his grossness. He is not that big, but he has become heavy through the chest. He breathes thickly through his heaviness. I sense the eagerness in his voice. My father is an expert on two things: shady business deals and the sexual motives of young men.

"He wants to get into your pants, that's what."

The remark stuns me with pleasure. My father thinks of

me as a woman. Jerry wants to get into my pants. Why else would a man talk to me? He rushes on, speaking with confidence, his cigar poking from the corner of his mouth.

"A punk like Benny Kay's kid. I see them downtown, by the drugstore, hanging around with that mocky friend of yours, Helen, and your Rita, that *shtilenke.* You have got to watch out for the quiet ones, let me tell you. They are out for what they can get. Do you know what I mean?"

I am very solemn, filled with awareness that I am having a heart-to-heart with my daddy. We go for months in the house, passing each other like ships in the night. Nothing more than a beep on his horn, a grunting "good morning" over juice or a sullen "good night." Who is Benny Kay's kid he should open the gates like this? What are my father's motives?

"Jerry Kay doesn't hang around the drugstore. I never saw him before. Anyway, all those boys are headed for college."

"Listen, kid." He is rough with me, direct. I am swimming in a sea of new sensations. "They go to college. They don't go to college. Take Jerry Kay. He goes to college. Five will get you ten that he is already planning to become a crook lawyer." He rises and straightens his belt, a very familiar action, the tug on the belt, the letting out of the belt, put on weight, take off weight, the belt, the tail drooping over past the last loop. My father is a natty man, custom shirts, gold cuff links, Whitehouse and Hardy shoes, Sulka ties, but he is weak on belts. Did he ever use it on me, his only child, conceived in his likeness to the stunning dismay of Marilyn Cooper and Sam Castle? What had they conspired when they brought me into this world? What had their plan been for me in the quiet wreck of their lives?

He lets off a long, perfectly formed ash from his cigar into the center of the ashtray, surveys me with a short, sweeping look, and walks out of the house. I hear him pull away in a feeling, very close, wildly intense. I'll never be convinced that that can be a bad thing.

John started to get dressed. I lay on the bed trying to remember to be good. I'm supposed to be in my new turned-off attitude.

"There's an Actors' Benefit downtown tonight."

John had put on his shirt and socks. The hair on his legs was fuzzy, soft, like the stomach hair. He ran his thumb and forefinger down the crease of his pants. I thought of all the men who have straightened their pants in this room, in this life.

"I have two tickets."

He stepped into the pants, zipped and buckled, combed his hair, flecked off a strand from the comb. "Have a good time." John is very good at keeping the dry manner. In the world of John Ames things are always as they are. And then here it comes, Old Faithful, the geyser of feeling rising from the deep unknown region. The lessons have not quite been learned.

"I'm inviting you. Don't give me a smarty-pants answer."

"I'm busy tonight."

I heard it. I was a grown woman. Don't violate the contract, Janie girl. He is a stud. You are a stud. The morning at the palace of love is over. Time to go to work.

"Call me."

"I'll call you."

He left and I surveyed the scene of the debauch. I was a tough turned-off chick, the new image. Live to fuck has replaced fuck to live. I've arrived at a *modus vivendi*. Who would I want to marry anyway? I love Richard Doyle, but who can trust an Irish alcoholic? And the years I've given to David Astor, trying to make a man out of him. Will he ever give up his faggy life? And my Jerry Kay. He is an old shoe, and a married one. Besides, if there is anything worse than an Irish drinker, it is a Jewish drinker. And Bernie. Two years of living with a man who sleeps before and after sex. And in ten years he will be sixty. Randy, my spade, is out. He is engaged. I would marry him in a shot, have a chocolate baby, and make the mixed scene. Just Randy and me and baby makes three. And the rest of the list, Neil and Leo and Ernie Weston and Paul Rabin and Mark and Hank and Lenny Faber, my internist from Jersey. They all came to this house for something.

I poured juice, made a cup of instant, dressed and left. The house was a mess. Who cared. Clean up tonight if I was up to it. I could have a girl come in, give her five hours, pay her whatever they are getting now, and have a clean place to come home to. Maybe she could wear a little white starched apron and cap over the black dress, Rosalind Russell's maid, or Irene Dunne's in a thirties comedy. "Miz Castle will be right with you. Won't you have a seat?" That kind of shit. A new life. What can marriage do for me? What has it done for anyone? I'm tired of love. I want to go to St. Croix in the winter. One of those guys will take me. Fly me to the moon, the islands, the whatever. I've turned it off, for good. I took the subway downtown and got to my building at ten. The janitor doubling as elevator man greeted me.

"Good morning, Miz Castle, going up?"

I am fifteen. I am standing in the recreation room of the Jewish Center. It is two days after another disastrous social from which I had fled in tears as a result of another rejection, my luckless scrawny body a hateful bundle under my mother's carefully purchased pale green empire dress with a little pink rose and little puff sleeves, all the way from Lord and Taylor's in New York, a dress designed to "discover my personality," another one of my mother's scheming euphemisms that she hoarded and doled out with a passion and talent born of her barely disguised contempt. I sit at the piano aimlessly punching out some tune, the end product of one of my father's designs for salvage, six weeks of lessons with some creep who taught me how to play guitar chords so that I could be the life of the party since I was so ugly. He didn't come right out with it, but I helped by whining and crying "Nobody likes me." And tap dancing was out, which I do very well, but that was too show biz. I stand up, alone in the empty room, a May sun sliding through the street-high window, and I try the waltz clog, the old East Side, West Side routine my daddy had taught me years before. When we did the waltz clog together it was all right. "Ladies and gentlemen, the dance team of Sam and Jane Castle. The father." Tap-tap-tap-tap-tap. "The daughter." Tappity-tap-tap-tap. I was nine. What could he have been? Thirty-five? "O.K. Now, Janie, move into it." This in a crooked mouth aside, the old Jimmie Gleason manner. He had a big, florid face and in profile he looked like a fat hawk with bug eyes. "And a one and a two, all around the town. Sam and Janie together. . . ." I looked like my father. Fishface the kids in school said, a rumor my father started himself, kidding me out of it by making the face, blowing up the cheeks with that casual cruel humor they both practiced on me, masters of the cutting putdown. "On the sidewalks of New York."

I am early for the Youth Canteen meeting. The war in Europe is over and we will meet to plan a celebration dance. I have a reason for my own celebration. The night before on the heels of my last defeat with a boy imported for me from Bristol, with my choking screams in my mother's anguished, desperate face, we decide on the nose job. I will have a sweet sixteen party with a new nose, a new face, a new personality. I sit on a folding chair near the piano, fingering my nose and my future. The door opens and a boy walks in. He is wearing a trench coat, belt pulled tight around the waist. He has black, wavy hair. He's handsome. I wait for panic to seize me before the inevitable moment when I fly into the Sam Castle banter, the shrill thrust of "personality" I have long been schooled in.

"Iz dis vere dey entertain for ze prisoners of war?"

It will be many years until I cultivate the icy Manhattan "pardon me." I giggle and curl my loafers around the legs of the chair. He walks around the room, hands thrust deep in his trench coat pockets, collar turned up.

"Are you the lady of the house?" This time it is the gravelly lisp of Bogart, who is very big as Sam Spade, and currently the rage as Bergman's lover in *Casablanca*. I giggle again and clasp my hands over my bony knees. I forget everything. I am Bergman and my lover has come. On the screen of my mind I see my face, alabaster skin, soft eyes, tender mouth. I risk a reply, his kind.

"I think you have come to the right place." I am appealing, mysterious. He stands indolently in front of me, a Bogie five o'clock shadow on his face. He sticks a cigarette, unlit, between his lips.

"I came here for the waters." He drags the last word out, in the sleepy, menacing way.

I am thrilled. I know the lines. My year with the Civic Theater is being acted out on the stage of life. I have heard the cue. "But there are no waters in Casablanca." I am Claude Rains, villain collaborator, nasal, unctuous, threatening.

He walks to the piano, sits down at the bench, turns around, lights his cigarette. He is smoking in a forbidden place. He puffs, inhales, shoots out a cloud through mouth and nostrils. "Then I was misinformed."

He runs a few chords on the piano. I see a school ring on his finger. A senior, unless . . . it is a college ring. He nods to me and I heed his call to join him at the bench. I walk over, a bobby-soxer, correct pleated plaid skirt, a yellow sweater over my just emerging breasts. (My father and grandfather stand on the corner of Grand Street and see me coming by. They whisper I was getting tits.) I had just started getting my period, a sophomore in high school. I sit at the bench next to the total stranger, my Bogie, my world turning over the Buick, big like him. I go upstairs to my mother's bedroom, take off my clothes, and stand naked in front of her full-length mirror on the door of the closet. I see a crow on a stick. The nose is long, with a bump, a whopper of a nose. My breasts are tiny hills, resting on see-through ribs. I am to meet Jerry Kay downtown tomorrow in front of Hamil's Department Store, near the lunch counter. He may want to get into my pants. His father owns a green Oldsmobile. I should be ready. I go to my mother's vanity and rub my body with bath oil. I search in her drawer and find a pair of lace panties, freshly powdered with lilac talc. I slide one of her brassieres over my bony shoulders and fill in the empty pockets with several pairs of her stockings until I am a perfect thirty-four. I roll a pair of her silk stockings over the oily legs, draw them up smooth and tight and knot them just above the knee. The dress I like best is a black moiré with a cross-over décolletage. The moiré rustles and glistens. I put on her lavender special-occasion pumps. I turn to the makeup arsenal on the vanity and work my way through the base, rouge, polish, lipstick, eyeshadow, liner, mascara. I have a good hand, being a senior student, a professional observer of beauty masks. Then a hat and the jewelry, rings, beads, bracelets, earrings. I stand again before the mirror—Marilyn Castle. I know how to vamp, the hand slung on the hip, the hooded eyes looking smoky under the hat, the head cocked at a slight enigmatic angle, the painted mouth parted in a pout. "Hello, Jerry." I sit at a proffered chair, cross my legs, show flesh above the stocking. "I will have a Dubonnet cocktail." I drink with my gloves on, black arm-length velvet. I am droll. I sip my drink, smoke, watch his sangfroid melt under my glancing eye. "Tell me," I say, gazing out into the bustling square. Cyclists are whizzing by, car horns are tooting, gendarmes are frantic. "Tell me, would you like to get into my pants?"

Chapter 2

JERRY KAY called me at the office. He wanted to see me at once. Could I meet him at my apartment at one. As I have discovered over the past twenty years, I have no resources when it comes to my first love. For other people the first adolescent crush was basic training for the big romantic wars to follow. Most girls are wise enough to know, even when they go steady, that growing out of love at an early age is natural and inevitable. We learned it from our parents, from the advice column in the teen magazines, from the manuals of love we peeked at on the forbidden shelves of our houses. Mr. Big was going to come, we all knew it. Real love, true love as we labeled it, would rise out of the embers of the first great heart attack. Mr. Elwood, the English teacher Helen, Rita and I loved so much, reminded us once of the phoenix story, and we supposed that the bird was a female, rising from the fire which consumed it, to live again and love again. Mr. Elwood neglected to tell me whether the phoenix had the same lover every time it came to life. I took the story seriously and made Jerry my phoenix, two in one together forever. The trouble was that he never heard of the story.

I made a few phone calls for my boss, a gruff remote man in his fifties who was a consultant for some out-of-town firms. It was a good in-between assistant's job for me. My time was pretty much my own, the work simple, the pay good. Best of all, there was no possibility of any office affair to throw me into hysterics. I wanted to give my new role a chance. I was learning that pursuing the life of pleasure was a hard job. I got into a cab at 12:30 and headed north on Third Avenue. Jerry's call sounded urgent. After a morning session with John Ames I wasn't able to muster the excitement I usually felt when Jerry called. The best thing about a good fuck is that it makes you feel good for hours after, not a profound thought but very comforting if you live often with anxiety and depression. My stomach was purring and there was a sweet looseness in the body. The Third Avenue stores flipped by lazily as my cabbie wove through the broad one-way street, like I used to ride the bump cars in the amusement park back home. The cab swerved to avoid a delivery truck pulling out of a parking spot.

"Goddamned jig." The driver turned his head halfway. "You see what's happening to this city."

There are no silent cabbies in New York. This one, fat, chewing a toothpick, was strong on the race issue. I waited for the story.

"I had a fare the other day. A pretty dame, good-looking like yourself, hails the cab from the sidewalk. I always like a nice fare. I pull up, open the door. She steps in. From out of nowhere this guy comes, pops himself in the seat next to her. I say, 'Hey, mister, don't you see the lady?' She says, 'That's all right. He is with me.' I take a good look in the mirror, and what do you think. It was a tan one." We stopped for a light and he turned all the way around. "I've been hacking in this city for twenty years, and I take all the fares, the drunks, the queers, it don't make no difference to me." The light changed and he jerked ahead, his hand mashed on the horn. "But it makes my blood boil when I see a white girl with a nigger. You know what I mean."

"They are people, like everybody else." I thought of my black Randy, ebony against the white sheets.

"The colored have enough sense to stay with their own

kind. Nine times out of ten it's the woman. Some cheap broad, you'll pardon the expression, out for a thrill."

"It's a free country," I said.

He offered a burning look in the mirror, hunched his neck forward. The dialogue was ended. I sat back and decided to try something else. When you have driven in taxicabs as often as I have you develop a queenly air. I have talked to hundreds of cabbies. It's a second life, riding in that big back seat, lots of leg room, hand on the strap, hearing the meter tick away. You get stalled, you always do, uptown, downtown, crosstown, and you talk. The talk is always intimate, even when it is hostile. There we are, sealed in the container, two of us, strangers in the night, and there is a charge of something. I'm never bored in a cab. One time it was a college kid working summers, and we ended up at my place. Just once. It was no good. Better to maintain the formalities.

"Do you have any children?"

"I've got three. My oldest is seventeen. I catch her like that I break her back."

"What if she falls in love?"

"My kid. With a coon. Lady, you must be kidding."

"It could happen." I dropped my voice, testing him. He caught the shift in tone.

"Look, I've worked with some great colored fellas, in the army, in the shop. I got nothing against them."

"Some of your best friends. Right."

"What?"

I tired of the game. He was another of that breed of shifty-eyed people. You even get tired feeling superior to them. Hey, Mr. Cabbie, I could say, I am Jane Castle, swinging career girl, who has made the scene with all of them, black, brown, yellow, not to speak of the shades in between. I know all about race relations, human relations. As the poet said: "I have known the arms already, known them all. . . ."

In the apartment I straightened the bed, opened the windows, threw dirty things in the hamper, put two martini glasses in the refrigerator, showered quickly, slipped into lounge pajamas, put some Brubeck on the machine, and waited for my man. Three months ago he had popped in, a Friday night before his poker game, with half a dozen Chivas-on-the-rocks under his belt. Some pussy and poker before the weekend domesticities in Westport. We had drunk and screwed, good sports, the brother-and-sister act, like sitting down to a bowl of cornflakes with a bit of casual family farting at the table. I had cried. How many times has Jerry Kay seen me cry? Then a Jerry joke, and the laughter through the tears. And a song. Time for a song before the pants go on, the hair combed, the jacket on, the hurried "See you soon, baby." A stupid thing from the Waterbury days. In the morning, in the evening, won't we have fun. I had a five o'clock appointment with Dr. Seltz. Does Jerry Kay try to rob me of my self-esteem with jokes and song? There's no business like show business. Jerry takes all, gives nothing, doctor, and even when I get sore I'm not sore. Is it because I see Sam Castle in him and I can't hate him. Think of all that guilt if you allow yourself to think you hate your father. But Jerry is not my father. He was my first hater. Ah. You keep Jerry Kay as a reminder of father-hate. No, doctor, love, not hate. Isn't there an incest taboo? I always thought my father wanted to fuck me. Get into my pants, you know what I mean?

Jerry arrived and I poured the cold martinis into the frosted glasses.

"Well, here's to a high noon," he said.

"You think so," I said. His eyes were puffy black pockets. The hair was gone at the top and a crown of skin showed through. Under forty, he looked seedy, past his prime. He drank quickly, put his glass down, and reached inside for my breast.

"Unh, unh." I pulled his hand away. "What's your trouble.

Something at home?" All the married men I knew had trouble at home.

"You want me to pay a little. Tell me a story, Jerry honey. O.K. Here is a story. I'm a lawyer, right. I have opportunities. It's too complicated. The truth is, I got my hand caught in the till."

"You did what?"

"No kidding. Look." He pulled up the sleeve of his jacket and showed me his right hand. I didn't see anything. "Caught in the till. It hurts like a son of a bitch. A little transaction, a business arrangement that is running into bad weather. What do you think this whole thing is about? Try to get him before he gets you. Listen." He poured another drink from the pitcher. "Are you ready?"

I sipped sedately. "I'm ready, dear." How could I tell Jerry how good I felt when he talked to me like this. We could have made it. I could have married that man.

"I'm reading Teilhard de Chardin." He shot me one of those old, whimsical, devil's looks, got you by two touchdowns. He was about to show another facet. Jerry was many-faceted, a shopper after things. Not deep, but very wide.

"That's nice," I said. I drank a little faster.

"Do you know about the noösphere?"

"Is that what the astronauts do?"

"Teilhard believes in some kind of unitary principle. It has to do with energy changes and the soul of man."

"That got you into trouble?"

"No, jerk. I hope it gets me out."

I poured more martinis for both of us. The record dropped and Tony Bennett came on. Fly me to the moon, fly me to the stars. Jupiter. Mars. The whole bit. Out of the past. "They're playing our song."

"I'm surprised at myself. The last guy to go for that shit. He has got something."

"What has he got?"

"I got something, too." He put my hand on his fly. He was hard, bulging through.

"Tell me your trouble. You got me home for something."

"You call this nothing?"

"Mmmm. It's something." I liked the drink. It went slipping down the crevices. I put my mouth down there, blew hot breath into the pantsies. My old friend.

"Teil is very hard. Kiss him."

I unbuckled and zipped down. His prick was stretching the underwear. I loosened it from its jail. I gave a little dry kiss and leaned back.

"Really, tell me what is happening. I'm going to make you put it away." Tony was still singing to us, telling us to make love while we're young. I watched his penis twitching with anxiety. I felt the full pleasure of power. Did I not see Jerry Kay, arrogant, selfish, a ruthless seeker after his own gratification, a man close to forty who has fucked dozens of women thousands of times, a vain, flippant man, smug and smooth, an operator—did I not see him the way I wanted him, pants dropped around his ridiculous knees, his foolish underwear caught under his balls, his rotten whiskey-corroded teeth hissing out bad breath that no sweeteners could mask. It was a joke. I wanted to ha-ha in his face. Listen, buddy, John Ames gave me the bang of my life this morning. I don't need your needs. You want me, do you? For twenty years you've wanted me. Some joke. Want a little more. He poured and drank. I poured and drank. Neither of us were alcoholics. I preferred grass these days anyway. But he is a daily, like Richard, two incipients. Anybody who waits for the click or the buzz or the bells, the magic moment, has got to be in some kind of trouble.

"I'm blue. Carol, the kids, are all right. I want to make a million in a hurry and play. I like good card games and beautiful women." He bent over for the mouth. Lips and tongue locked as they always have done. God, we were practically man and wife. "I lost out on something that might have made me a million."

"So there will be another deal. You will make your million. All I want is a piece of it. At least set me up in the style I am going to be accustomed to." I really didn't want to work any more. What about the courtesans? Nobody ever knocked that life.

He threw me a hard look, mean and bossy. My father's eyes, without a doubt. Cruel is the word, downright cruel. Frightening. I was a girl. I had fear. He had no right to demand anything. Screw him. But he had all the rights and privileges that go with the office of first love. Squatter's rights. Carrying his drink he stumbled into the bedroom. He was bombed at one o'clock on a Monday afternoon. Soon my next-door neighbor, Charles, would be up and the smell of pot would start. He was a free-lance writer for the mass magazines and he grew his own stuff in the backyard. So far it had been hands off. He owned a very light-skinned, very beautiful black girl. I waited, sipping my drink, feeling no pain. I wanted to sleep. I am out of my twenties. John Ames had depleted me. But I had my obligations. To turn down Jerry Kay would be an act of self-rejection. Am I a Puritan? Do I need a Jerry Kay as a permanent symbol of my sins? Where was the smashing kid in the trench coat, with the black eyes and hair? I could have married that man. And then what? Didn't my father say a crook lawyer, and I would have to give him a very long leash because he would take it anyway. A life of cheating, of heartache. But we would have lived in style. I would have seen to that. My mother had taught me the tricks of style and grace. That woman would have been proud of me.

He was in the bed, smoking and reading *Variety* when I slid in. I put my hand over the lower organization, and we kissed. "What's new in *Variety*?" he said.

"Same old thing."

And we sang, in the old way. Every morning, every evening, ain't we got fun, not much money, Oh! but honey, ain't we got fun. I slipped into a comfortable position and took his very long, very hard thing, still the biggest of them all, into my jewel box. Tired, I loved him. Let him fuck me if he needs it. I was loose and sweet and loving under him, then over him, and alarmed and pleased he saw the act of accommodation. The vanity leaked out of this very vulgar man, and he loved me good. For a few minutes we had it. It wasn't too late. It is never too late. He came, and leaned his head on my chest and I cried. The tears were salty as I licked them out of the corner of my mouth. Even now it wasn't too late to tell him. What could it cost me?

"I love you, my baby."

He lifted his head and through the bad teeth and spoiled face I caught a flash of innocence. He was going soft inside me. I grabbed his ass and held him in. He put his head in the cradle of my neck. He was checking his watch. I didn't know what time it was when I met you. Bullshit. He always knew the time. "I love you too, baby."

I pushed him off. "Don't do me any favors."

He slid off the bed and began to dress. Jerry had tried for years to train me to hardness. "You asked for it."

"That's just what I was thinking. I won't do it again. You won't, either."

He stood in front of me, knotting his tie, a rep with a stain in the middle of the blue stripe. His face was relaxed. "Janie, you're threatening me."

"You bet your sweet ass I am." I felt the day beginning to come down around me. One fatal slip, and the bad feelings, waiting in the wings, rush in. Did I really love him? That wasn't even important any more. But I had to make him pay his dues. "You rush me up from the office in the middle of the day. It costs me two and a half bucks for a cab. You get me high on martinis, give me your little bang, and then run off until another crisis comes up. I don't even know what the crisis is."

He took out his wallet and put a ten-dollar bill on my night table. "You could have said no in the first place." He sat on the edge of the bed and smoothed his hand along my thigh. The hair on his lower knuckles were little tufts of black. I was crying. "Right?"

I snapped a tissue from the box next to the bill. "Ten dollars for cruelty to animals. Right?"

"That's the baby. We had laughs. Right?"

"Lots of laughs."

He kissed me on the cheek, one of his goodbye specials, and left. Downstairs Ella Fitzgerald was singing about a paper moon in a cardboard sea. I had faith in song lyrics. Through the banality came the real truth. It wouldn't be make-believe if you believed in me. After twenty years I was still trying to catch what it was about him that was so appealing. I remember when I had a job for Donald Allen, who was just getting started. Jerry was still living in Waterbury, trying to make it as a small-town lawyer with big-town ways. He came to see me at the office. I had a feeling of status when he walked in. I had a man coming in from out of town with a beautiful camel's hair overcoat and a very natty hat. He breezed in like Frank Costello. Some girls like going out with the captain of the football team. I like going out with the head bookie. He had a stylish manner, not exactly flashy but it wasn't classy either. That was what my mother liked about him, just enough class to make the flash exciting. And there I was sitting at my little gray steel thing and Donald Allen was nothing then, but he is president of the League of New York Theaters now, and I introduced my man to him. I was Tallulah Bankhead.

I dressed and took a quiet cab back to the office, paying him with Jerry's ten. I liked the excitement and theatricality Jerry created around him, the whole business of being a big shot. It is phony. It has nothing to do with anything, this flashy kind of worldly behavior, but I was intrigued by it, because I still hadn't learned the true value of a *menschy* guy who didn't have to flash his sapphire pinky ring around. I am still intrigued by this kind of man, even though I have discovered he is basically hostile to women. If I were to walk into a room and there was a guy who came on strong and funny and handsome I would go for him instantly. With Jerry, underneath it all he had a good ethic which I liked. He was always ready to stand by his actions. He always took a position and kept it. He has never lied to me and there were plenty of times I wanted to hear the "I love you, Jane" with a deep look in his black eyes. But he did not do that. Take it or leave it. So I took it and I have taken it. What his honesty amounts to is that he can't help but treat women badly. What he really likes is the poker game, the company of other men. Dr. Seltz calls him a clinical homosexual. There must be a joke in it somewhere.

I am wearing black suede high-heel pumps with ankle straps, completely closed, with four-inch high heels. They are my Minnie Mouse shoes. I have on a Ceil Chapman hand-me-down dress, an ice-blue faille with a huge flared skirt designed to make me look fatter. The skirt is very long. I am wearing a fitted jacket with covered buttons. My mother has dry-shampooed my hair, following the doctor's orders to be careful on these first crucial days after the operation. I am walking in Central Park with Jerry Kay, who has come down from New York University to escort me to the theater. My nose is swollen and bulbous but the hook is gone, having disappeared under the hammer of the great doctor from New York.

"No solids for a week, Mrs. Castle," he warns, no jarring of any kind.

"I don't care about the thousand dollars," my mother says. "We don't want to go through this again, do we?"

But the week is up and my mother sits in our room on the

fourteenth floor of the Croyden Hotel, chain-smoking her Chesterfields and playing solitaire, while I take the first steps to freedom. I have a new nose, I sing to myself. I am prettier, or I will be as soon as everything settles. The doctor has given his approval for the theater trip. The three of us will go, Jerry, my mother, and I. In the hotel room my mother and Jerry have planned the strategy of how to maneuver me through the crowd, get me seated, and get me home in one piece. They have put me in a chair near the window and I look out over the park while they relax over a game of gin rummy. They play the game rapidly, Hollywood gin, with the boxes, my mother keeping score with quick decisive strokes of the pencil. It has always been this way with the two of them. Jerry is witty, with little flattering asides. He is nineteen, she is forty-two, and they are lovers over the gin table. He calls her Marilyn from time to time in a gruff way, impersonating my father. My mother laughs occasionally, a husky, cigarette laugh, and I see that she loves him. She is still very beautiful, and she primps a little. With my father and their friends she is aloof. She has never come down from her palace on top of the hill. Jerry brings her out. She chatters aimlessly under his spell. I am completely forgotten. I jump up and declare that I am going for a walk. It is a few hours before theater time. Jerry gets up and we leave the room with my mother dealing to herself. Her head is bent at a familiar angle, although the room is strange. She is an absolute master of that lonely game.

We walk down a path not far from the hotel. Jerry keeps checking his watch. He fails to hold my arm and I walk gingerly on my four-inch heels, keeping my face to the ground for cracks and stones. "We won't miss the play." I am tart, superior, since I have made up my mind to play the game differently, with a new nose and a new personality. When you are over sixteen, I reason, you must take hold of your life. Distracted, Jerry doesn't answer. He has come as a special surprise to see me, but he doesn't see me at all. The doctor has cautioned me not to cry. Something about swelling membranes and discomfort. I am through crying. We circle around a fountain. People are sitting on benches near the fountain, some with heads back to catch a little of the breeze-blown spray. It is a warm, muggy June day. I think of the accusation of my closest friends, Helen and Rita. "Why are you such a crybaby, Jane?" And it is true. I am shoved out of the house, age seven, and I sit on the front steps crying. In the schoolyard at twelve I stand in a corner. Helen comes up to me. "What is it now?" "They won't play with me." I run home from a confirmation party at thirteen. The wrong boy wants to kiss me. Nobody likes me. "Marilyn," my father says, time after time, with disgust and frustration, "is that damned kid ever going to stop?"

In a few weeks I will be looking in the mirror and it will begin all over again, the first sixteen years wiped out. The doctor has worked well. It will be a good nose. Two days ago Helen and Rita came up to the hotel, and we had a picture-tearing ceremony. We ripped up the old nose and scattered the pieces out of the window. A new life. I see Jerry throwing sidelong glances at me. He is a sophomore at NYU, a college man, living in the city. I love him beyond belief. We share the knowledge that he has laid me, and I know I am the first of the girls in my crowd. I remember very little. He has fucked me. What does that mean? All I want is his tenderness, his love. My father is suspicious of Jerry and will make a scene when we return home.

"What is that punk smelling around you for. I'm not laying out all that money so he can mess around with you." For months after the operation my parents are in a bad mood, quarreling about petty things. The house is charged with anxiety and hostility. They talk about money. Business is slow. I am a weapon they discharge on each other. I want only Jerry, who has stopped coming to the house.

We drive down to the theater in a cab, Jerry and my mother sitting stiffly on either side of me. My mother pays and we enter the theater. It is five minutes to curtain time. The play is *A Streetcar Named Desire*, and we have come to see Marlon Brando. I forget everything in my excitement. The theater, I have decided, is to be my life. On the way down to the ladies' room I stumble on a step. My mother shrieks and catches my arm. Her face is blanched with terror. If I fall, the face will be smashed. She herself is living within a circle of terror, her own life sour and unredeemable, in and out of hospitals, kidney, gall bladder, hysterectomy, gastrectomy. She imagines me crumpled at the foot of the stairs, her own fragile vanity shattered forever. I catch the banister and laugh.

"It's O.K., Ma. I'm all right." I put my hand to my nose.

"Your nose," she says, distracted, stunned with nameless dread. I have never seen her so terrified. We return to the seats and Jerry strokes her hand as he helps her to her seat. I see his eyes in the dimming light. They are warm, full of concern for my mother, who sits and stares at the rising curtain.

"Your nose," she says to herself, barely audible.

Jerry and I exchange looks. How can we save this woman, who is frightened and lost on the day I am found? The curtain goes up. I sit back and move to the side away from my mother's rigid hand which is gripped around the armrest. For a moment I feel a sweep of joy, free of her pain. In the darkness I gently finger my new nose. The skin is inflated and tender. I trace my index finger down the bridge. The hook is gone. I feel that I am free.

Chapter 3

My analyst's office was in Yorkville, on the corner of Park and Eighty-Sixth, in a building of analysts. On the nameplates at the front entrance the M.D.'s outnumbered the Ph.D.'s. Dr. Seltz was an M.D. His plate, flanked by two Ph.D. plates, looked good in shined brass, like the polished names of the Fifth Avenue stores. For the first several years in New York, I used Milt Slazenger, Ph.D., with an unimpressive plastic nameplate, one of those things you see with D.D.S. on them, except that Slazenger was no dentist. He had carried me through bad days, my crutch. Once I called him from Nantucket from a telephone at a beach bar, in tears because the guy I was with all evening had walked off with a man.

"He's a faggot," I screamed into the phone, the noise of the crowd billowing around me. "Dr. Slazenger, what am I going to do?" waiting for the miracle words, the balm to soothe my tender, sunburned brain. And the advice came, crackling over the long-distance phone, something about courting rejection with the wrong kind of man, hadn't we discussed this many times, his voice at midnight without a trace of irritation, and hanging up, I wondered whether it was exactly the irritation I was seeking, my masochism riding through me like the waves breaking on the Nantucket shore. And again waking him in the middle of his August vacation

45

in Maine, this time for no reason except for the maddening loneliness of a hot summer weekend in New York. "Hello, Jane. Yes, it's very pleasant up here." He wasn't angry. They never get angry. I mentioned something about pills, and the voice grew stern, forbidding, not being able to play the game of the city. Go ahead, he might have said, in fact he did say on one occasion of threat, angry with my self-pity. "It eats away. You don't have to force me to care. I care."

And like that, year in and year out, holding up on payments, lying to him, chaining myself to a rock of self-deceit and expecting him to free me, realizing dimly I was my own vulture eating at my vitals. And then at last, he was moving his practice to Jersey, I declared that I hadn't transferred, that was it, I had never let my hate-love out on him, very cool about it at the very moment my own father was near death from cancer.

"Isn't that what it is all about?"

Playing the game to the bitter end, not veering one inch from the prescribed course, he said, "Is that what you think it's all about?"

"Don't give me your tricks," I shouted, startled by my own passion. It was a palace revolt, but the emperor had already fled.

Now here I was again, in my second year with Seltz, two years of mapping out real territory, staking a claim that was delivering the gold. He sat opposite me in a leather chair, feet crossed on a footstool, nice-looking, with an ordinary academician's face, soft-voiced, slow-moving, a two-mile-an-hour man with a slight Southern accent, a novelty and a relief from the New York Jewish-Vienna crowd. My chair, upholstered in a tasteful subdued fabric, faced his. A daybed stood unused in a corner. Who lies down anymore? All around the city, in pleasant leathery dens in tall buildings while the madness of the city went on, hundreds of people, sitting in twos, were plunging into their anxious lives, looking for keys to their destinies. When I walked into the building I saw four women come out of the elevator. Right now as I was facing Seltz, other women in other rooms in this same building were facing their wise men. Right now other women were sitting at the beginning of the hour stone-silent opposite silent stones, obstinately refusing to yield to the painful relief of the first shattering of the silence, clutching to their bosoms their raging passivity; or sitting down, pouring forth the bad juices of the accumulated day, looking for nothing more than to get the shoes off the aching feet and the gas out of the aching heart. Two or three times a week we make our way in cabs and subways and buses on a pilgrimage to the secular confession boxes, tell me, father, tell me, I have sinned, a female army of walking wounded; then popped out again into the nightmare streets, home to the flat for the cocktail and a night out to apply the lessons learned. How many times have I followed the instructions! On how not to jump into bed with a man. The Slazenger line: "I don't think I know you well enough." I tried it and the guy didn't come back. This is the priestly advice, but I believe it, because where else is the support? There is no father, there is no God as far as I'm concerned. There is only your doctor, who is god the father, and if his name isn't hallowed mine is mud.

I couldn't get started. He charged me the fifteen-dollar poverty rate and I watched my money tick away as he sat in his chair, legs crossed, hands folded in his lap. The facial expression was Standard Analytic: the poker face and the thoughtful, concerned eyes as if he had a gas pain and was trying to mask it in polite company. I shifted in my chair, pretty much used to opening silences but they are never comfortable. Stu Jennings, a lighting director I knew, told me he walks in, sits down, and says, "Well, how am I, Doc?" Some months ago Dr. Seltz and I had a conference. We agreed that I would refrain from bringing in the day's news each visit, wasting thirty of the fifty minutes. "Try to remember your dreams, Jane." The tone was big uncle. "Keep a little pad by your bedside. When you wake in the morning, or even at night, jot it down."

All I had in front of me was the day's news, no dreams, only my life right now. I wanted to talk about my new self-image. I selected my bright, brittle manner for openers.

"We made a deal, right? No Today show, but I'm bothered by something that will probably plug into the past. I mean I'm through wasting my time here talking about Richard this, Richard that. That is over. I'm not going to get caught with my pants down, ever again."

That brought him out of his chair. We laughed.

"Which resolution number is that?"

I knew why I didn't want to talk. I wanted him to think well of me. How many things does a patient suppress to promote a good image? But it's exactly for that reason people go to the shrink, to break through the fake shit, the face before the world. Everything outside of me was the world. Arnold Seltz was the world, a mask to meet the mask. I lived in a whirling sea of suspicion, deceit, mistrust. I couldn't trust myself. How could I trust the world? Look at him sitting there, wise and filled with mistrust, not really believing anything I say. Yet I carried his word everywhere, the gospel according to Saint Arnold. He gratified his ego with silent cunning. I thought of the endless dark hours with Slazenger, with Seltz, men who probably led fucked-up private lives, but in the office nothing more than a face, a voice, a posture, witch doctors of the mind, caring for nothing but the science of feeling. What did they know about real feelings, real pain, real suffering. Did anyone ever imagine a suffering psychoanalyst. Freud died of cancer of the throat, but do the pictures show the anger, the dread?

"I have a very strong urge to make it with a woman." My lips were very dry. I waited for the sensible rebuke. He moved

his hands from his chin and opened them. The signal meant
to go on. "I have finally discovered that sex is a pleasure. I
enjoy it." I paused because God knows there is nothing more
exciting and ominous than uttering the forbidden. I wanted
to say it straight, but I looked away, embarrassed enough to
take the edge off. "My cunt is twitching. I think of nothing
else. I thought maybe I'm a nymphomaniac, but now I want
a chick."

"Go on."

Go on. What was I supposed to say. John Ames promised
a threesome.

"Am I a lesbian?"

"Forget the labels. Just go on."

The tone of his voice had picked up. Oh, Arnold, you
waspy looking Jewboy, what do you know about the ways of
the world.

"Well, I'm not a lesbian. I'm not dykey-looking enough.
And I like the company of men, right. But I've never felt
this way before. I have slept with an awful lot of men, some
day we will take a count. I feel that loving a woman is a liberation. It is the pure act, sex for its own sake, no man to
hang me up emotionally. I have waited half a lifetime to be
free. Insecurity, vulnerability, lack of self-esteem, aren't these
things prisons? A woman is like me, no male genital threat,
no big phallic narcissim, that's the phrase, isn't it? What did
my father ever do but throw his big fat ego around. Primp
and strut and make loud noises, Janie, come down at once,
Jane, stop sniveling, Jane this that, and Marilyn, what was
my mother but a betrayed beauty, a woman of grace and
courage. . . ."

"And loud and sarcastic and hard. Your words." Seltz
stretched his hands behind his head, stretched his legs out on
the footstool. What did he make, fifty, sixty g's a year, just to
listen. A remarkable profession. Jesus, I could go into it. I
have good perceptions.

"But my mommy was a scared woman, and she married a weakling."

"How do you know that?"

"Contempt. She married beneath her station. But she loved him. She loved Jerry Kay, who incidentally dropped by today, who is a carbon copy of my father. Brutal men, completely self-involved. Why did she love the man she despised? Why do I still love Jerry Kay, who shits on me? . . . I don't know what it was. But the brutality. It is sadistic. I don't mean he beat her. Weak men don't do that. She beat him too in a million ways. They murdered each other. They had me and stopped cold. They saw their product. I have hated myself all my life. Where did I learn that? I was lucky. They could have had another child, a pretty sister for Jane. I would have killed myself. Now it is just a matter of enjoying the pain. If they beat you long enough you learn to wait for the pleasure of the pain. That's the pleasure principle, right. A human being can't stand that much pain. You become a masochist. That is my revelation for the day."

He handed me the tissue box and I blew the snot away. I closed my eyes and waited for the throbbing to subside in my throat. A heavy head. Good session. An emotional bang. Clean out the tubes. In one hole in the morning, out the other in the afternoon. What would the night bring? A face loomed before me, a man with horn-rimmed glasses and a moustache. I am in his car and we are driving away from a building. It is the Jewish Center and my cousin Suzy is getting married. I am drunk on two glasses of champagne. I am wearing one of my puffed-sleeve jobs, a junior cocktail dress, subdeb cut. I have a modest décolletage, my breasts tiny grapefruits, which the man is eyeing. We pull into a wooded dead-end road. He turns off the motor and looks at me. It is Seymour Arbeit, married to a second cousin of mine in the furniture business in Hartford. He opens his fly and pulls out a hard penis. It is the second time I have seen a man hard.

My father, a hot summer morning, stumbling to the bath-room, naked, thing sticking out. "Do you know what this is?" Seymour asks. He lifts my hand and places it there. I am faint with fear and excitement. He asks me to hold it which I do, the way a girl holds the end of a baseball bat the first time. I grab it very hard. He instructs me to loosen my grip and to move my hand up and down. I try this but he is not satisfied. He puts his hand on my head and begins to force me down. Just give it a little kiss. No, no, no. I take my hand away and ask him to drive me back. He turns to me with a funny look. His glasses are big and steaming. You little cock teaser. He lifts his arm as if to strike me. I throw up my hand and shrink to the corner. Mamma, mamma, I start to cry. It is the gesture of my father, the back of the right hand raised, the ring on the thick, fat pinky flashing in the shaft of sun knifing into the car. Don't hit me. Hit me.

Dr. Seltz stood over me, his bland face showing concern, faking concern. He sees six or eight patients a day, kleenex boxes, how much real concern can he show? Which is O.K. with me. I don't want anybody's pity any more. What is pity but false concern hiding contempt.

"Is the time up?"

"We have time." He walked to the window overlooking Eighty-Sixth Street and stretched his arms and yawned.

"I don't blame you," I said.

"It happens."

In the silence my stomach growled. I could have a bologna and Spanish onion on pumpernickel with mayo. I like to spread the mayo evenly on both slices. When I'm very hungry I don't cut the bread. I like to bring the whole thick sand-wich to my mouth. Wash it down with a coke with ice. Soda was forbidden in my house. Coke rots your teeth, my mother said. Once when the circus came to town I had a soda and cotton candy. My father shared it with me. I have no other memory.

"If I have a woman I don't want to feel guilty."

He returned to his chair and folded his hands under his chin. "Isn't that a way of escaping?"

"Escaping being a woman?"

"Don't you think so?"

"But I'm always having to prove I'm a woman. No man has accepted the proof. Marriage is the proof of womanhood. That's our society. Get married and go to the supermarket for the big box of Tide."

"You want that?"

"I don't want the Tide. But the concept may be that inside the box of Tide is the prize, the package of self-esteem. Marriage tells you that you are wanted. I don't see them knocking down my door. I might as well try a chick. Who needs marriage? Some guy to get his rocks off regularly. My father married my mother. I don't know if I want to repeat the crime."

"You don't want to marry?"

"Yes, I do want it." Sometimes I hear myself and I have to laugh. The impossibility of telling him what it really felt like. I get so hungry for love that I eat onion sandwiches. And then there is that pit of fear in the stomach, as if panic itself were an object. I've got a piece of panic caught in my chest.

"I could have married Bobby Green years ago. I could have structured a relationship that would have ended in marriage. He was crazy about me. I mean he wasn't in love with me but he could have been made to be if I had been a little more standoffish, a little less buddy-buddy. How do these things happen? Burton Lipsky is married ten years already. What did she do? He fell madly in love with this little *pischerkeh* Jewish kid. Nonsense. She played with the tip of his thing for a while, and the rest of the time she would not until he married her. It is true. Marriages are not made in heaven."

"They are made in hell."

We laughed. "Don't you know it." I felt the hour coming

to an end. I was just getting into gear. Talk about structuring, doctors created the fifty-minute hour because they knew the patient comes alive in the last few minutes. "My mother, and I swear this is true, never instilled in me that feeling of being married, how important it was. My guy from Jersey, my Dr. Lenny Faber, most girls would have sat tight, been a little less available to him. They would have pulled a few little trickies to get him. Most girls have a security instinct like trained killer dogs. I have no frame of reference for that kind of behavior. I operate on the survival instinct, where you have to go out and earn your living. I don't stalk my men the way these girls do, give the guy a little bit of boob, a hand between the legs, maybe let him slip the thing in once, but that buys a trip to the Copa, and a lot more. I was never trained for that.

"I could have had a decent marriage with Lenny Faber. We wouldn't have had a bad marriage. I could have hooked him with my cunt. I could have given a simple kind of guy like this the idea that I was the hottest box in the Western world. If I had been smart I could have kept him off and if I had made screwing something terribly special I could have married him. I could have had these guys, not to speak of two or three others, Barry from New Haven, for instance. Yes, I want to marry, but I don't want Bobby Green or Lenny Faber or Barry from New Haven. To find a real human relationship is the thing that is difficult. I think I might have it. I know I have it with David Astor, if he gives it half a chance. I love David Astor. But these girls who fall into things, get their picture in the *Times* right away out of school, they don't know which end is up. Are they ever aware they are missing it, are there some people who don't really feel it or need it, and the house, the box of soapsuds is enough for them. Or does everybody have this semistate of despair?"

Dr. Seltz stood up. "We'll continue next time."

Which of course was a lie, but I didn't mind. Next time I

will come in with a new load of laundry, and we will end up at the same place, the laundry still in the washer. But the secret was not in the final action of spin-dry. It was getting the stuff in there and agitating, back and forth, back and forth, working the dirty goods around and around. Clean laundry you get with that box of Tide. (When I was very young, four maybe, my mother used a brown box of Kirkman soap chips, in the tub, on the board, cigarette ash hanging long, smoke slipping up into her eyes, hair falling over. She would stop, knock off ash and chat with me. The room was warm with hot water and damp soap smell.) I had the tickets for the Actor's Benefit in my bag. Two one-acters with some people in it I knew. It had been a good day. Maybe David would go. I could even try Seltz. Arnold, theater tonight? Two on the aisle, compliments of a producer friend. I won't eat the onion sandwich just for you. We could stop for coffee.

"I'll have a check for you next week."

"That would be good."

"I'm up to my ears in debt. But listen, we talked about that." I got a swift message from outer space, a heart seizure. The I.R.S. man tomorrow, the bank loan due next week.

"We'll work it out," he said.

He probably said it to patient after patient. We'll work it out. Jerry Kay said if I was serious he could work something out for me. He could get me twenty-five dollars a pop. I really could stop working if I wanted to.

I left the building of the shrinks and walked down Eighty-Sixth Street toward Second Avenue. The block between Lex and Third, the Times Square of Yorkville, gives me the willies because I know they know I'm Jewish, and none of us has forgotten a thing. Basically, it's not any different from walking any city street in spring and summer. Either you are so familiar with the streets and the path you take from one place to the next that you walk in a state of forgetfulness, a very internal walk almost as if the sidewalk itself were your bed and the storefronts your family; or they are strange, uncomfortable, curious, in a kind of exotic, nightmarish way. On these streets the faces are blank and hostile or lecherous and the sidewalk presses up against your shoes and you feel the concrete eating away at the leather and behind every store window somebody is waiting to lure you in to break the monotony of their gray, dead lives. The funny thing about Eighty-Sixth Street is the cheery atmosphere of hostility. Everybody is ready to wait on you, rubbing fat hands smoothed by pastry dough, pouring hearty enemy beer into poisonous crockery steins, wrapping your package of wurst under bright fluorescent lights with murder in their obsequious hearts. It is a food street, a grocery, bakery, restaurant-beer-hall street, with the smells from busy open doors spilling out in a blend of aromas, aphrodisiacs, frightening come-ons to partake of the bounty of the German people, who are announcing to all visitors that it was all a mistake, look how clean and healthy and productive we are, try our delicious wiener schnitzel, our sumptuous Dusseldorf torte, our bratwurst, come in young lady, wiping hands on the clean apron, lovely weather we are having, a nice day for the master race, *hein*?

I turned the corner up Second Avenue with my package and stopped at a fruit and vegetable stand for two Spanish onions, a couple of green peppers, and two good-sized cucumbers, very firm to the touch with a good green shine. I knew the owner, Tony Vassario, who had taken over the store when his father had a stroke, and his wife Rose, both young, American-born, waiting every morning for the ice truck to crush two large blocks, dropping three or four wooden buckets of ice onto the sidewalk in front of the shovel-type food scale, then spreading the ice evenly in the trays inside the store, and the two of them, opening crates of celery and lettuce, packing them neatly into the ice, both in long butcher aprons,

packing and joking, the store swept clean, no leaves or anything, like the broom guy in the barbershop next door, always sweeping when I passed, looking up at me with a little
nod of recognition, I didn't know the guy, but we knew
each other, me walking by with a celery stalk sticking out of
the top of my bag, him standing near the barber pole eating
a peach, just around the corner, what was it, three blocks up
Second Avenue, from the Eighty-Sixth Street murderers. Still
it was a life and nobody bothered me, so why should I knock
Eighty-Sixth Street Germans and praise Second Avenue Ital-
ians. Look, the Mafia are no angels. Who was it that ran my
father out of town because he couldn't pay a debt?

The shoe store near Ninetieth Street where I was having
heels put on was run by a Mafia type. I don't know his name,
but he would take my shoes, grunt something about the next
day without giving me a ticket, and disappear into the back.
One day I asked him how business was. I had been coming
there for three years without a peep out of him, and I really
like to dish with neighborhood people. It's my life. I walk
those streets every day. I know every sidewalk crack. He
grunted a "can't complain" in a thick, grubby accent, and
threw a little smile out of that big water buffalo face. He
started to go to the back and stopped, turned toward me.
"I'll put Neolite heels on these. No extra charge." So what
was this Mafia-shmafia, this guy probably had a wife who died
and he lived alone in the back of the store and every day he
would come to the front and dust the showcase with cardboard displays of Cat's Paw heels, and bang nails into shoes,
the nails jutting out of his pursed mouth, hammering his
loneliness into every shoe, nailing himself into my life.

The huge deserted Ruppert brewery covered a square
block between Ninety-Second and Ninety-Third Streets. In
the spring coming from the doctor I sometimes walked down
Ninety-Second from Third Avenue, past the hulls of scavenged cars and through the debris of broken Pepsi bottles.

Pasted on the windowless dingy red brick walls was the clown's face announcing the circus, the old ones from the year before and the year before that and the new one, this year's clown, same as the last, the grinning mouth reminding the empty lot with the cyclone fence across the street that the flying whatevers were going to thrill you with the greatest show on earth. Pints of empty Gallo bottles dotted the gutter, lying flat in their beds alongside the curb. I never saw a broken Gallo bottle, only the Pepsis and the Mission Beverage bottles that the guys drank in the auto body shop, the only business on the street. Everything else had been abandoned years before.

I stood on the corner of Ninety-Third and Second waiting for the light as the cars came galloping down the avenue, matching their speed to the staggered lights. The Ruppert building itself with the name Jacob Ruppert and Sons fixed in stone was an incredible event in Manhattan. It was the fortress of the old neighborhood, defending the seedy, slummy section from the onslaught of the developers. At one time the brewery must have been something, with the trucks rolling in and out, day and night, in the heyday when the Ruppert name meant Yankee Stadium and Babe Ruth. I remember seeing a picture, I think it was in a collection of famous New York people, old Jake and the Babe at a contract signing. But the brewery itself deserved the picture, standing there, a monster warehouse without windows, watched over by the Second Avenue residents, the old ladies and men, and some young ones too who quickly fell into the habits of the old, arms folded on their pillows, leaning out of their windows, watching the army of shining cars charging downtown, speeding away from the gritty smeared streets of Ruppertville. Who could blame them in this age of urban renewal? Over on First Avenue a mammoth low-rent housing project was going up, and the river was there and the Drive, everything closing in on this last piece of decaying uptown. I took comfort from Jake Ruppert's red bricks and dead beer, and I liked the unforbidding laundromats, leave it at nine, pick up at six, with their bundles heaped in the window and the busy lady owner who seemed to take her cheer from the dancing laundry in the machine, and I liked the Greek restaurant on the corner and the newspaper-candy store next to it and all the dumpy little nickel stores on the Avenue. For all its rattiness, the scarred tenements and broken, neglected streets, there was a life going on. Ninety-Third Street, my street, which had exactly three small apartment buildings renovated for people like me, was lined with worn and beaten brownstones, with the usual business of crowded, overcharged Puerto Ricans and a mixture of whites, mainly Lithuanians and Poles, some Irish, a few blacks, all poor and grubbing, with a lot of stoop-sitting and banister-leaning. I was scared plenty at first, the single attractive woman in the rapist's den, but those were my crummy values. I lived on the safest block in the city, aside from breaking and entering, which was a universal problem because of the addicts, but nothing like down in the Tompkins Square area. Whatever it was, it was my street, and when I crossed the Avenue and stepped to my side of the street, my turf, and I caught a glimpse of the sky above the river down the narrow street framed by the iron railings, I felt as if I had come back to my family.

As a matter of fact, across the street from my house was a little mama-and-papa grocery, a real hole-in-the-wall run by a heavy, wheezing Polish Jew who looked like a cross between Khrushchev and Mussolini, and a skinny little wife with rimless glasses, both of them dressed in heavy cardigan sweaters made of iron, with thick close-knit stitches, cutting the butter from the tub, slicing ham, filling the eggbox, the apron flecked with bits of pumpernickel cut from the ten-pound loaf of Moishe's brand that he carried exclusively in the neighborhood, that I was addicted to, except for my diet days. "What's the matter, no Moishe's today? You're a Jewish girl, yes." Most of the time mama and papa, like all the other storekeepers I knew, lived in that world in the box, the store their life, the goods their children, keeping those impossible hours, seven in the morning to midnight, seven days a week, devoted to the milk and the bread and the eggs, the store always rich with warmth, not that they were warm, two *grubenes* my grandmother would say, puting down the vile strain of Jews with some oath or other, but they were there, keeping their little factory going, eking out a living in the old way, throwbacks to a depression style, right here in the middle of flaming New York, where across the street stylish careerists like myself lived in the new mode, the world of pot instead of pot cheese. Every day I bought something, including occasional special items, imported oranges from Israel sold to god knows who, the Spanish families couldn't afford them, but they disappeared, along with a fancy hybrid melon, which he cut open and offered slices from to the customers. "Hello there, girlie," on good days, and on bad he merely nodded in that gross, thick-minded way that is developed by a class manner, cutting across ethnic lines completely. (Once in a great while I would go into the *bodega* around the corner, and peppy as the P.R.'s are, this guy also had the same nod, sullen, unmindful of the customers, a look that protected the cheese and butter in the glass case behind him.) Papa extended a little credit on short money days, threw in an extra slice of this or that, the wife chatted with me about the weather, at which time I played one of my superfavorite roles: Lady X from the town house in that good blend of condescending noncondescension, Princess Margaret visiting the poor orphans. It was in that mood that she broke the sound barrier one day. I was wearing something new, hair washed, and she offered a "have you got a fella," not at all trying to be snoopy, these people really took care of their butter and eggs, but obviously seeing something in me, some drift of pain through the elegance, or the look I sometimes let sneak over me when I'm playing Lady X, furtive, a shadow over me, my mother's desperate eyes in her wedding picture. "You find me a nice one." Taller, I bent over and patted her dusty brown cardigan, assuring her that we shared a common fate as women.

In the apartment I put the stuff away in the refrigerator, undressed, turned on the air conditioner, straightened the bed, and lay down, pulling the sheet over me. Eyes closed, the lids were heavy against my eyeballs, lead weights of fatigue. On shrink days I felt the drain. In the life of the single woman there are spaces, pockets of time filled in by blank-nesses which have a peculiar shape and weight of their own. The one science course I took in college taught me about volume and mass, I remember nothing else, mass of something displaced in a volume of something. And in these periods at home, most often in bed before going off into the half-hour nap, the abstractions contended with the real things. It was volume and mass and shape, snapshots of nothing in my mind's eye, set off by bursts of colored light. You live with that, the silent fireworks in the head, a nothing as palpable as Jerry Kay's selfish prick. Then the lights go out, the mass disappears, the volume collapses, and it is goodbye world for a while.

Helen, Rita, and I are sitting on the stone wall outside the tennis courts. Rita, as usual, is quiet and superior. Janie cannot join the club unless she knows a dirty joke. At ten I know a lot of dirty jokes, but Rita insists on a real joke, not the bathroom and underwear kind. Helen's joke has been accepted and she sides with Rita. They make me sit several feet away while they discuss my fate. School has ended and it is a week before camp for me. Helen and Rita will spend the long summer together at home. I promise to come back with camp stories, with presents, real Indian moccasins, anything they want. First tell us a dirty joke. I try a very old bathroom joke, something about bubbles here, bubbles there, bubbles in the underwear. No underwear jokes, a real joke, they giggle. Rita gets haughty. "If you can't tell us an F-U joke then you can't join the club." We all know the word and we have said it out loud many times, but the club rules forbid the use of words until initiation is over. I try an old joke with fart in it. We giggle. Helen looks at Rita. Rita turns her face away. "That's no good." Helen agrees. "Come on, Jane, a real dirty joke." As usual I feel something creeping inside me which I identify as a wetting-the-pants sign. "Let me into the club and I will buy you something." They are interested. "How much can you spend?" Rita asks, weighing the offer. "Can I get a jewelry box?" Helen, poorer than us, thinks of an immediate purchase. "I can get five dollars if I want to." That brings us together. We plan to spend the five I intend to steal from my mother's purse. "No," Rita suddenly decides, "a dirty joke is the rule. You can't break the rule." "You can't break the rule," I mimic, almost sticking my tongue out, but we are too old for that, too aware of our emerging femininity. In desperation I reach down and pull out the Johnny Fuckfaster joke, about the boy with that last name and the girl who yells at him in warning, "Johnny Fuckfaster," and he answers, "What the hell do you think I am, a locomotive." I am in the club and we sit on the wall in our shorts and sneakers kicking at the wall and telling all the jokes we know, and then Helen asks, "When they fuck do they really put the penis in the vagina?" We all know that is true, but we don't believe it. However, I am the acknowledged master of sex information, my parents of the younger, worldly, faster set. "Of course they do, right in the pee pee hole." Helen is aghast. "That big thing. Doesn't it hurt?" "It doesn't hurt a bit," says the expert. I am aware of the noise in my parents' room and the moans from my mother, not very often lately, because the pain is too much. But we are

confused. If fucking is pain and having babies hurts, why do
so many people want to do it? Once again I am consulted.
"Because it is the will of God." Rita and Helen go to Sunday
School but the will of God is not in their book. I have learned
that from Mary Stella who learns in church that many things
happen because of the will of God. I don't talk sex with Mary,
but the will of God must have something to do with it, else
how can there be so much pleasure with the pain? We discuss
the problem and decide that if you are married you can have
a baby and have fun. The problem gets too weighty, and we
dash for the court to play tennis, my long, skinny legs carrying me ecstatically over the grass and on to the court. I don't
care if my mother thinks that Helen is a mocky because her
father is a nothing butcher, and that Rita is beneath us because her uncle is a house painter. They are my friends. We
are a club, a secret society of three. We dance on to the
court and start to play, Rita and me on one side, Helen on the
other. I am just beginning to play and I am like a starving
bird pecking around in weakness and confusion for the life-
giving crumb. Helen hits vigorously, with confidence. Rita
returns the ball according to her character. She lobs the ball
softly, patting it with the racket in that already delicious
feminine way I am to envy for years to come. I am eager to
please. I lunge at the ball, feeling all the parts going awry.
I miss the ball. We try again. The ball goes off the wood. I
swing over the ball, under the ball. I keep trying, the ball a
dizzy blur in front of me. My father's words are in my ears.
"You have got to fight to get anywhere. Be a fighter." Advice
to a seven-year-old. Be a fighter. Helen's face across the net
is impatient, Rita's is turned up in an annoyed frown. I
swing harder, I swing faster, I miss. Frantic, I set my teeth
and try again, I swing harder, faster, harder, faster. Johnny
Fuckfaster. I flee from the court in tears. As I turn up the
street I glance back and see the ball arcing lazily on the
shadow-speckled court, the two girls moving back and forth

as the popping sound of the ball reaches me a moment after the stroke. I stop and sit on a stone wall in front of a strange house. I will steal ten dollars from my mother, somehow. Five for Rita, five for Helen. I walk along the street to my house thinking about the club, but it is no good. In a very secure recess deep inside me I have a feeling lodged. It tells me that nobody loves me. I pause for a moment, taken by a sudden intense vision of the future, a feeling of knowing something definite and permanent. I will have to buy my way, I will have to pay. I see Rita. Everything will fall to her, the soft, beautiful Rita my father secretly desires. I see Helen. She will push herself into good things with her aggressive innocence. And I, walking along, ten years old, my eyes wet as usual, my bony knees brown with tennis court clay, my skinny arms hanging out of my blouse, I will have to pay. I see that and a wave of bile rises in my throat, sour, choking. When I get home my mother is there, early from the office. Annie, the maid, is gone. "Have a good day at the court?" she calls from the kitchen. I want to run up to my room, but today I am not in the mood for pity. I am a member of the club. Be a fighter. My vision has sustained me. If I am to pay I must prepare to be hard for the world. "O.K., Ma." She looks through the open door of the kitchen, a stunning woman. "Why don't you wash up and come and have a cold drink." Her voice is gentle through the cigarette hoarseness. I look at her in surprise. She has a little space between her teeth and when she smiles the beauty is marred, broken into, and she is something else, like me, somebody who has to pay. I kiss her impulsively and run upstairs to clean up.

Chapter 4

BETTY SNOW had the adjoining apartment on my left. She moved in a year ago with her husband, Lester, a media man for a middle-sized ad agency, one of the upstart outfits with the funny TV ads. Lester was a Jewish boy, educated in the New York system, changed his name when it was still fashionable, married Betty, the daughter of an alcoholic mother and a vague plumbing supply salesman from Pennsylvania, the family nominal Christians. After occupying the apartment for several months, where I would occasionally see them tending their flowerpots and their little piece of garden, both dressed in neat Sunday gardening clothes and drinking Bloody Marys in between plantings, Lester disappeared after a violent quarrel, which Betty later told me was nobody's fault in particular, just the culmination of three years of a mistake, you know, one of those routine cases of Manhattanitis, incompatibility of character and culture, a disease whose only known cause is the pressure cooker of city life, which steams the juice out and leaves only the garbage. This is the way life goes on for all the Snows around town, people picking at the garbage dump of their relationships, rummaging around in the tossed-out parties and movies and theaters and restaurants for something to salvage, wondering after all what the banquet was supposed to be for. And then, separated, sitting around in the apartments of friends on the handsome sofas from Georg Jensen or the found items from the Salvation Army, counting all the broken marriages they know, looking out of sooty windows onto hostile, aimless streets, trying to unearth, with the courage of the second cocktail, the roots of failure, so maybe another little shoot could be planted somewhere and flower again in the face of the heavy odds of the contaminated city atmosphere.

I fixed a drink for Betty and myself, the last of the J&B, two rocks in each old-fashioned glass, poured the whisky, stirred with a finger, clinked glasses, and we heaved a mutual sigh.

"The papers have come through. Lester is giving me rent money. I'm satisfied. He really is a sweet guy."

I would be Dr. Seltz. Time for a little role reversal. "Why the divorce? How many sweet guys do you know?"

"Things weren't really that bad. It's just that we didn't have anything to say to each other. I worried about that when we married. What would we say to each other."

In her black minishift she had one arm propped against the back of the couch, her cheek in her hand, legs curled up. She was twenty-seven, looked twenty-two, a pretty blonde with distracted green eyes, with a good figure and sensational legs. I looked at the legs showing full length from under the high-riding dress. Her twangy Pennsylvania voice ran against her good looks. She was a medical technician in a clinic downtown. She spent her days typing blood samples.

"I know how you feel."

"You do. Jane, do you get that feeling you're turned off, like nothing adds up? You've been around."

I saw the problem right there. Betty was about ten years younger. I was her mentor, her housemother. I liked the role, but that boxed me in.

"Lester didn't give you anything. He kept it for himself. Am I right? You married a spoiled Jewish boy."

"My daddy said he was dependable."

My nap had refreshed me and my skin tone was up. She was talking and I was making plans. That's what the men do.

"Was he dependable in bed?" Up to now we had avoided that topic. Increase the pressure, just a little. I sat on the couch at the other end, my hand propped on the back, like hers. We were bookends. If I kept taking out the books I would have to keep pushing the bookends closer together. A strand of hair fell over her eyes. She didn't brush it back.

"He took care of himself, if you call that dependable."

"He didn't wait for you."

"Jane, you know how it is. I don't like being rushed."

"I wouldn't rush you." I dropped my voice into throaty confidentiality. I was selling black market jewels. Betty swung her legs off the couch and let the dress ride higher. She was giving me a good look at top of stocking and panty girdle. What would my next step be if I were a man? I had enough experience with all kinds.

"Could you freshen this, Jane?"

I took her glass, leaned over and kissed her cheek. Up went the darting green eyes. The kiss might have meant congratulations now that the divorce is final, or isn't it fun to share our agonies over cocktails. I brought back some house label rye sitting on the shelf among the other dregs of bottles. I must have had fifteen bottles of things, mainly cordials and aperitifs, each with an inch or two left. The good stuff disappeared. On the shelf next to my treasured Grand Marnier, which I would bring out when the timing was right, was a box of candy, chocolate-covered cherries lying there since Leo Stein's visit to commemorate the summer day five years before when we sat on his fire escape down in the East Village eating a bag of cherries and spitting the pits out over the railing to the yard below. We kept score, penalties if you hit the railing, points if you cleared it.

"Sit here." I pointed to the high-backed wing chair, a

favorite of my father's that I had had sent down from Waterbury after his death. It was comfortable, red plush, a king's
chair. Betty moved to the chair holding her drink and put
her head back. I stood behind the chair. "I've got a surprise
for you. Close your eyes and relax."

"Jane?"

"Don't worry. Just lean back and relax. Good. Now, open
your mouth as if you were in the dentist's chair. Not too
wide." I was the dentist, soothing and efficient. That's it,
Jane, this will only take a minute, the hands firm and clean
smelling. Don't drill me too hard, doctor. Now, now, the voice
is pitched a fraction higher. It will be over in a minute. Just
open your mouth, not too wide. That's good. And the cold
steel of the drill pressing against the corner of the mouth. I
took a candy from the box and held it close to her mouth.
Eyes closed now, remember, we don't want to lose the surprise. Head bent over the patient who crosses her legs and
tightens her hands on the arms. Sweet breath of whisky as the
faces close in. Remember doctor, only a minute, you nice
doctor, don't hurt me too much. Take it out if it hurts. I
hold the candy an inch from her lips.

"Are you ready?" My voice was music purring over her
clean, fresh skin. My lips were close to her cheek. Tiny waves
of heat moved from cheek to lips, lips to cheek.

"I'm ready." The voice cracked, a tremor moved through
the body.

I slid the chocolate-covered cherry between the good
medium-full lips. "Surprise." She opened her eyes as she bit
into the candy. What did I want to find? The exchange of
looks, eyes that never meet now met, an eye-on collision.

"I didn't know what you were going to do." She couldn't
keep the fright out of the coyness. A scared chick from the
coal country. What could she know about anything? It was
about time. I felt nothing like this with John Ames and
Jerry Kay.

"What did you think I was going to do, put my tongue in your mouth?" I felt fluid moving down below. Either I was peeing or coming in my pants.

"I just didn't know, Jane."

"You wouldn't mind kissing me."

"I just don't know, Jane."

"Would you like to try a kiss?"

"Jane, I think you're rushing me."

"I like you, Betty."

"I like you, Jane."

"Would you like a chocolate-covered cherry?"

"Not right now, thank you."

"I have some good grass. Would you like to turn on?"

"Not right now, thank you."

"I have never touched a woman, Betty."

"What do you want me to do?"

"Close your eyes. I want to give you another cherry."

"All right."

"Here is the cherry."

Our lips met, slightly parted, very dry.

"It's a good cherry."

"Yes, Jane."

"Open your legs just a little."

"I don't think I can do that."

"You don't have to do anything."

"My legs."

"Your beautiful legs. Just a little."

"I can't do that."

"Try. Just a little."

She spread her legs. The skin was creamy above the stocking. Firm, creamy, smooth thighs. I put my lips to the thigh.

"What are you doing?"

"Kissing your thigh."

"Lester will be home soon."

"Lester doesn't live here anymore."

"Lester doesn't live here anymore."

Her legs were stiff and trembling. I stood up and went to the couch. My legs were rubber, my stomach heaving up in my chest. I was hot as a pistol and I was scared to death. Waves of passion and anxiety swept through me. I was a body without will or consciousness. Who was this Jane? Where did this heat and terror come from? Betty was still in her chair, her head back, eyes closed, legs in the same parted position, dress well up above her crotch. A woman. A man. A cunt. A cock. Tits and balls. I swam in a flame of parts. Surely, Dr. Seltz, it is a rationalization, or do I mean sublimation? Surely I am acting out. Isn't that another way of letting go? And I wanted to let go. Who put the Spanish fly in the minestrone? I put my hand on my crotch. It was wet. I was a sea of libidinal juices, a fountain of sensuality. The bologna on pumpernickel wandered into view.

"Would you like a sandwich?"

Betty opened her eyes. The green eyes were glass balls.

"Don't you worry, dear. We ain't done nuthin' yet." What the shit, a little pass is good for the system, increases regularity. Bologna sandwich on cunt, hold the grass. She got up, came over to me, held my cheek between her hands, gave me a whither-now look, and hugged me. I was touched.

"You are a beautiful woman, Jane. You're not afraid of life. I wish I knew what it was all about. I admire you." A peck on the cheek and she was gone. Goodbye, Betty Snow. Next time it is going to pour.

I like sharp knives in the kitchen. At home at Sunday brunch rimming the platter of cream cheese and lox were thinly sliced tomatoes, a series of red wheels that my mother cut with great care. I do not remember a thick slice of tomato or a tomato wedge. Thin, thin, paper-thin. It was the principle of thin roast beef, it tastes better. Thin orange slices were for highballs. Oranges are cut in wedges or eaten whole. Hoffritz has this marvelous array of knives. My choice was the kind that tapers from a broad base to a narrow tip, the chef's quick-chopping knife. The Spanish onion often as big as a grapefruit. The very sharp, broad base of the knife, with one single pushing motion, or at the most two cutting motions, detaches the slice from its parent. It lay on the cutting board, the circles fitting inside each other perfectly. I spread the mayonnaise on a slice of bread, slipped the onion on with a spatula, repeated the operation with the other slice of bread. On each slice I placed three pieces of bologna, then the tomato, thin, then five slices of cucumber, thin. I took the right-hand unit and flipped it quickly on to the left. I poured the warm Pepsi over the cubes in the glass. The soda fizzed quickly to the top. I bent over and vacuumed in the overflow, waited until it settled, and poured more until the glass was full. I brought the works to the table. Ravenous, I took big, full, man-sized bites. Tomorrow, next week perhaps, I would go back on the diet. I secretly understood that any diet I used was simply an excuse to go off it, to have a food binge. And I would diet that way, two or three weeks of pills, or a new gimmick in the latest paperback by doctor somebody, or weight watchers, or *McCall's*; the no-fat diet, the all-protein diet, the meat-only diet, the low-cholesterol diet; waiting like a patient tiger to leap upon a Monday, catch it by surprise with pounds of bacon and cheese and ham and potato salad. And leap off again, slinking into a corner, shamefully licking my chops and vowing starvation, for three days fasting on black coffee for breakfast, yogurt for lunch, bouillon for supper, up and down the roller coaster, eat and starve, a maniac of self-indulgence and self-denial. Once I asked Dr. Seltz if schizoid tendencies could be directly manifested in food habits. It wasn't mere quantity, he observed, but intensity. Oral gratification is of course a kind of infant return, one of Freud's classic stages. Food hunger is love hunger. Seltz might not have said just that, but that was because he had the disadvantages of most professional advice-givers. No experience. Arnold Seltz lived in Riverdale with a family and noise in the house. He says oral gratification but what does he really know about the lonely pickle and the sad celery and the forgotten swiss cheese. I don't keep pets, but if you live alone you must keep something. When I'm hungry I eat two thick sandwiches like some cross-country truck driver, grabbing the terrorized food with his black meaty hands in some Joe's Diner. Who could live in Schrafft's? What kind of life must the single woman have if it is watercress on gluten bread?

I bit into sandwich number two and began to dial David's number. I could have called Stefanie, but she would start vamping at the theater, don't I know Stefanie. Besides she had herself a new guy. I pressed the cutoff button. The Pepsi was pressing against my chest. I let out a loud burp. What the hell, Janie, you only live once. What are you but a burp and a fart in the bigger picture. I dialed the number. Three rings. On the fourth it would be the answering service. The voice on the other end, David's, faggy, the tone of a little girl walking the plank, full of wonder and fright, but behind it that selfishness. Hello, I'm David Astor, come in but don't mess up my life, I want to save it for myself if you don't mind. Fools rush in. I rushed. I had post-pumpernickel hiccups. I swallowed air, held it, burst it out. David, hi, did I tell you that Stefanie is seriously thinking of marrying Howard, her new beau. I'm worried that she is going to leave me at the store with the tax man. I'm seeing him tomorrow, we're supposed to go together, and now she is pulling this crap about a trip, I don't think she means it but she has an absolute penchant for screwing things up. I mean she invented the word irresponsible. Jaystar Productions could be still alive but I couldn't handle her *shtick*, running off with that other guy just when we were ready to put the unit on the road. I love Stefanie, we have great rapport, I know you're busy, I don't want to hold you too long, the thing is I will really be up the ying-yang without her promise to stick with me on the tax settlement. You think I should push to postpone this thing with Howard. Why she picks on sadist types, which he is, I'll never know, she certainly has a gift for self-abuse.

David's voice came back patient, tolerant. You ought to consider dropping the relationship entirely, hasn't Stefanie ultimately tried to use you, Jane? Get her off your back, she is really a bitch, friendship, what is that when you spend your life obliging her all the time. And by the way, could we manage to have some dinner tomorrow night, maybe the Italian place across the street from me. I want to talk about our arrangement. If you come in with me, if we can work out a sensible setup. It would be a blessing. The work is just coming in from all sides. I may have a bite on the *Huck Finn*. Tomorrow night, then.

I think I'm free. I'll meet you at your place for a cocktail. David, I have two freebees tonight for the Ricky Chase revue, Jill Jackson, the girl I used to manage, she's in it. You're not too tired are you (honey)? Not a good night for you. Listen, David, think about the weekend. Maybe we could go out to the island, I can get Stef's car. Ciao.

Ciao. Ciao. Ciao. Six, seven, eight years now. On again off again Finnegan. Ciao David. But no more hysterics, not for this girl. The ball game will be played differently. Last week we had dinner here. I invited him but it is the last. No more operating in the old pattern, "I've got tickets to this or that, let's go." Unless he asks to see me I have no reason to ask him. That is the principle I must operate on. I can do it. It takes a lot out of me and it makes me a little nervous, which is projected to him. We had a long talk the other night on the phone, very open. He was very concerned about my being happy, and I said something about "Well we have to sit down and talk about this business thing" and he said, "I want to see you anyway," which is always his pattern, I've got to push, push, push. And then he said, "But we don't have to keep the two things completely separate." And I said, "Well, we don't," and I said, "Listen, we have no problem, sit back, relax, and enjoy it." I was very strong, but I'm waiting for signs. That is the great thing about David now, he is different. He leads a very interesting life, busy with TV appointments and scheduling his clients for auditions. When he came to New York eight years ago he was a nothing kid from the sticks. It is now a life I want to share. I used to be concerned about what guys he might be seeing, but it's not a world that really threatens me. I know those people, I've been there before, the gay people are no real threat to *me*.

Now I have this new self-concept. He has got to take the initiative with me, I'm not going to be the devouring woman again and go back into the same bag. I am moving into the acting-out stage. If I hold back a little, he has got to wonder where I am a little. I understand it intellectually, and now comes the bit test emotionally. He wants me, he will call me. I will not touch that black box again. It is the simple principle of holding off and I'm going to do it. I will sit right here and eat my bologna or my chicken or my whatever. I am not going to eat my heart out.

I called Pat Seeley and we went down to the theater, the Greenwich Mews on Thirteenth Street, nestled alongside a church on a restaurant-filled block. Pat was a very tall, very lean, very bright girl, a whiz of a script girl, who worked for everybody because she has this marvelous even temperament. We had a funny relationship, the kind you pick up at college, you meet a girl who is not your type at all and the friendship is sustained in a how-the-other-half-lives manner, maintaining a healthy sense of unease, never quite comfortable in the talk but very comforted by the knowledge that you have busted out of parochial relationships. She was good for me, a Monday-night-at-the-movies friend. This time it was a show, a typical revue, speedy little blackouts on Fun City grime and

crime and spoofs on nudity with nude actors spoofing themselves. Pat remarked on how rapidly any kind of new wave
finds itself parodied. And there they were on stage, the men
now, with pants dropped to show hairy asses and the girls
taking off their things, including Jill Jackson, who was a bit
dumpy for naked flesh, but she was a game one with a loud
talent, I could have managed her to the top maybe if we
hadn't had a falling out over a silly summer stock show. The
only person I saw at the theater was Bruce Merz, an assistant
director, who was ready for a show of his own. "Hello there,
Jane." He had a big announcer's voice and made like old
buddy talk, which was in fact true, you couldn't count on a
three-week affair for much more, good style, not afraid of the
pocket, especially a rustic Connecticut restaurant, the Old
Grist Mill or some such name, and a reasonable guy who
made the attempt at least to satisfy the woman, the booming
voice lowered to a tender note, "Are you ready, I'll wait for
you," which of course I wasn't, but it was a good fuck every
time, very conventional, he didn't have busy hands, he was a
visiting salesman, we both knew it, and wondered where the
first flash of heat came from. I could have married Bruce,
what would have been so bad, we were in the theater, he was
a man, I'm not concerned about the size of his thing, just
that he didn't put me down or look for the selfish score, at
least he hid it well, stayed for coffee afterward, gave me
some money, which I took, and who knows I may need him
someday.

After the theater we took the subway uptown and stopped
for coffee in the Greek restaurant near my apartment. We
talked a bit about somebody she had seen at the theater, Pat's
coffee sitting untouched as she shredded a paper napkin. I
admired her hands, long and somewhat bony, good hands for
showing rings.

Pat made long strips of the napkin and twisted each strip
into a ring. We walked out, each wearing a paper napkin

ring. When I got home I put the rings in my jewel box, an inlaid silver affair handed down from my grandmother. When my mother died I inherited the box and the jewelry, mainly pearls, which my mother was a nut about. I got into my nightgown, light cotton baby dolls, it was a pretty warm night, brushed and washed, turned on the Johnny Carson show, got into bed, and promptly fell asleep. When I heard a tapping at the door I snapped out of my doze and found Lou Costello squeaking at Bud Abbott. I went to the door and peeked through my one-way viewer. Richard stood there with his attaché case and red eyes. I undid the door chain, unlocked the two locks, the clicks echoing loudly in the silent hall, and let him in.

I met Richard Doyle in a way I would not recommend to every girl in town, and it certainly wasn't my technique, standing in line waiting for the bus up to Connecticut. When I travel, bus or train, I develop a travel glaze, cultivated by my parents' rules for getting along in the world, number one of which is never talk to strangers in any moving vehicle, my father a big abduction specialist, I think he kept clippings of kidnap-rape incidents. A second rule was, never cross your legs in public, ankles only, legs to one side. They thought maybe I was Princess Shit or something. But here is this guy standing right in front of me, a knockout, the prince half of the team, a living cliché of the handsome Irishman, complete with premature gray hair, twinkling eyes, and that healthy glow of complexion that in fact is whiskey pink. Neat, regular features, almost pretty enough to pass for a fag. He could have made a living as a men's wear model in the Sunday magazine. He started some inane thing about the weather and he maneuvered me into the seat next to him on the bus. He was going up to New Haven on a case, he told me, and what was my calling in life? By this time, of course, the rule book had gone out the window because I was being made a pass at by the best-looking guy I ever met. And I was at the end of nothing, Jaystar having folded and David Astor in hiding once more, and months and months since I split up with Bernie Wasserman. Reeling out spools of charm with the blue, blue eyes very direct, cheerful, this guy had me hooked before we got out of the city limits. Later I got the whole business about the wife and the etcetera. Sitting there in the gathering dark I felt a sweetness, a heavy-scented oil streaming through my body. Could I tell a guy I had met only minutes before that this might be it, that as I was talking a furious hive of activity was going on upstairs, a buzzing nest of fantasy, an end to the crafty men and their destructive relationships, forcing on me their damaged egos, and in its place a honeypot of love, because, I had to face it, Richard, the handsome Irish prince, was a delivery from the gods, popped right into my lap, an incarnation. And incarnate, he was discreetly letting me see the bulge in his crotch in one of these shiny sheer summerweight grays, the bumpy spot shining a little brighter, the bulging pants disturbing the starchy neatness. He was the kind of guy who stayed crisp in wilting New York days, with a smile pasted on his even, glistening teeth. And that is what he has relied on, the charming Irish twinkle teeth, the ingenuousness of his whiskey manners, the guile, the absolute, treacherous guile, like running river water over jagged hull-ripping rocks, behind the manners, guile to keep him afloat, what a discovery to me later, another Jerry Kay in Hibernian clothing, loaded with his needs, spotted all over, underneath the pressed pants, with the sores of selfish, gross, utter need, coming to Jane Castle, the living tube of Unguentine, spread a little Cream of Jane on the need spots and off again, you Jerry Kay, you John Ames, you Richard Doyle, to the good woman in Upper Creepsville for another week or month of lies, licking the Carvel's with your 4-H Club kids, making nice on the suburban lawn. It was a Port Authority bus, Trailways number six hundred forty-two, the driver of the vehicle a Mr. James McInerny, the poipetrator of the crime Mr. Richard Doyle, accused of driving an unregistered, unlicensed, defenseless white female to an early grave.

He walked in past the mess, three different suitcases from three different weekends lying around, both hampers bulging with stacked clothes, and me, exhausted, sticky, my hair stringy. In the year I had known Richard, a year of midnight appearances with crooked tie and glassy eye, and morning departures of the original anal man, making me feel my messiness was a capital crime, a year of frantic bed-straightening, bathroom-cleaning, hair-fixing, chin-waxing, fearful that a misplaced hair would lose me this blue-eyed devil. I made the decision. Let him see that this is the way I am, I have hairy places, I smell, I make gas like everybody else. He grabbed me in the rough, direct, needy way.

"You've been drinking."

"No, not really a lot."

But it was obvious that he had. He held me and began to cry. Boy, he was the biggest crybaby I have ever known. "I certainly didn't mean for it to be like this," he said.

He was beside himself. My big rule from that second was, keep your big mouth shut for once. Let somebody else show his hand before you start anticipating and projecting. To distract him I said, "Why don't you come out to the terrace?" On the terrace he started to cry again. He grabbed me. My next-door neighbor, Charles, who was working on his book, a biography of a minor movie star who fought back, looked out and there was this guy holding on to me for dear life, and sobbing how he missed me, how he didn't know how much he missed me.

An envelope fell out of his pocket. It was addressed to a Mexican law firm. I thought, "She has run off to Mexico and divorced him." No, he was just handling a case for his firm. Richard didn't tell me why he came and I didn't ask, proud of my shut mouth. I got him a glass of water, something to quiet him. He wanted to leave.

"Give me five minutes to get dressed." Screw it. It's a hot night and he's coming in the middle of the night and while I'm very glad to see him I don't have to look like hotsy-totsy from *Harper's Bazaar*. I'll do the best I can, but the important thing was to get him into a cool place, because he was burning up and very distressed.

As we walked over to Third Avenue I felt beautiful. I didn't resent him for a minute. I didn't needle him. It's great for the ego to get the man to come to you. You feel strong enough to do anything. He was leaning on me and I was thrilled. "You know I haven't changed. I've got all the same things wrong with me that you didn't like before." I kept the appeal out of my voice. He walked ahead, mumbling through a clogged nose that I was the best there was.

We found a place on Third Avenue, Rigby's, one of these upper East Side saloon saloons, where they knock the plaster off the wall and put a brick wall there, and it's supposed to be a hippie spot. It's late Monday night, only a couple of people in the place. Behind the bar is a very interesting character by the name of Tony Eagen, an uneducated guy, very handsome, with a lot of class, and he's been around. I dug him. We sat at the bar. Really a very tacky place. And there was a girl there, a twenty-two-year-old from the neighborhood, a real Irish character, a funny chick. Evidently she was Eagen's girl for the evening. Richard was already pretty tanked and when he drinks he gets tense, hostile, the id in the bottle ready to jump out.

Vicki, the girl, was dancing on the bar. And we are sitting there, probably the two classiest people this saloon has ever seen, we're very open, very gregarious. She is up on the bar doing a go-go girl thing like they do in those bird cages, and Richard is trying to get this chick to take off her clothes. He is like a prosecuting attorney pressing his point. Some bad kind of eroticism in him comes out, a fag thing. He kept telling her to take off her sweater, making himself obnoxious. While he was fussing with her, out of the side of his mouth he was carrying on with me, how marvelous it was to be with me. Tony Eagen was very cool about it. He kept serving us the drinks, a Scotch Mist and three or four shots of Scotch for me, doubles for Richard, who was reaching up, not exactly pawing this Vicki, who had a great pair of boobs, touching her, and the jukebox is blasting some fucking rock-and-roll number and the bar lights are shining in front of us, that dim red-orange color that makes you feel drunk even when you're not. And Richard kept this double thing going, fast hands with the dancing girl, and telling me how much he missed me.

"It's at the wildest times that I think about you," he said, intimating that he has had some wild sex scenes in his place in the Village since the separation from his wife. And he intimated about how his good looks gets him into any sack he wants, including some strange ones, meaning who knows maybe a gentleman friend. Mr. AC-DC. Finally reaching up, and succeeding in getting his hand under the sweater and Tony Eagen's fist, like a handcuff around Richard's wrist, you could hear the crunch of the bones, removing it from the offended creature, who never stopped dancing, a vacant smile on her face, probably floating on hash or something.

Then nothing would do but that we would take a drink home with us. So the guy poured a double Scotch and put a piece of wax paper around it, and we walked down the street at three o'clock in the morning with the glass of Scotch.

"Are you going to take me to your house?"

"Yes I am, and you are going to sleep and that will be the end of it."

"You have to get me up very early."

We got in the house, the Scotch dripping out through the wax paper, and he puts it on the night table. I helped him off with his things. Dead drunk he still had the presence to hang up his jacket, fold his pants correctly, neat to the bitter end. And he fell asleep. I was exhausted and I fell asleep right away.

So everybody was sleeping. And I dreamt about him and there was a knife and a cup of blood, a nightmare. I woke and went to the john to pee and look for my aspirin. I heard a terrible crash. I ran back in. He had fallen out of the bed. And he knocked over the drink we paid two dollars for. The stuff was dripping over the night table, the wax paper still on it, drops of Scotch like blood in a Poe story, onto the rug. "Richard, are you all right? Did you have a bad dream?" He never woke up. I helped him back into bed, and he was out again like a light. Shortly after that he woke up and we started to have sex.

Now it is true that I had had a busy day, and my cunt was a little sore from the activity, but when you're in bed with a man you love sweet juices flow down, oil the engine up again. And we went at it. We did everything we had ever done, the entire repertoire. He stayed hard, but he couldn't come.

"I'm uptight."

"Well, you had too much to drink."

"It's not the liquor. I'm just too uptight."

We did a little bit of this and a little bit of that, one from Group A, one from Group B. I licked him a little bit, he's not nearly as big as John Ames or Jerry Kay. He is about the same size as David Astor, who is probably the smallest I've had, which probably accounts for the whole fag problem, in Richard as well as David. And I fall in love with them. He has this thing where we are side by side, with our legs sandwiched, very nice because we can look at each other, and we like to look at each other, it's comfortable and nice. And I did a ride on him like he's never seen, sitting on him, the homestretch of the Kentucky Derby, rocking the horse, shuddering the bed, the headboard squeaking so loud I was sure it got right into Charles's book next door. And he kept saying, "Well, if you would come, I would come" as if he were making a deal in the judge's chambers.

"I don't think I can," I said, but I knew that I was holding back because I wanted to be made love to, and because he was sleepy and boozed up and not really making love to me. Lots of positions, left side, right side, him on top, me on top, dog fashion, if there was a cat position we would have done that too. And he stayed hard, which must go for the longest hard-on in history. Every once in a while he would go soft, and I would suck him a little, looking up, not at him because he isn't like John Ames who puts a premium on looking, and seeing the gray early light in the window, falling on the bed, that beginning-of-creation light, the two lovers on the golf course in *La Notte*. Through all this he was testing me to see if I would still be free with him. Part of it was the rigidness of all the other sex he has had, with people who have to be in exactly the right position or they can't have sex. You could call it the pillow-under-the-ass school, probably from some dumb manual.

So finally, the freedom train arrived, but I wasn't going on board until his signal. He fucked me in the ass. This was the culmination of the hours. Would I let him do it, for the right reasons this time. It was the thing I had objected to before. It was the thing he had used as a whip before, at his own guilt, saying to himself, "Get the jar of vaseline and fuck Janie in the ass." Well, I never said this, but "You go fuck some fag cunt in the ass, not me. On the other hand if you want to fuck me in the ass because that is what people do, men and women, that is O.K." And so I let him because that was the culmination of hours of loving. Maybe you could call it a reward for good behavior. And I liked it, I've always

liked it, even when it hurts, which it does when you haven't
done it much. But John Ames has fucked me in the ass, and
he has a big cock, and I'm loose there, I guess the sphincter
muscles are not so tight after a while. So when Richard gave
it to me up the ass after two hours of fucking without coming,
we were both very excited because we both knew this was it,
exhausted as we were. And he gave me everything he had.
I'm on my knees with my head down on the bed, my big ass
jutting up in his face, very much like the doctor's rectal
examination when he sticks the finger up, except that the
dick doesn't move around like the finger. He entered me without trouble, no vaseline, which might have made him suspicious. John Ames hadn't done that in the morning so I felt
free of worry, Richard saying, "Somebody else has been
fucking you in the ass" in the tone of father bear, but he
didn't. I don't know what I like about it, but the dick up the
ass allows for a certain freedom to use his hands, which he
does, moving them around my breasts. I have good ample
ones with big nipples, Janie Cow. And the hand along the
belly, and fingering the pubic hair, working the hand down
around and in the cunt, timing it I think to give me a clitoral
come when he comes. And best of all is the feel of his body
against my ass, and the dick up, up in there, and maybe he
wraps his arms around my body as if he were a little boy again
asking his mommy for a piggyback ride.

I think there is a dependency in it, in addition to the other
thing, the fag thing, and there is very definitely the eroticism
coming from the sense of perversion. It is in one sense purely
an erotic act, very impersonal, a long hard thing into an
animal hole, and in another sense it is an act of gratefulness,
see you are letting me do this to you, how vulnerable you are,
how you are letting me victimize you. And with Richard this
long night, the sex was beautiful in that the eroticism was
out in the open, we were operating on the same level. He
wasn't trying to hide his desires and I was throwing my ass

in his face like I knew what to do all along, come on baby, shove it to me, I can take it. And we had the feeling of love, a very strong love operation. He kept shaking his head and saying, "Incredible," all the booze out of him, the mask off and his body next to mine, pliant, yielding, the flesh opaque and slack, all the Irish vanity washed out of him, and a small, sliding delicious feeling of love in me, seeing him vulnerable. What we like to see best is the vulnerability, so we can lick around it.

We dressed and had a glass of juice to chase the wool out of the mouth, but it would need major surgery to hide the puffy eyes and the chalky look. But I didn't care. He had come to me out of need and gave me love in the idle, wasted hours. So what if he was a handsome, drunken Irishman, with a Jewish wife and two kids, who knocked down doors in the middle of the night for a bang and some tenderness. He wants that, I'll give it to him. How much different is he from David Astor, both unable to sustain anything, both basically hostile to women, and they can take a woman for just so long. And those are the kind of men I fall in love with. Bullshit. The new day has come.

So we left the house. There was a big downpour. We walked down Second Avenue in the heavy rain. He used my umbrella which meant nothing, so we got wet a little and we talked nonsense. And then he said goodbye, and I said goodbye, and I said not a word of "Will I see you again." I did not ask. Of course he said nothing. I said nothing. And at that moment I felt absolutely no compulsion to get in touch with him ever again.

Part II

Chapter 1

FROBISH CO.
Forged and Seamless Welding Pipe Fittings
Large Diameter Flanges—Welding Necks
Weldless Rolled Rings—All Contours and Sizes
CUDAHY, WISCONSIN

Sunday, January 23, 1955

"No man is an island
entire unto himself."

Dear Jane,

I was very happy to receive your letter even though it was
not a pleasant one to write. Darling, I know it is difficult to
make a decision when sacrifices are concerned and I don't
want you to feel our love is forgotten. I love you very much
but I won't stand in the way when it is the moral considera-
tion to be with your father.

I've been moping around today like a lost dog—who lost
his favorite bone! When I look at the postcard of the Tip
Top Tap I get all warm and soft inside. When you mention
that word *Sex* I go into a spasm of pure ecstasy—nearly anyway. You have the knack of appealing to me so much I can't
think straight for wanting to caress you. Yummmm! Here,
here, get off that subject boy, or you'll be in a sweat without
anyone to relieve the agony.

You know, hon, I don't fall in love easily, as witnessed

by those trying times we had early; conversely, I don't fall *out* of love easily. Kinsey says it takes a man 6 mos. to forget a woman and it takes a woman about 3 mos. to forget a man. I fully intend to keep our love alive as long as you'll have it. There may be obstacles, such as the Jewish acceptance of our marriage. Did you think I was blind—your ritual is important to you. But I remember a conversation when you said, "There is only one God, how you worship is unimportant." This reminds me of a time back in old '49. I was about to marry a Detroit gal, but at the last minute she changed her mind about religion. Her mother's return to Catholicism on the deathbed was so impressed on the girl's mind that in the final analysis she figured she would not quit her ritual. Jane, if there is anything similar in your plight to the above-mentioned, tell me. I want the tooth, the whole tooth, and nothing but the tooth, said the lawyer to the dentist.

Going to close now, have to do some reading on Magnetic Iron. You know, "Joe knows," I'll have to tell them someday. Hurry back as soon as you can.

Yours alone,
Dale

Cudahy, Wisconsin. November 1954. Cudahy is a small suburb of Milwaukee and one mile from the Milwaukee Airport. Airport traffic goes through but it is a small town. The big industry is the meat-packing plant. On certain days the smell from the slaughterhouse beef hangs like vomit over the town. Cudahy is connected by regular trolley service to Milwaukee. On the corner where the trolley arrives from the city stands a brand-new library building. I am the assistant librarian to a dumpy lady who keeps other dumpy ladies posted on the latest best sellers. It is the year of *The Egyptian* and *The Power of Positive Thinking*. It is my first job after I have graduated from the university. I live in a rented room in a house with a very strange lady who talks a lot. The room has a back stairway which I sneak up to. I want to avoid the talking lady. At first on weekends I take the bus and run up to Madison to see Jonathan, dragging the tail end of four years in the dust of our relationship. It is almost over, and we both want out, but in my terrific isolation I cling. Occasionally I take the trolley to Milwaukee and look for good restaurants I can't afford and shop for clothes I don't need. It does not occur to me to go to a temple in Milwaukee on a Friday night. "If you're living out of town in a strange place, go to the *shul*. You will find there your own kind."

Instead of a temple I begin to frequent a restaurant not far from the library called Wendt's, which has a bar and a regular dining room. Every evening after work I go to Wendt's and sit at a little table for two with a red-checkered cloth and eat the ninety-nine-cent blue plate special, soup du jour, tossed salad, chopped sirloin or salisbury steak. Occasionally I have a cocktail and stare out the window through the matching red-checkered curtains and wonder about the immediate future. I have taken the library job in order to prove to my parents that I am free and brave and independent, that I must be close to Madison and Jonathan, that I must resolve once and for all where we stand. In the month at home before my return west my parents and I fight every day. Why, they argue, can't I settle down at home and find someone here, meaning, don't marry the gentile, and saying it too, "If you marry a goy, there will only be heartache," my mother's own heartache visible on her nicotine fingers, and strained face, only two months before the final strain and the overdose. And flight, the zooming westward out of the black night of the Hartford airport and dropped into the blacker night of Milwaukee into the single upstairs room and the shiny new library to catalog and order the tasteless books for the stiff-faced Lutherans with their wire glasses.

And the voices of the restaurant, hello George and Mac and Myrtle, how's Bill and Bob and Glenda, voices jovial and joyless, eyes furtive, glancing at the girl with mousy hair and harlequin glasses drinking a cocktail all alone in the dining room like some person from the East, probably a New Yorker, she's over at the library with Miss Hazel. And the way I am dressed. A shopping spree to Milwaukee, a getting-even-with-my-parents spree, an-I-need-to-feel-good-so-I'll-buy-spree-at The Boston Store. I light a cigarette, another Eastern danger signal, but Wendt's is a bit faster than most places in town, so O.K. we're sophisticated people here, and sip the drink and send the cigarette smoke out in a thin jet stream, my head tilted up in my version of sangfroid. My outfit is a purple tweed suit with a long skirt and long jacket with a peter pan collar, a very tailored job, and I wear gunmetal gray metallic sling-back high-heeled open-toed pumps, which I change into, leaving in the library the sensible low-heeled square-toed grandma shoes favored by librarians.

One day, in the very same outfit, I stop at the bar and Pop Wendt asks me if I would like to eat in a booth near the bar, not usually recommended, I understand later, to unescorted females, but seeing that I have become a regular I might like the change. So I change to the bar and smoke my cigarette and drink my drink and think the usual thoughts of a solitary person in an out-of-the-way place. When will the package arrive, when does the telegram come, when will the discovery be made, when will I taste all the riches of success, what kind of Hollywood will I be welcomed to, dissolved out of the gray bleak reaches of this impossible country. Will Pop Wendt's be the Schwab's drugstore? Is there not the agent who will spot the beauty of this Lana Turner? Say, why don't you drop down to my office, here's my card, I've been looking for you.

A second martini appears in front of me. It is followed by a man in a business suit. He is young, a face I have seen at the bar as I pass into the dining room.

"May I join you? Martinis like it when they have friends." He waits with grinning expectancy. I look at the drink and

I look at him. He doesn't wait for a signal and slips into the seat opposite me. He is smooth and pleasant, a bland voice, the kind I imagine m.c.'s the weekly Rotary luncheon that is a big event in Cudahy. He tells me his name is Dale Albright and that he is assistant purchasing manager for Frobish, he is a regular here, and he has been looking at me for days and I did look just the slightest bit lonely. I notice that his nose is a little red around the edges and the eyes are set together too close, a little beady, breaking up the featureless good looks. I sip my second drink and I am a little loose.

"Do you always have an eye out for lonely girls in restaurants?"

"When they look like you do."

"It's a very nice place you have here."

"Best place in town. They don't make them any better than Pop Wendt. Right, Pop." He calls to the bald man behind the bar who is drawing a beer for another businessman type. "Right," Pop calls back, not having heard the remark.

"He is very nice to me," I offer. At twenty-three I am new at the game of pickup, uncertain of the right tone to strike. I want to be a proper lady, and I rely on banalities to get me through. Dale gets up, goes to the jukebox and puts in a coin. The lights begin to move. He returns.

"One of my favorites." It is the McGuire sisters. Mr. Sandman, send me your dreams. He sings along off key, attempting a more intimate look, slight, but I catch it. I am very much out of practice. On my trip home last month I date Jerry Kay and a boy from New Haven, a big redhead named Bruce. Apart from that it has been only Jonathan all through college. We eat dinner and he suggests a roadside dance place I have seen but pass by as being too vulgar. It has large irregular chunks of colored marble pressed randomly into the concrete. Montero's, the light glows steadily in the Wisconsin sky. We go in and sit at a table near the dance floor. On weekday nights it is quiet and the three-piece band fills in for the big weekend crowd. Dale orders two rye and gingers, the band plays "Three Coins in the Fountain." Dale is a very good dancer. I can demonstrate my father's teaching. We try everything including a tango, our faces pressed together in that serious, studied way we have learned from the movies. Jea-lou-sy, why did you pee on me, da dum da da dum. . . .

"Jane, you're a swell dancer." We are in a fox-trot and he holds me close but not tight. I appreciate that he is not a grabber.

"You're not so bad yourself." I think I remember the line from a movie with a tough girl role, Gloria Grahame maybe, saying, "Hey, mister, you're not a bad egg." Then he takes her up to his room, smashes her around. Usually we see her in her slip in front of a cracked mirror, crying. Mr. Sandman, send me your dreams. We smile at each other.

"They're playing our song." He is not a bad guy, a sense of humor, pays attention to the amenities. I am very sensitive about the amenities. I am thinking about the proper behavior when we leave Montero's.

"A penny for your thoughts." Dale's warm, eager face is close to mine.

I let out the coquette in me. "That's for me to know and you to find out." He clutches me tighter, but I ease myself away, feeling his hard pants pressing into my skirt. I resolve to give him nothing more than an outside feel. The drinks have settled in. I feel sexy.

"Let's go someplace and find out."

In the car he drives leisurely, one hand casually on the wheel, the other draped over the seat. We sit close enough for leg to brush leg. The radio sifts out lush strings. The November moon is a suspended white ball. The road sign says, "Kenosha, 20 mi."

"That's my hometown," Dale says.

I see other signs, Racine, Waukegan. "Isn't Waukegan. . . ."

"Jack Benny's hometown. Lake Forest is something." He points to Lake Michigan on our left. "That's what I want, a place on the shore."

"I've always dreamed about that."

"Maybe Mr. Sandman will send you your dreams."

In the lovers' lane we neck. His breath has a nice smell of whiskey and I open my mouth a little to his insistent tongue. I push away the hand that has fallen on my leg, but my touch is firm, not punishing.

"I don't think so," I say, feeling the remark foolish.

"You're right," he says. He tries again, resting his hand on the outside, pressing the tweed against my skin. I push away again.

"What exactly do you have in mind?" I turn on my hard, saucy manner, Anne Dvorak as Belle whatever.

"You did come for a ride."

I feel good, but a little scared. The plaintive note satisfies me, but men can change, get wild with desire. They snarl or they breathe very hard, get resentful, how can you cause such suffering, such pain. Bruce from New Haven gave me that, the crucified note, a nice handsome redhead with the world in front of him reduced to agony, until the inevitable passion spread through me like a virus, and I let him do it, big with red-haired balls, popping his damned madness into the vessel. I am the vessel. A receptacle.

"Not tonight." Satisfied with the promise of future reward, he drives me home. We find out that he is living down the street. I feel an involuntary jerk of excitement, down the block, an apartment, the lover's bed, breakfast, the movies. We stand in the dark recess of my back door entrance and we kiss. He starts to move against me and I know he wants to come, but I stop him and send him home. I hear the car grinding explosively, not angrily, and then leap away from the curb.

Upstairs I undress lazily. There is heat in my body. I lie

on the bed with the yellow night table light burning under the waxy-looking shade, and run my hand along my leg and around my hair and then a finger inside. I have a mirror which I prop up in front of me and watch myself in action, my counterpart in the glass, legs spread and drawn up, hand working in the hairy mass, and I try to think of a man, but I can only watch the girl in the mirror fulfilling the absurd need, all so ungainly, grotesque, laughable. I am hot, hot, god am I hot, the heat shimmering out of my cunt, and the release, and I fall back and stare at the shadow the light has cast on the ceiling. I am overwhelmingly aware that I am nowhere and alone.

I soon discover we have an illicit relationship. He has a girl, Wanda, and they are on the brink of marriage. I am a home wrecker, he tells me, a femme fatale. And there is the Jewish question. On the second date we meet at the restaurant and we drive directly after dinner, the amenities dispensed with, to the lovers' lane, the Wisconsin moon this time a bite of white in the sky, and he fucks me quickly. I am unable to tease, to hold off, to jockey and maneuver and manipulate and drive them wild, wild, what do they do, these women who hook their men, but zipper the pussy and get the ring. I am only worried that in his excitement he will come over my dress before he puts it in. (In the 1948 green Olds Jerry Kay and me in the front seat, Helen and Cliff Wilson in the back, Jerry's enormous, violent prick all the way up me, my left leg hooked over the back seat, almost kicking Cliff in the head. My bobby socks are rolled down. Helen tells me years later that she didn't know what we were doing in front.) We share a cigarette in the dark. In a car some yards away we see the red glow of somebody else's cigarette. Is it before or after? Dale asks me about my life, and I see that, spent from sex, he is still interested. Heartened, I blurt out a good deal, not everything. I am thinking of the men I have known, and my nose, which I decide to keep a secret.

"I never went out with a Jew before."

"Are we any diffrent?"

"What do you mean?"

"You know, down there."

He has thrown his rubber, wrapped in my tissue, into the bushes. Zippered straightened, and combed, he is a rooster. I can see he is proud of his score.

"You are tremendous, Jane."

"Now you can say one of your best friends is Jewish."

"At Frobish we have one, Henry—"

"Forget it."

We are always alone. He picks me up in front of my place now, and we drive to roadside places on the lake drive and we drink and we dance. We go to a motel attached to a tavern and we screw. He takes me to the Allerton Hotel in Chicago one weekend. In the hotel dining room with waiters in monkey suits hovering over us, dishing out stuff from gleaming silver tureens, we sit opposite each other rigidly, like visiting firemen from the boondocks. I am wearing a black cocktail dress much too old for me, a hand-me-down from my Aunt Claire. He is bossy to the waiter who drowns him with ironic politeness. We have gone too far from Pop Wendt's. On the way up to our room, Mr. and Mrs. Martin, he is sharp with me about my dress, my hair. The sex is bad and we fight. We drive back along the shore in silence on a treacherous, icy road. The relationship becomes rocky. We even argue about politics. He likes Ike, I think Ike is a dope.

"You New Yorkers are all alike."

"I'm not from New York. I'm from Connecticut."

"It's the same difference."

"You want to get into my box, that's what you want."

"You *are* vulgar, aren't you."

But we continue because he wants to fuck and I, I can't stand the little room, I can't stand the library, I can't stand the grubby little town with the odor of dead meat sifting into your gut. We go out New Year's Eve, alone, to a place called the Tip Top Tap and we drink a lot. On the dance floor with the boob hats and streamers dripping over us we lock together and move like drugged marionettes around the floor. I think of Jonathan, and Dale slips and calls me Wanda. In the bedroom we sit on the edge of the bed naked and drunk. Outside our window the neon sign flashes on and off, Tip Top Tap . . . Tip Top Tap. The red light splashes into the room and I mumble through my tears that nobody loves me. Dale lurches to the bathroom, throws up in the toilet and falls asleep on his knees, his head resting on the toilet seat. I sit in an armchair near the window, my legs propped on the sill and watch the lights. Downstairs I hear the band playing good night ladies. The steam heat from the radiator hisses in the corner and I pass out in my chair.

Sunday, March 13, 1955

"Be ye the master of your faith
And the captain of your soul."
—Longfellow

Dear Jane,

My letter may not come as too much of a surprise to you, but I did want to explain why I have accepted this proposed way of life. I tried, in every way, to get you to say that you and I would be married regardless of your mother's death. In my attempts I wanted some idea of how long I would have to wait for you. And you held back that encouragement which I seeked, to tell me it was worthwhile. I called you on Monday night asking for some insight into your reasons for not making plans for us. Wanda asked me on the following Friday how I felt about a May wedding. Jane dear, I couldn't continue living in a state of doubt as to your intentions. I feel that you accepted the martyr position, out of love and devotion to your parents.

Fortunately for me, I had Wanda to fall back on so that my outlook is not shattered. She wants me now, very much, thanks to the real competition from you. Plans for the wedding are all cast. Church in Kenosha, reception in the Women's Club, best man is my brother, ushers, catering, singer, organist, etc. is all set. It will be a 3/4 white ballerina, white jacket wedding. All I can say is, "What happened. . . ." Wanda is not letting any grass grow, that's for sure. It's not right for me to write complete details about a marriage to someone else, but I hope you understand why I am resigning to my present circumstances. And don't make any buts—she is not pregnant. I don't have any idea how our first experience will be. She has passion and we will be happy, Jane. It's a stable life and I always wanted one, deep down. I chased Wanda for six years more or less. When I was ready for marriage you appeared and thoroughly confused my schedule.

Forgive me Jane, if I have disappointed you. I will think of you tenderly and hope that you have some luck, especially in your hour of need. And tell your father he is a man now, that you have a right to live separately from him. Listen to the line from Longfellow. I don't know much about poetry, but this feeling is a true one. Take courage, be the master of your own faith.

My good wishes for your future, in whatever you do. The gang at Wendt's says hello and wish you the very best.

Lovingly,
Dale

P.S. I've made the break from Frobish and will go in with Taylor in a week. He is the biggest pipe man in the region.

Chapter 2

THE FEDERAL OFFICE BUILDING at 250 Church Street was another one of those anonymous concrete boxes designed to punish the civil service workers. The penitentiary architecture had a double effect: It frightened the people going in on business and it made the employees prison guard sadists. Trapped by their own choice, they were worse than jailbirds. Another feature of the civil service style is the Eichmann mentality. When the guy in that box grabs you and you are cut and bleeding and you plead for mercy, he sticks the knife in a little deeper, shrugs innocently, and says, "But I only work here. I carry out orders." At Church Street they act like the guys who draw your beer on Eighty-Sixth Street. They click their heels, bow at the waist, and deliver the poison brew with the moral scruples of a water rat.

I met Stefanie in front of the building at five of nine and we took the elevator to the Group Eight Section, Internal Revenue Service, eighth floor. Some joker in somebody's administration shoved in that service euphemism. At your service. Zonk. At your service in a steel-partitioned glass-topped cubicle was Morton Katz, IRS man.

"How do you do, Mr. Katz," we chorused.

Katz was a smallish man with a smallish hook in his nose, a smallish moustache, horn-rimmed glasses, nice black hair, only promising to thin out. A pipe and a smallish smile went with the package.

"Spelled Katz. Pronounced K-A-Y-T-Z, as in dates." He turned to the folder on his desk. "Mrs. Fedder, Miss Castle. We have here our forms, your 1060A for corporate income, your J-form for personal liability, and your 1000-XL financial statement. Since you are filing a personal bankruptcy statement we can forgo your TF-101 assets statement, which we can take care of in the provisional section of the 1060A. Personal liquid assets, up to twenty-five percent of the adjusted gross income, are of course protected under the rider clause in your 1000-XL." He removed some forms from the folder, placed them on the desk, and folded his hands on top of them. He wore a white shirt, sleeves rolled up to mid-forearm. A gold band circled a tufted finger.

"You know what the figure is, I presume."

I waited for Stefanie. She had a good, throaty, businessy way about her. "Mr. Katz, we came down here to straighten our affairs. This thing is hanging over our heads."

"The figure is fifteen thousand dollars. You girls really tied one on."

"Drank it to the bottom, Mr. Katz," I said.

"Kaytz," he said.

Stefanie shot me a trouble signal. Cool it.

"We're looking for a good lawyer we can afford," I said.

"Fifteen thousand dollars. That's a lot of shellac," he said.

I had heard these guys were man-eaters. He looked like pie. "We intend to pay every penny, Mr. Katz," Stefanie said. He pushed one of the forms toward us.

"The J-form is kind of a promissory note. You understand that you are personally responsible for the failure to withhold the tax of the employees of Jaystar Productions, Inc. The place for the signature is at the bottom of the form where the X is."

Stefanie and I leaned over and looked at the form, without

touching it. It might have been a hand grenade. "I don't think we can do that," I said.

"We would like to consult a lawyer first," Stefanie said.

Katz picked it up and shrugged. "The lawyer will tell you that you must sign the J-form. It declares your indebtedness, but it acts as a waiver against. . . . I don't want to use upsetting language. You girls have played in the big leagues."

"Against what?" testy Jane popped out.

"Criminal negligence."

"Gee, Mr. Katz," Stefanie said.

"It is, after all, something like stealing money." He shook his neat black-haired head. "Fifteen thou. That's a caper."

"You've been watching television shows, Mr. Katz," I said.

"That's a lot of varnish, Miss Castle." He took off his glasses, breathed into each lens separately with a short hah, and wiped with a handkerchief.

Sober Stef offered a tissue. "We'll take the forms home and study them. I don't think we can sign anything today. Don't you agree, Mr. Katz?"

He put the glasses on and leaned back, arms behind his head. "Ladies, we live in a world of forms. Without form we are, so to speak, formless, eh. In the beginnning the world was without form and void." He leaned forward. "You should see my wife."

"We have outstanding notes. I have people I want to pay back," I said.

"They paint these interiors green, apple green," Katz said. "It is better than prison gray." He put the folders in a manila envelope and handed the envelope to Stefanie. "All right, outstanding notes. Maybe we can work something out. I am responsible for a region. I'm Morton Katz, Assistant Director, New York County, East Side Region. I can make deals. You have a list?"

"Mr. Katz, I believe in loyalty. We have people who went down the line with us."

"We can study the forms at home," Stefanie said.

On a sheet of paper Katz wrote at the top: Jaystar Productions. Notes Outstanding. "Shall we start with the largest debt?"

"I can't give you any first names, Mr. Katz. I have to protect my people. You might start running them down. You understand my predicament. We put two hard long years in getting that package on the road."

"Tzvai meshugenahs," Stefanie said.

"Girls, I have a busy day."

So I rattled off the list: Mr. Miles $5,000; Mr. Levitsky $1,000; Mr. Gordon $1,500; Mr. McNeil $500; and so on, and he scrawled in a neat accountant's hand, trailing down the page names like a list of war dead posted in my heart, a battleship of names swamped in a tidal wave of dollars, the maniac phone leaping in my sweating hand, the cab rides to this one and that one, my voice cracking with earnestness, but cool, we've got a winner here Mr. Miles, I've got contracts for a quarter of a million already, they're eating us up in the west, and the miraculous check for $5,000 from a total stranger, *chutzpah*, they'll have to invent a new word for it. The trip to Waterbury, borrowing against my grandmother's will, Tom Bayer $2,500 against the will, Jack Weingarten $2,500 against the will, Sid Levitsky, coexecutor of the will, $1,500; and Adrian Foster, whose father owned the Graybar Building, whom I had been friendly with, a dilettante playwright, $165 for my rent one month, my Aunt Claire $165 for my rent another month. In one week I borrowed $200 from Noni Fay, just before she broke with her husband, $300 from Bernie Wasserman, we were already finished with the affair, guilt money for sure, Lenore Wein $100, Michael Bean $100, and he made me suck his dick, my friend Michael Bean, and Vince Padilla, from Gulf, doing the industrials, and Gene Warner $1,000, he needed a tax loss, and Viola Savage, ready to go into the hospital to have a breast removed, no, it was a hysterectomy, Lila Waxman had the breast removed, $50 from her for food one week. And like the rock of Gibraltar, Gene Gordon, $100 here, $100 there, Gene, Gene, I'm uptight, $500 toward the end, not counting the $500 for the abortion.

"Is that it?" Katz stopped writing.

"That's a lot of house paint, Mr. Katz."

"Don't forget my ten thousand, cold cash," Stefanie said.

And $2,000 from my father's will, the last bitter legacy, disappearing in one month, a dead man's money that would give me life. Sam Castle, I was going to dance on your grave, Jane Castle of Jaystar, another Jean Dalrymple, a Cheryl Crawford, two more thousand for that score.

Katz glanced at his watch, but he had one more thought. "What were you doing with this outfit? Off the record, you understand."

A little oil on troubled waters. Stefanie began the tale for the regional director. "The plan was simple, the idea was good, the acts were right. Hit the college towns with a package of four entertainments. Buy the package for $5,000. Who did we have? Jane, who did we have?"

"We had the Korchnoi mime group, authentic White Russians. Hung around the Russian Tea Room. Knew all the Serges in town. Could outmime Barrault."

"And the black gospel lady, Sister Maybelle Turner." Stefanie shook her head. "Mr. Katz, Sister Maybelle, she could blow the house down with her voice."

"And she took a cut, a big one, when the bookings weren't coming through. Sister Maybelle is a real domestic. She wants carfare and all that."

"There was the Shakespeare Portfolio Group. They had these big lecterns and they sat on stools, in modern dress, and they read from these big black reader's theater notebooks. House lights, footlights, spots, the works."

"The big nut, the real problem was the Composers' Revue.

Very good stuff, the best from Berlin to Rodgers and Hart, Cole Porter, the works. But six prima donnas like you wouldn't believe. That was our big mistake."

Stefanie hacked out a heavy smoker's cough. "Are you going to begin with our big mistakes? Jane, the man hasn't the time."

Katz rose and shook hands. His hand felt as if the flesh had been wrapped around an armature. I could feel the wires. Tough little Morty Katz from the Bronx, with a wife who has run to fat. For goodness sake I could reduce the debt, maybe wipe it out. Have him over for dinner. In the coffee shop across the street I put the question to Stefanie.

"No good, Jane. Tampering with federal property. I don't trust 250-Church people. Saul had a little run-in with the feds some years ago. They were polite as hell, but they gunned for him."

Saul Fedder was Stefanie's ex-husband, who produced big shows for summer crowds. He was doing the August Shea Stadium rock-and-pop festival starring you name it.

"We could give him some wine, cheese and crackers. We can't pay the man what he wants. Give him an opportunity to lose the evidence. What's fifteen thou to the big, rich government."

We ordered fresh, good-looking Danish with our coffee, a cheese for Stef, almond paste for me. She was on her fifth or sixth cigarette, just like my mother, the perennial butt in her fingers. "He'll hound you," she said. "They tried to collect a small back-income debt from Howard, and they got him, something like $190, which he didn't have at the time. The man never let up."

"Who do they think Howard is, Joe Louis? Stef, I can't take this shit. I'm getting too old. Maybe Howard knows somebody."

"Maybe Richard could help us? You got yourself a nice Irish lawyer."

"I had. I have to tell you about last night. Richard rang the bell at midnight. It's been months."

"You slammed the door in his face."

"Baby, I let him in. What would you do with Howard?" Howard Milman was a staff musician for NBC, who always had ideas for big shows, a very scrupulous guy, who ended up in the back row because he was too careful. He was careful enough to manage a wife and kids in Connecticut and Stefanie in the city. Howard was working with David Astor on the *Huck Finn*. They were a good team, except that the thing was going a half a mile an hour. The romance with Stefanie had been carefully arranged. Introduction by ex, Saul, Stef and Saul's breakup a classic of goodwill, no hard feelings, right. Howard kept his cello in Stef's apartment because she was closer to the studio. He also was trying to work out his marriage and the shrink was eating up his money. Still he gave a thousand to Jaystar without too much urging from Stefanie, a decent guy when he controlled his sadism.

"I've been trying to work this thing out with Howard and Dan. I'm such a schmuck. That's what you and I have in common, be good to everybody. Dan is such a baby, he's not even thirty, acts twenty. But I have it for creative people, I must be around creative people. My mother said to me when I married Saul, 'You're marrying trouble with a capital T.' "

"Saul is creative?"

"The way your Bernie was creative."

"I never said Bernie was creative. He knows how to work around the theater. I've done that. I'm not creative."

"Creative people have a special view. They have the artist's ethic. Dan comes down from Woodstock on weekends, paint on his arms and in his eyes, good long hair and a sweet manner. I feel good with him."

"So what happened?"

"Howard you know goes home to wife on weekends. I've been living on a tightrope and I don't know how to get off.

Friday Howard is off. Friday night the Woodstock Wonder
appears, with his dungarees and his guitar. Sometimes it is
that close. I'm a one-man woman, Jane. How did this
happen?"

"You want it to happen."

"It happened. Howard has been suspecting something. Dan
must have left an old sock around. Howard smells him. Howard takes the morning train in from Wilton, the financier's
special, and usually goes directly to work. I fix Monday dinner for him. Sunday night I get a call. 'I have to get my cello.
I have to take it down to have it fixed, right now.' It's Sunday night I tell him. 'Where are you going to fix your cello
on Sunday night?' 'I have to get my cello right now to have
it fixed tomorrow morning.' Dan is sleeping. I could have
got him out of bed but I didn't."

"You structured it, Miss Masochist."

"Jane, I'm coming apart at the seams. I feel the skin sepa-
rating."

"So Howard Hero shows up."

"I let him in, and I said, 'There's your cello in the closet.'
But he has to go to the bathroom. Now you know my place,
in order to get to the bathroom you have to go through the
bedroom."

"And the Woodstock Wonder is in the bedroom."

"Hiding under the covers. Would you believe it. Howard
starts for the bathroom. 'You can't go in there,' I tell him.
He gives me a murderous look and whacks me in the face."

"I don't see anything."

"An open hand, across the cheek."

"And Dan leaped out of the bed and socked him."

"Are you kidding? He was a mummy. Howard might break
Dan's painting hand. He took his cello and walked out."

"Sunday night."

"Right. Last night he called, and I tell him about Dan. I
don't care about Dan, so why am I sleeping with him?"

"Why are you sleeping with him?"

"He's single at least. Howard will go on forever with that woman."

"So it's splitsville."

"You don't know Howard. He wants to go away with me for a couple of days, patch it up. That man loves me, Jane."

"Stef, he needs a place for his cello."

Stefanie hopped into a cab to get to a recording date with Sister Maybelle, who with the loyalty of the domestic had kept Stef as her personal manager after Jaystar folded in '67. On the E train going back to Newmark's office I looked at the ads in the car. One of them said come to the park for a summer under the stars with the stars, Peggy Reese's name down at the bottom under the weight of Tony Bennett, Ella Fitzgerald, and the rest. She had quit the Jaystar tour to have a baby, the beginning and the end of the company. What had gone wrong?

I was making $140 a week with Barnett in 1965, plus very nice bonuses a couple of times a year, one of the best agencies in town, they had properties from way back, practically a shrine for the musical comedy field. But it wasn't enough for me to be a glorified secretary, plus I wasn't able to live on it. I have a bad sense of the dollar. I needed more money and I started doing things on the side, handling the Oscar Hall musical down in the village across the street from Folk City and the NYU math building. I had become friendly with Stefanie, who had some money to invest, it was the settlement with Saul, the first year of the breakup. One day we started working out budgets on a series of plays at low prices in colleges, and the plan went quickly, too quickly. We were both so eager to do something big, redeem our lives really, and we worked like blazes, perfect harmony in the planning stage. I was at the end of the relationship with David Astor, the first time, discovering that I had repeated the error of David Vogel. David Astor was just beginning to work on his *Huck* libretto. The trouble was that he was looking for a live Jim for himself.

So we doodled with the budget and wrote the brochure in September and October. Stefanie had Sister Maybelle from before, and on a trip to Stratford, Ontario, we met this guy Jason Witte, a big hot shot from Canada, who said he'd come down and do the Portfolio, and originally I had worked with the Korchnois, Alex and Viva, when I took my first shot at personal managing in '62, and through Oscar Hall we put together the Composers' Revue and the whole business under the name of Jaystar Productions. So then we had the Shakespeare thing and we had the mime thing and we had the Maybelle Turner thing and we had the Composers' Revue. We were going to make Jason Witte a partner, but he didn't want to work, plus he was really stupid. What we should have done was stay with what we knew best, me and Alex and Viva Korchnoi, Stefanie and Sister Maybelle, mount a modest package, test it out for a year. But no, I wanted to be a *gantze macher* producer. Stef had her dreams of glory. This was before Howard Cello. It was another creative person who was shaking up her cojones. Always running off. Zip, to the Catskills, zap, to Puerto Rico. I was still working at Barnett, doing my business on their phone, dishes piled in the sink at home, a roach's paradise. By the end of November I had Alex and Viva and the mime troupe in the house pasting the brochure and Saul Fedder made us a great blowup. If there is one thing I know it's brochures.

The bookers' convention came to town and we were a big hit. We entertained them, a huge party at Stefanie's house. I made eggplant casserole till it came out of my ears. These people buy only from people like Hurok and William Morris and Columbia Artists Management, but everybody entertains them and free tickets here and free tickets there. And we were running around dishing out eggplant and using brochures for napkins, giving the spiel a mile a minute, right into the convention we push, I was very pushy, antagonized everybody there, who were we, a little unchartered airline with one engine missing selling trips to Miami for twenty dollars.

Then we sat down and did a huge mailing from *Lovejoy's*, checking off every school with more than a 750 enrollment. We got our first reply card, some guy from Ohio Wesleyan wants the whole $5,000 series. Sol Hurok move over. Just then Stefanie went off to Las Vegas, patching up a thing, and that was the beginning of my resentment, my doing all the work. By this time I was through with Barnett, living off the severance and the first of the borrowed money, god the icebox, leftover cheese hard as a rock and green olives floating in a half-open jar of muck, moldy tomatoes, a container of half-and-half, the spout slightly open, stinking up the machine. The whole house could have dissolved in ferment. Then in January I went out to Madison, Wisconsin, to a regional convention, my first shot at the hinterlands, but really old territory for me. It was ten years since I had said goodbye at last to Jonathan, and now I wasted no time in calling him from the same booth at the University Student Union that I used to call him then; and my heart in my mouth again, you don't erase four college years, practically married, just like that.

Instead of some impossible magic words, "I've been waiting for your call," he was stiff and polite and I rattled on and I walked out of the booth with a "good luck on your venture" squishing in my gut. So I went to see Jack Neally, an old friend, a hack television writer for a local station, a big fish in a little pond with a big home and a big car and I got pitched on king-sized martinis and went back to my hotel room and repeated my old pattern. In my drunken hysterics something happens to me, the air of resistance runs out, a plug pulled out of an inner tube. I pick up the phone and the wire is a black umbilical cord and the food of mother life is going to come rushing into my ear and through my arteries. I called Jonathan again, his wife answered, my voice cold and urgent, "This is Jane Castle, may I speak to Jonathan please," and the brittle bite of his voice cut through the sleepiness, "What is it, Jane, are you in trouble?" "No, I just wanted to talk, I'm sorry I called, didn't mean to wake you," and I drop the phone to the cradle, cradle, that's a good one, and wait for morning. Who was she, another bright-as-a-penny blonde who dropped herself into the gumball machine and came out with the prize, with a home on the lake and four Presbyterian kids, husband the ace director of *Our Town* west of the Mississippi.

I left the convention in Madison and went to Iowa for a week to cover colleges. Stefanie had done Indiana and had come back with nothing, which ended her selling career. I rented a car, and hopped college towns for a week, over a thousand miles through the bare flatland, just the eastern half, from Dubuque to Cedar Rapids to Iowa City, then all the way to Des Moines in the dead center of the state. I didn't get to Sioux City or Council Bluffs, too far west, and saved the last trip for Fairfield and Parsons College, which had a national reputation as a diploma mill, lots of new buildings and hard sell and nobody stays more than a year, the turnover is terrific. I arrived in Fairfield on a Friday with $12,000 worth of contracts in my bag, and I put up at a snazzy motel, a Holiday Inn type place, the last word, thirty a day, with a big frosted-glass sliding-door stall shower with good hot Iowa water pinging off my skin, and I gave it all I got, somewhere over the rainbow, the vibrato shaking the walls, and a towel wrapped around me, doing the hotel room bit, on the bed, phone in my lap, reclining against the headboard. I dialed the quick-fingered way, index finger thrust into the hole and held there through the return, almost forcing the dial to go faster, jab and return, nails clicking against the hard black metal dial. And the face the way the actress sets in the wings before going on stage, first the deadpan indifference of the pro, then the cue and out you go with the pasted smile, the audience going along with the put-on, illusion bearers all of them. The clock in the clock-radio anchored to the night table read 4:45.

"Hello, Mr. Bunsen, my name is Jane Castle. We met at the convention last month. You might remember I gave the eggplant party and you said some good things about the brochure. You have a thousand-seat house. Mr. Bunsen, I can give you the full guarantee, isn't that nice. It's a great series. I've just come from Des Moines, they're buying it, in Cedar Rapids they're buying it, in Dubuque I sold the series. I have to confess I didn't think Dubuque existed until I took this tour. I haven't seen anything until I've seen Fairfield? You may have something there. You can pick me up around seven. Fine Mr. Bunsen. Bink? O.K., Bink, see you later."

I let the phone rest in my lap and closed my eyes. I thought of Mr. Bink Bunsen for a while, the five thousand for the package I was sure to sell him would go into the folder with the other contracts. A busy week tasting winter Iowa corn. Mr. Bink Bunsen. What the hell. What was Stefanie doing but treating herself to some pretty crummy dishes, what was Howard but a baked potato. The trouble is that when you close your eyes and start thinking in strange hotel rooms a million miles from nowhere you are liable to start looking at the black void and see the spots and stripes and colored flashes, fourth of July exploding in your head, nothing really menacing, no big atomic blast, just some fireworks, and I let the Roman candle burn itself out before I got up, dressed, made myself up and prepared to meet the man of the hour.

Since there was no such thing as a typical booker, they came in all shapes and sizes, I had to tailor my style to fit the needs of the occasion, in this case the Parsons College sand-and-grit operation, cultivating my best silver-plate manner, the New York *bon vivant* funning it with the country cousin, trading him up, not me down, dressing up the Fairfield Motor Lodge and Restaurant with our class. Bink Bunsen was an ex-phys ed instructor turned administrator, who had never seen the inside of a New York theater until he got a free pair to *Mame*. A burly guy with stubby fingers just managing to cradle his old-fashioned glass, really a perfect fit for the fraternity pewter tankard, that is if they had discovered the existence of pewter, which I doubt. Not my type at all, a grosgrain bowtie reserved for annual sports award dinners, a clip-on to boot, a real prairie Neanderthal who grew up throwing the shot put from cornfield to cornfield.

"I wonder if I can get a vermouth cassis." I had already bagged my contract before we had finished the first handful of mixed nuts the waitress had dumped on to the formica table. Bink lit the candle with his Zippo lighter, looking at me to see if he had committed a *faux pas*. He snapped his fingers twice and the waitress hurried over. She would ask the bartender.

"We're still catching up with blended rye whiskey. You go a few hundred miles west and the only thing you can get is a Dr. Pepper."

"I had a Dr. Pepper in Mobile once."

"We imported it."

The waitress said no they don't make that, we have rye and scotch and. . . . "I'll have a Jack Daniel's on the rocks."

Bink nodded to the girl. "Old Jack has had his baptism in this place. The college hasn't been able to bring in any hard stuff. We've got just about everything else."

"And Jaystar Productions, too."

"I'll drink to that." He waited for my drink and we clinked glasses. He held his drink lightly in the stubby hand, and I saw a touch of poise in the density. He talked about the Parsons Theater and how he fell into the job, he was really the assistant dean of men, having gone to administrator's school in Chicago to move out of the bind of the physical education program.

"I got tired teaching volleyball to these kids. Most of them have paid their way in. It's a dropout college."

"They'll go for the Composers' Revue."

"I sure hope so. Jane, is it all right if I call you that, we've got a bunch of kids with m-o-n-e-y, and they'll spend it. You send that promotional stuff and we're in."

"Like Flynn."

I knew it but did he. Another Jack D. on the rockies and I began to substitute cocktail cozy for career brittle. The funny thing was I didn't even like the guy, so what was I thinking about. I had his signature in the bag, the week was a success, Jaystar was on the way. And Janie sat in a building with plastic tabletops and flowers in the dead center of the universe listening to some locker room sadist talk himself into a night of free love. I accepted it, more's the pity, what featureless image spilled before my eyes, what combination of vanity and fear conspired to seize the day with a stranger in the night. Miss Jerko I was not. I drank my drink and brushed his finger and kneed his knee and turned all his opaque need into pinpointed desire, his blocky body lifting off the chair after the fourth or fifth, the waitress replacing one after the other with gum-chewing efficiency, until he escorted me out of the lounge and down the path, his legs slightly bowed, walking the springy simian walk of the athlete, his pants hiked over his shoes, revealing, god bless my poor Jewish soul, white sweat socks.

"Where did you think you were going with those things?" We were in my room with a bottle of Daniel's, two glasses and ice. I could go back on Saturday, train connections were right, so it's Bink Stink in room 14B don't bounce on the bed you'll break the springs.

"My socks?" He sat in the company armchair, leg crossed over leg, smoothing the socks.

"Your socks."

"I have a fungus, to tell you the truth. But it gets better when I'm drinking."

"Then you had better pour yourself another drink, hadn't you, Mr. Bink Bunsen."

"And another one for you, Miss Jane Castle."

"But I have no fungus." A roar from the wide mouth, followed by a belch. He was the monster of the midway.

"It grows like wildfire around here. It's practically an epidemic." He splashed whiskey in the two glasses, the dark brown liquid anesthetic filling the tumbler. He undid his sports award bowtie and unbuttoned his shirt. Brown apey hair rode over his belly like prairie grass. David Astor's smooth boy-body superimposed itself, my hairless David, a nubile boy-man, sacred sweetness of flesh with tender little sucking balls. How could I get away from this gross man. The first grab surprised me. He held me the way he held the old-fashioned glass, the way he probably balanced the shot put, firm and considerate of the object to be drunk, thrown, or fucked. He zipped me down and I slipped out of my things and he dropped his jockey shorts.

"You are a nice man, nice man."

"I bought the whole package, didn't I?"

"Every penny of it."

"Why don't we drink to that."

Glasses met, booze flowed down, my fingers numb, body nerve-deadened. Here comes the Iowa Special. He was into me, still managing to preserve that ballet-like daintiness graceful heavy people have. And then much harder, the full bulk in thrust. I uh-uhed and ah-ahed and he grred and oofed.

"I can feel the Bunsen Burner."

"Stay with me, baby."

I could have stayed all night. I wasn't coming and I wasn't going. Rosalie the Receptacle. The springs danced, the mattress squeaked, and he sent the flame-thrower across the scorched and barren land. (In Cedar Rapids I had lunch with the booker, rimless glasses, tight little desexed face, corn voice, "Miss Castle, a pleasure to meet you," his Miss Castle the lady from the church bazaar.) The room was a deserted barn with shutters in the hayloft banging aimlessly in the sudden squally wind. When Bink Bunsen left a little bit later I noticed that he had not taken off his socks. Was it possible that he was hiding the devil's foot? But then I wouldn't have been able to recognize it anyway.

We went into production in the summer of '66 and still raising money and still booking and in the fall we put the show on the road. The snowball started down the hill. We had overextended ourselves and Stefanie was goofing off left and right, Howard and whatnot, and I put in these hours, I persevered, persevered, I became a monster, just horrendous, the witch of Seventy-Second Street, where we had an office in an old fleabag Sam Spade building. We simply did not have the organization to handle everything, and the loans increased. I had a $2,500 telephone bill on my back, we were calling everywhere, making half-hour deals to California. Who could stand it. Alex Korchnoi began to act up, he wouldn't take a cut, $800 a week he was getting, and the prima donna from Composers' Revue, Peggy Reese was the bitch on wheels, wanting this and that, won't work here or there, finally getting pregnant with Joel Wornick, who was already Mr. Big, *she* gets the man. I kept borrowing and finally Stef and I said, screw it, and we didn't send in the quarterly withholding. Fifteen thou. Taxes for Vietnam. Fuck 'em.

Chapter 3

I FIXED HIM the sandwich from the bowl on the sideboard, fresh Bumble Bee tuna on bakery rye bread, seeds, and a glass of Diet Rite Cola on the rocks. He sat in his office, the door open between us, swiveled to the window, hiding his left hand, the little finger of which was lunching on his nose. From the rise of his neck I knew he wouldn't turn until I called him. He picked up the phone and called Baltimore, trying to keep his voice low to punish me. Later he would accuse me of eavesdropping, which was part of my job. When he talked to his girl friend he shut the door and that meant hands off the phone, but the thing had fizzled, a woman of thirty-six, and he was back from Europe a week early, waiting for action, irritable. Newmark was a bitter, angry, hostile man, and he would make me pay. The SEC regulations had come through, Baltimore had told him. Nothing to do now but play the market. Everybody has a broker. Merrill and Lynch and Shearson and Hammill and Edwards and Hanly. Baltimore had no use for him so maybe he could buy and sell a little and get over his heartbreaks.

"Call Baltimore," he called out, his back still to me. He had just finished talking to Baltimore, but I wasn't going to say anything. I picked up the phone and started dialing. He walked past me. "I'm going to lunch."

"Aren't you going to eat the tuna fish, Mr. Newmark?" He walked right past me and out the door. I ate the tuna sandwich and drank the soda. I called the telephone company and told them we were not getting incoming calls and I wanted it cleared up right away. I'll get your file and call you back, the girl said. No, let me talk to the supervisor. The supervisor said they were working on it, we'll call you back as soon as we check your file. No, let me talk to the business manager. I will not hang up until we get satisfaction. I waited, cradling the phone in my neck and picked at a hangnail. Newmark walked in with a toothpick in his mouth.

"Where is the tuna fish sandwich?"

"I ate it."

"You ate my tuna fish sandwich."

"I'm on the phone, Mr. Newmark. I'm trying to straighten out the phone service."

He walked to his chair and swiveled to the window. "I suggest you hang up."

"Are you telling me to hang up? I don't want to hang up. I'm getting the business manager."

"Hang up. And don't yell between the rooms."

I hung up.

"Did you tell them you would lose them their job?"

"I raised hell, Mr. Newmark." I was standing at his desk. He was still facing the window.

"Now you're learning what I taught you. Put up coffee."

I went back to my desk and I heard him talking to somebody about another girl. I went back into his office. "Why are you annoyed with me?"

"Where are the paychecks? I told you to have the paychecks ready when I came back from Europe."

In the long night with Richard I had forgotten to bring the paychecks. "I left them home."

"Go get them."

"I can't go now."

He turned toward me and cracked his knuckles with a

backward snap. Aimless, nervous man. A friend of Arnold
Seltz. Next week Seltz would get an earful.

"Is the petty cash up to date?"

"Yes it is, Mr. Newmark."

"You came in at a quarter of eleven. You've been coming
in at quarter of eleven for four months, ever since I hired
you. How can I run a business when my secretary comes in
at a quarter of eleven?"

"I told you I would be late. I had some important personal
business downtown."

"My business is your personal business."

"Shall I call the phone company back?"

"No, I'll do it myself."

"I'm in touch with Mr. Hagge. I can settle it."

"I'll call Mr. Hagge."

"Is there anything else?"

"Nothing else. Make out a check for yourself for the rest
of the week."

"It's Tuesday, Mr. Newmark."

"I won't be needing your services anymore."

I walked out of the office and threw things into my bag.
Also some extra pads, pencils, a box of staples and a Swingline
stapler.

"Don't forget to leave the key to the sideboard."

I went back in and dropped the keys on his desk. I opened
my purse and dropped three quarters on the desk. "For the
tuna sandwich."

He shrugged and turned away. "Put the other paychecks
in the mail."

"Special delivery, Mr. Newmark."

"You've learned nothing. Miss Castle, you're only as good
as your last mistake."

Like your girl friend, I almost said, but I realized he would
have to put in for unemployment insurance. "I'll try to
remember that."

I went downstairs to the Automat next door and had a

pineapple Danish and coffee. The nickels lady overchanged me a nickel and I slipped it into my purse. What could it be but a good omen after that disaster upstairs. The lunchtime rush was over and old people were scattered at tables reading the *Daily News* or, clustered in twos and threes, arguing over the relative merits of competing cafeterias. "The vegetables here are always fresh," a lady in the group near me said. "Well, they have a large turnover," her friend said. "When I first came to New York," the third lady said, "a ham sandwich was fifteen cents." "That's nothing," said the first lady, "I remember when it was a nickel." "It was never a nickel," said the third lady, "anyway I don't eat ham." "It's awful," the fresh vegetable lady said, "I get my check and it goes in a week. A bag of groceries. . . ." "A bag of groceries," the third lady said. The large turnover lady was quiet.

Outside, the early afternoon sun was bright on the people walking by the large front window. Red lights stopped all the traffic and people moved in waves across the streets. They looked like a moving square. How many of those chickies swinging their mini-butts could claim they have been canned in the middle of a Tuesday afternoon? I looked in my bag to check my cache. Cash my check? I could do that and go down to Ohrbach's and pick up a few accessories before I met David for dinner. I dunked a piece of Danish into the coffee. In my first job when I came to the city working for Charlie Silver, doing the Chevy industrials, I was let go for a legitimate reason. There was a slack season, besides which I came on too strong, practically telling Charlie and his boss, a famous fag Shakespearean, how to run the show. And I was let go by Donald Allen at the Provincetown Playhouse when I was house manager and ended up $1,000 short on the books, in addition to which I was already into my personal managing with David Astor. That was in '62. Then there was the job with Columbia Artists Management, the same pattern, efficient, superqualified, I was a regular Miss Brisk, but I always wanted more than the job asked for. If I was a secretary I crowded the business manager or the editor or the producer. I know how to do that Miss Jones, I'll take care of that, Mr. Smith, give me a piece of the real action and I'll show you how to run this horse race. And I did do it once at Barnett, when my boss, Walter Weinstock, had to go away and he sent me to the contract negotiation with 20th Century on a hot property, a big musical, and I gave them his position just as he had directed me, and when he came back I gave him my interpretation of the facts as well as the facts, who was holding out and who was being tough, and I got a $250 bonus for that.

So you manage the books and you write the brochures and you make out the payroll and you introduce artists and you read scripts and type scripts and you do a little play doctoring, and you get your own children's show off the ground and you produce a little, direct a little, sell on the phone, get into the loan business, travel on hot days and snowy nights to out-of-the-way launching pads and you wheel and deal and sell your soul right down the river. David was saying something to me about the human condition, he's elbow deep in Camus and Sartre and that sort of thing, the risks one has to take to test the full extent of your being. And he put the question to me once, is it the tragic or the absurd, because you must take your pick, you can't slice the bacon two ways. I saw my mother's beautiful, haunted face and it spoke tragedy, but then Handsome Sam Castle, who knocked himself unconscious in a pool room the very day of his big hoofing audition, what can that be but wild absurdity, soft shoe Sam, take if from the top, Janie girl, and a one and a two, I could cry. Did I need Mr. Al Newmark's *shtick,* the vanity of an infant and the mind of a shrewd pea, dishing out abuse like Halloween candy, throwing handfuls of chicken feed in my face. Were those people moving down Forty-Second Street in a trance going someplace important, heading for their destiny on smooth, greased rails? Bullshit. They go in somewhere and tank up on a couple of lunchtime martinis and eat a plateful of fantasy and stumble out into the stinking streets to their air-conditioned nightmares. Fifty bucks a week for the next six months, I'll take a little sabbatical, get an ounce of grass, clean my apartment, turn on a little, and wait for David to take me on the Honda to endsville.

I stood in the middle of the ground floor of Ohrbach's trying to decide where to attack first: a head-on assault to the scarf counter, or maybe a little flank attack to costume jewelry, or I could bomb in on the handbag sale in the far corner. Gloves and stockings were out this trip. I had in my purse the ammunition, $150 in crisp new ones. That awful man had done me a favor, a little 'oliday 'e had given me. I should have been spending the time chasing down a good lawyer. Morton Katz was not going to let me go that easily. But I operated on a pretty consistent principle, satisfy the need and the ethic will take care of itself. I was a latter-day Sister Carrie, a smart little cunt who always followed the scent of blood. Hats were piled in front of me. I started for them but veered over to the sandal sale. Perhaps an ensemble for the beach. Why not celebrate the liberation with beach accessories and then get David to take me on the bike to Jones Beach. I bought the sandals and dropped the package in my Ohrbach's shopping bag. Schemer. At the hats table I tried on a few and found a huge navy blue floppy straw hat. In the mirror I vamped a little. I carried the hat in my hand, covering the sales ticket. When you shop at a counter in a department store and you leave the counter with the item in your hand in order to stop at another counter to purchase another item, you leave the first counter with the item conspicuously in hand. See, you are saying to the man or the machine, I'm really buying, I have it right here in my hand. And I found myself on the second floor in front of swimsuits. Nothing unique, no eye-catcher, just a black tank suit, low-cut in the back for a little style. In the dressing room I put my dress on over the swimsuit, gathered my shopping bag, picked up my navy blue straw, and headed downstairs. Near the escalator a table of bathing caps, and leaning against the table, a store guard. I stood next to him and fingered a few caps. Underneath my dress the swimsuit itched. I carried the blue straw casually, recklessly. The matador is in the ring and the horns come very close, slashing his jacket. Toro, toro. I saw a red velvet cap. I waved it in front of the guard. He shifted his weight and yawned. I tried it on in front of the round mirror on the showcase. The matador in red velvet. I carried it in my hand past the guard. In front of "Irregular hose, 98¢ a pair" I dropped it into the shopping bag and walked out. I stood in front of the store waiting for the man to come out. A garment-center salesman type walking past, stopped, loitered, went on, and came back.

"Don't I know you from somewhere? Concord? Laurels?"

I gave him a Castle superspecial. "Have you got any problems?" He shook his head and walked on. I waited another minute and walked west on Thirty-Fourth Street. I saw it as an experiment, which it must have been because I was ice, not even now, some distance from the store, coming out of shock into the severe post-theft palpitations. Ice. I have a basic belief about myself, that I have the nature of an experimenter, I explore the unknown, a lady of the bizarre. I have the capacity to take the risk for show, to say, I know what it is like to do a threesome with John Ames and a chick, to try a fifty-dollar trick with one of Jerry Kay's clients, to steal a few buttons here and there. There I was with twenty-five dollars worth of stolen goods and a million dollars worth of danger. Hey, they nudge each other, a little elbow in the ribs, there's Jane C., a woman who likes to walk on the edge. I risk because I know my motives are good. Mr. Ohrbach is giving me a few bucks of free goodies because he is a character builder. I wouldn't do it in Saks Fifth. Ohrbach's is a psychologist's rat warren. Saks is a guilt-maker. Who was I responsible to, anyway? What restraints did I need? Who was I to be good for? Was I not ready to smoke grass and hash and have a try at a woman? Was I not ready to do in the government for $15,000 as well as that phone company for $2,500? Have I not slept in the strangest beds on the shortest notice with the oddest cats? If I walk in with the hat and say look at me, and they do, then the weight of me is felt in the world. I copped a bathing suit at Ohrbach's. Right under my dress. Janie, you didn't (my gay friends would love it). I did. I did.

I stopped at a phone booth and called Richard. Hello, came back the why-are-you-calling-me-in-the-office-again voice. Then remembering his p's and q's, hand over the mouthpiece, how are you. I'm all right I told him, almost dizzy with my businesslike cool, but I went to see the tax man and we had papers to sign. A Puerto Rican chick with spiked heels, high-riding bosom, and a beehive hairdo stood outside the booth shifting from one foot to the other. If you have ever stood outside a phone booth, or inside, the look exchanged between the two is intimate, the I've-got-to-go-to-the-bathroom-to-wee-wee-look, a shared plight. For a second, looking at this tan lady, I felt I had more in common with her than I did with the man on the other end of the phone. Richard said he would try to get someone to help us, and if not, he might look at the material himself, don't call me I'll call you. I needed action, I said, because Katz was a Jewish J. Edgar Hoover. I started to hang up, but wait, a last remark, Richard it was great this morning, just great, the fatal crack in the voice, unlatching the love box, old Pandora Castle. And I got it back quick, ungrudging, great, he said, the best bed I've fallen out of in my life.

I took the Sixth Avenue bus uptown. At Forty-Second Street a wino was sitting on the bench in front of the marble statue of a Latin American hero. Just below the drunk was a puddle of wet. As the bus moved away I saw a young cop stop, look, and walk on. Talking about how to learn to live in this city, it has taken me these ten years to learn how to look, and it is a tonic to get out of oneself. I've sat in buses, subways, cabs, and mulled my fate, analyzing my relationships over and over, circling in on myself as if I would catch myself by surprise, the great discovery right there on the bus, this is what you do, develop self-esteem, or that is what you do, give nothing away and force his hand. Weary of self-preoccupation I began to look around. It became therapeutic. I looked out now and saw a fat lady driving an air-conditioned Cadillac, her legs swung open, showing garter and flesh. In the bus a man opposite me, in his forties, no ring, with an attaché case on his lap, was doing a job on my legs, up and down and away went the eyes. I opened just a little. That would make the attaché case rise. A delivery boy with an apron, riding frantically with the big delivery chest in front of the bike, almost swerved into our bus as a car door opened on the street side. This was on Fifty-Third Street. On Fifty-Seventh I got out and started west toward David's. I would be early. In the Ritz Thrift Shop I tried on a few coats. The man knew I was horsing around and he ignored my officious tone. In the apartment I had a mink coat, my mother's. I wore it to the theater a few times, a swell from Park Avenoo. (Marilyn, wear that goddamned coat or I'll throw it out. My father, irate, shoves the coat under her nose. My mother, in a striking tinselly sheath, draws back. Sam, I don't want to. It's too heavy. What did I buy it for you for? I'll wear it, don't worry. She goes to the ball in a silver fox cape.) In the showcase outside the Russian Tea Room a menu announced borscht and sour cream and blintzes. Alex Korchnoi's hangout. I drank straight vodkas with him one night, Viva Korchnoi sitting there hair pulled back ballerina style, a handsome spoiled couple. Alex was one of the very few who never made a pass at me. It was the most successful business arrangement I had made. That crazy bankrupt Russian superiority, a noble arrogance that is laughable. They really were gifted amateurs, superb performers who missed that last bit of flair, that willingness to undo the ego in public, to protect nothing but the performance. The gifted amateur always acts as if he were more than his medium, the professional knew that he was only his medium. In front of Carnegie Hall an old man played the violin, scratching out an unrecognizable tune, an amateur grubbing for nickels. Opposite him the Carnegie banner announced the debut of a young violinist, whose face stared out in the standard hands-on-instrument-three-quarter-penetrating-eye look. Another gifted amateur in the making. They will spot him and wipe him out, and he is the old man with the winter overcoat with a paper coffee cup in his coat pocket ready for the change. I reached in my purse and unwrapped my good omen nickel from the Automat and dropped it into the cup. The old man nodded and continued playing. The tune sounded like a Hungarian rhapsody. David had the classical background. I had never really gotten past *Scheherezade*, my opera repertoire consisted of *Carmen*, maybe *Aïda*. Like everyone else I knew, we owned an old Caruso record, the great tinny voice, which my father joined in his rare moments of exuberance, *vesti la giubba* . . . except when I heard it as a kid it came out jewboy.

"Janie Castle." It could have been old Enrico's voice on the shellac, the piercing whine of a voice trapped in a tin can. It was Roger Voisin.

"Hi, Roger." We stood on the corner of Fifty-Seventh and Seventh.

"Jane, where did you get that impossible hat?"

"You ain't seen nuthin' yet." I yanked up my dress and showed him black rump. I told him about my purchase at Ohrbach's. Roger was the kind of man you like to reveal things to because he could never threaten you with anything. Even his darting, gossipy tongue was harmless.

"I never did anything like that."

"I need an accomplice. Want to come down with me next time?"

"What if I got caught?"

"Didn't you ever steal anything from your mother when you were a kid?"

"My mother? No, she gave me everything."

"Roger, that's where the trouble is."

"You mean if I stole. . . ."

"What do you think?"

"She gave me baths."

"That's nice."

"I was fifteen before she stopped. Jane, she used to wash me, you know where."

"Roger, that's what I love about you."

"I just don't like, you know, talk about unpleasant things."

"Have you seen David?"

"Not for weeks. We had a spat."

"About what?"

"What do people spat about? Money, for one thing. Anyway, I've had it with David. He's so busy being a big man these days. And he has got this thing with Pam Haber. I suppose you know about that. He never has time for anyone."

"Was he with her this weekend?"

A cab came zooming up to our corner and a tall, leggy model with a huge bag stepped out. "Carnegie Hall?" she asked.

I pointed across the street. She legged it across, flapping her bag beside her. "Now what has she got that I haven't got?"

"No bosom," Roger said.

"Another titless wonder."

"I told you I haven't seen David in weeks. But my guess is that he was out at Pam's place in Jersey."

"But she has a husband, kids."

"Not anymore."

"So that's it."

"That's only half of it, Janie girl."

"What's the other half?"

"You'll have to find out for yourself. Where are you off to?"

"To find out for myself."

"Tell him he owes me forty bucks for that piece."

"Tell him yourself."

"We're not talking."

We embraced lightly and brushed cheeks. His fattish ass jiggled under his Brooksy suit as he headed down Seventh Avenue. "We'll have lunch," I called out. He turned, waved, and walked on. Roger spent most of his time running around peddling handcrafted costume jewelry, a kid from Indiana who came to New York and went to the Art Students League and found out he couldn't paint. Which, incidentally, took care of an awful lot of people in town. What David saw in him I couldn't understand, but David was a waif gatherer, a junk collector of human odds and ends, who had no conventional sympathies at all. He found Roger in the same way he had found and reclaimed Winnie White, an alcoholic lyricist, a small girl with pneumatic breasts who had gotten a song in the top ten many years ago but had faded. Now she was working on the *Huck* thing. David had given Roger Voisin a shot at the costume work, and he had Howard Milman working on the *Huck* score with him. Howard couldn't exactly be called a reclaimed project, but he was of the failed artist breed David liked to befriend. And what was he reclaiming with me? Was I a used fiddle sitting in a pawnshop window waiting for the rightful owner to come and possess me? The truth of the metaphor is that David was the only one to play on the strings of my heart, send the music soaring through my senses. If he could do that with me maybe he had that power with silly little Roger Voisin or dumpy little boozer Winnie White, or Pam Haber, I knew who she was, a bored Westchester mother with a good voice, three golden kids, and a husband who tinkered with car engines. David's motley.

I stopped for coffee at a luncheonette around the corner from his apartment on Eighth Avenue. The five o'clock rush had started and the streets were choked with honking cabs and swiftly moving people jostling their way into buses and down subway steps. Nobody lingered. Let me out, they screamed silently, away from the poisoned streets, I want to get home, maybe there will be something in the mail, you have won the free trip to whatever, up, up and away. The coffee had a day-end taste.

"What did you put in this?"

A tired colored guy behind the counter washed glasses. "Want another cup?"

"Never mind."

"Made it fresh this afternoon."

I watched him work. He took a glass from the sudsy water, followed it with a one-two motion over the bristle brush sitting in the same suds, a rinse in the second tub of clean water, the cold tap running into that tub, then over, face down on the stainless steel counter, water dripping down the glass and back into the clean tub. He repeated the action with his right hand keeping his left in the soapy water. I was alone at the counter. The store manager was counting receipts at the register. Behind the glass-washing man the day's leftover desserts: half an apple crumb cake, one slice of custard pie, two bowtie doughnuts, a quarter of a tray of rice pudding.

"May I have some rice pudding?"

He gave me a generous portion and slid the dish to me. Surprisingly, it tasted fresh. I ran my spoon around the pudding, sipped my coffee, gazed outside at the crowded streets, and thought of the other David.

Milly Whelan and I went to a barbecue at Bob Tracy's house. I was still going with Gene Gordon but we weren't getting along well. He was complaining about loud clothes and I was complaining because he began to take me for

granted and he was running to get Fay Rosen a pack of cigarettes and not asking if I needed any. I never could stand
for that. I came alone because Milly told me, you gotta meet
this guy. And I waited. And I sulked. There were hardly
any parties, from childhood on, when I didn't sulk. I was
not having a good time, I was not reaching anybody. I was
looking for too much out of the situation. And everybody
was talking. "David is coming." Milly was telling me, he
knows how to order wine and he's witty and charming and
I would love him. David, David, David, David. Three hours
later when the chicken and the shish kebab had been eaten
and we were already sitting inside wondering what to do next
in walked David Vogel, a skinny, scrawny, sloppy, homely
man. He weighed a hundred and twenty pounds soaking wet
and wore expensive sloppy clothes. My god, I thought, this
is not what Milly was selling. But it turned out quickly
enough that David was witty and charming and we played
charades and I felt easier. It became obvious to both of us
that we were communicating.

On the first date after that we went to see *The King and I*
and the big song of the evening was "Getting to Know You."
It was a very soft quiet evening. Once a little later he took
me to a park in Hartford and we walked in the grass and sat
under the trees and talked and had hot dogs, a very quiet
day. And we kissed and he held me in public. I was as tall
as him and a few pounds heavier so I never got over the peculiar sensation that I might smother him. But it was public
affection. Very soon there were no quiet times. We were busy,
he was very busy, a Hartford lawyer, phone calls and plans,
who was going to meet who where when why. And then
Milly and I went to the Cape with Bob Tracy and David was
to meet us, shortly after we were dating regularly although
not steadily. Gene Gordon was still in the picture and beginning to act up. And I sat in a Falmouth, Massachusetts, version of an East side bar, lots of singles, people having fun, and

watching the door and waiting, knowing he would never show. I was in love by this time two dates can be enough for a love junkie, and feeling deep down that was my lot in life, to sit on a bar stool in a swinging place and watch for the open door. He showed up Sunday afternoon with a story about having knocked a kid off a bike with his car. He was cut, bruises all over his face. Later, much later, after it was all over, I thought, cuts and bruises, he must have had some weekend on Fire Island.

Then I threw a party for Andy Raskin who was getting married. Andy was a close friend, a buddy, whom I had screwed one night downstairs on my couch. I told David, five to eight, for cocktails. Gene Gordon came and Jerry Kay and all my friends from Waterbury. I was going to show off my man. David called in the afternoon and I said, "Where are you, it's time for you to come," and he said, "I thought you meant five to eight. I wondered why you would start a party at such a funny time." I didn't know that he was probably looking for an excuse not to be on time, the pattern was just beginning. My man showed up and Gene Gordon was mulling around trying to be nice, but I wanted Jerry Kay to like him. I wanted Jerry's approval because my father was indifferent, really interested in getting me out of the house so he could carry on with his Bernice, what was it, just about a year after my mother had died. And Jerry got into a big politics argument with David, two very clever lawyers from Waterbury and Hartford, and I stood on the side beaming, my men quarreling over me, which of course was not the case.

That same night, after everyone had gone, Gene Gordon sat out on the stone wall outside my house making a fool of himself over me, which was just what I have always wanted, but all I thought was, how terrible, how disgusting. I should have understood it then for what it was and grabbed him. I should have said, "All right, if you will marry me." That's how every girl has gotten a guy. But no, I was totally immersed in the moment, my David, whom I hardly knew and who was already breaking appointments and coming late. Soon after that, a few more dates, lots of affection, necking, we went to New Haven and told his parents we were going to be engaged. The same night we went to his place in Hartford, his own apartment, and I took a shower and came out with a towel wrapped around me and a towel wrapped around my head and he put his arms around me and kissed me, and that was it. I went to sleep without being touched. The next day we drove home and told my father, who allowed as how that was kind of fine.

We were both riding the same wave. It was the greatest twenty-four hours of my life. I guess my enthusiasm must have carried him along and made him feel he could bring it off. I was in love, we were in love. I was going to get my picture in the paper, a ring, everything I had dreamed about was going to happen to me like it had happened to everybody else. My father had good perverse insight and bought me three of the most obscene nightgowns I have ever seen, real transparent teasers. I think he knew all along that David was . . . not right. As much as he couldn't stand Jerry Kay he would have preferred him to David Vogel. We went house hunting. We had to turn down an expensive house that was the image of the Elm Street house. We found one I liked which we could afford on a private street on a crescent, and it pleased us both that it was in the gentile section of West Hartford, not on the "reservation," the rich Jewish section. He was ready to buy, but there was a delay here, a delay there. It really was the beginning of the end.

Little by little, day by day, things started to happen, evidence started to build up. I was an engaged girl with a rock on my hand and I had status and I was going to catch up with my childhood friends Helen and Rita, both married. A couple of months had passed and he hadn't touched me, barely a finger on a boob, and I had a good pair. I thought, he respects me, doesn't want to jump me like every Tom, Dick, and Harry. That's what real love was, the woman on the pedestal. I was uneasy. Calls started coming from Hartford. Canceled visits because of clients, late work, and then when he came in he was tired or had a headache and he would fall asleep on the couch and I would sit in my dark living room watching a Late Show with him stretched out, his hand over his head.

One night we were invited to a party in New London. David always had an adventure ready, he structured adventurous situations. We were going to New London and then leave the party to drive to Boston to see friends who were in the cast of *Pajama Game*. I took the bus to Hartford and waited for an hour for him in the bus station looking like a leftover from a New Year's Eve party. I wore a fifty-dollar black cotton dress with a very low square neck showing good front, long tight sleeves, and a princess line, and a pair of very expensive backless shoes with open toes and rhinestone-studded heels, a Herbert Levine shoe, the very height of fashion. We drove to New London to a beautiful house, loads of the best middle-class people. They were waiting for him and we were late. "Oh, there's David," a big fuss over him. He was so gregarious, so genial, and he drank and flitted around, dragging me with him, he seemed to be saying, look, I can do it too, showing me off to the men.

We took off for Boston at one o'clock in the pouring rain. You drive, he said, and he gave me the wheel. It was a two-lane highway with one thing in the middle and I drove all the way to Boston. He was sound asleep, curled up in the corner, out cold. He hadn't had that much to drink. It was treacherous. I was terrified, huddled over the wheel, wiping the windshield, peering through the wipers to get a view of the road, the rain smashing against the windows. When we got to Boston I was absolutely exhausted. He was ready. He stayed up all night. We never checked into the hotel, we never got near a bed. He had structured the whole thing to avoid a confrontation.

A week later I was at his apartment, changing the sheets, playing house, being a regular *balabusta*. I loved the feeling of it. The domestic scene meant the life of acceptance. Clean and cook and soon watch the belly swell, tripping the sound "my man" off my tongue as I hummed over the dishes. I was a born homemaker and I had a guy. The phone rang, emergency, David's mother was ill, her heart, come at once. He got behind the wheel, his knuckles white with terror and we made the trip from Hartford to New Haven in thirty-five minutes, racing down the Wilbur Cross at fantastic speeds. He drove like a maniac. When we got there she wasn't that bad. She wanted her David, my son the lawyer. Back to mother's nest. I was up to it. I was the daughter-in-law, right. I fed her chicken soup and hovered around like Florence Nightingale while David sat on the edge of the bed and held her hand.

I should have gotten the signal then, but what did I know about such things. Then I heard from my Aunt Claire who knew a man who was in partnership with David in a vending machine business. She said that I should watch him, something wasn't kosher. I slept in the bedroom with him, there were twin beds, and I knew he could get an erection, but it was small and tough to maintain. I fooled with him but we always stopped. He kissed marvelously. I loved him.

There was a guy in the Waterbury Civic Theater by the name of Tod who hated me. There were whisperings, rumblings, "Oh, Tod knows David Vogel," blah, blah. I didn't quite know what they meant. Finally Jerry Kay, old faithful, came to me and said, "You don't look happy." "I'm happy," I said, but I had to tell Jerry, of all people, that David had not touched me, it was now over three months. Maybe he wanted to keep me pure for the wedding night. But who knew any bridal virgins?

"He's got another friend," Jerry said.

"What do you mean?"

"Tod from the theater."

"Tod from the theater?"

And we went on like this, word jockeying, skating on the edge of the issue. For as a matter of fact when you fall in love with a homosexual is there anyone who wants to bring the news? It is like a next-of-kin telegram. I never faced him with it. We didn't even have a quarrel. Somewhere in the early spring, just when the forsythia bushes began to dot the countryside with splashes of yellow I gave him back the ring. We talked about how premature it was. We were in the house on Elm Street. My father was off again with his Bernice woman, and David and I were alone. The overpowering surge of love had dwindled to nothing. In its place was the chest pain, a heavy gnawing thickness. This skinny little charming faggot wanted to marry me and be a good lawyer and satisfy his momma. What remained for me, haunted me, haunts me now, is why did I fall for him? And now turning the corner of Eighth Avenue and Fifty-Seventh Street, a dozen years later, I reached out again for my fate.

Chapter 4

THEY WERE at the piano when I walked in. Winnie White was singing in an ice cream soprano, leaning over David who sat up, back straight, sleeves rolled, pencil in his ear. They were working on a song, "Free Again," which they intended to use as the theme for the *Huck* show. Winnie and David sang:

> Free again, free again
> The two of us together
> Free again.
> In any kind of weather
> Going down the river
> We are free again.

Winnie's banal lyrics were rescued by the melody. David had a good ear for the open, sunny melodic line, which he frequently crossed with a flinty, hard-edged sadness out of the classic folk idiom. David played and sang Jim's solo:

> Luck has brought me Huck
> The blackest white boy I ever seed
> He'll take us down to Cayro
> Where the river leads
> To free-dom.

Winnie sang Huck's part:

> I'm darned afeared of Miss Watson
> And the Widow Douglas too
> And I'll fry in hell I know for sure
> But Jim is a man and I am a man
> And I know what I must do.

Together: Free again, etc.

"I'll fix drinks," I said. David nodded and continued playing. I took out the ice tray from his utility refrigerator, the half-sized jobs built in under the stove in small apartments. My body filled the cavity of a room. David switched to Pap's song, "Call this a govment," with his own lyrics, harsh and biting, ". . . soon the niggers will have a vote/ What is an honest man going to do/ What is this country coming to." I brought the Scotches in as David ended with a flourishing chord and, deepening his voice, a booming "What is this country coming to. . . ."

"Isn't that the speech from chapter six, with Pap and Huck in the cabin?" *Huck Finn* wasn't exactly my kind of book, but I had done my homework.

Winnie picked up her drink and sat on the piano bench next to David. Her feet brushed the floor. David took the pencil from his ear and made some notations in the score. His compact back muscles moved under the Banlon shirt.

"I think it's chapter seven in my text," Winnie said.

David swung around. "We need a last act song, a closing solo for Huck, in front of the curtains, maybe."

"Hello everybody," I said, lifting my glass.

"Hi," David said, offering me a quick smile, forced. It would take him an hour to make the adjustment. All our meetings started the same way, as if I were packing a derringer in my handbag. Someday I would bring one.

Winnie sipped her drink and ignored my greeting. She

was the queen of bad manners, but David had explained over and over that she was a social cripple.

I stood up. "I'll get the book." I started for the bookshelf. The wall groaned from ceiling to floor with books. He was a crazy, eclectic reader, the kind of man a woman would have to keep up with if she married him.

"Don't bother," David said.

"Is it chapter six?" I asked.

"I think I want the Huck solo at the end. Maybe something like this." He sat down at the piano, struck a few chords, and began:

> I've seen this civilization,
>   and it warn't very good
> I'm going to light out, I have to light out
> For the territory ahead . . . .

I walked to the bookcase and lifted out a copy of the book. "It *is* chapter six," I said. "That's a great speech."

David continued fooling around with "The Territory Ahead."

"The duet sounded great," I said, still fingering the book.

"We need to clean it up a bit," Winnie said, still giving me the chapter seven look.

"How's this," David said.

> I've seen lyin' and cheatin' and stealin'
> And a man shot down in cold blood
> Human beings don't seem to have feelings
> I'm going to light out for the territory ahead.

"Marvelous," I said. "David, it's terrific. On the duet, there's a line that has been bothering me." Janie the play doctor was making a house call. I heard me but why should I stop. "When Jim sings, 'the blackest white boy I ever seed,' I don't think that is quite accurate."

"You don't," Winnie said. She sipped her drink, reached into her purse, pulled out a cigarette, lit it with a snap of her lighter, and dropped the lighter back into the bag. I really had nothing against Winnie. We had settled that score years ago.

"Huck really isn't that committed to Jim. He's all bound up in the morality of the white society he is escaping. Jim is too. He might think Huck is the blackest white boy. But I'm not sure he would say it."

"I think he does say it," Winnie said. "May I see the book?"

I handed her the book. I had come for an evening with David, drinks, dinner, and if he was right, a night of lovemaking. I loved his tense, lithe body. I knew it loved me. Winnie turned pages.

"You could switch one word for accuracy," I said. " 'Huck is the *whitest* white boy. . . .' That's Jim's kind of thinking."

In bed with Randy the first time, the delicious shock of the glistening black skin against the white sheet.

David sat on the couch, really a sofa bed with maroon rope tassels and antique wood pineapple knobs in the corner, his biggest piece of luxury in years. He looked out over Eighth Avenue. Winnie closed the book and put it on the piano bench.

"I have an appointment downtown. I'm late."

"You could keep the line. It isn't all that bad," I said.

"We're writing for a modern audience," David said in a pinchy voice over his glass. "It's like Shakespeare in modern dress. I don't think the audience could take Jim the way Twain saw him."

"I think you're right, David," I said.

Winnie stood up. "Any other suggestions before I go?"

"That dress looks great on you," I said. Usually she looked like an upside-down bowling pin, but the white cotton she was wearing drew in the top-heavy torso.

"It's a knockout, Win," David said.

"I'll see you guys later."

"You've got a great show here. They'll be crazy not to buy it," I said.

"We've worked very hard. David?"

"Like fiends," David said.

"I'm going to talk to some people," I said. "Donald Allen will look at it. He hasn't done a musical yet, but he's ready."

Winnie left and I took David's glass to the kitchen for a fresh drink. I made it a good double on two healthy ice cubes. I brought the brimming drink back.

"Hello there," I said. David took the drink with sullen fingers. My role was to ignore. Ignore and conquer was my motto. "Did I have a day today. I'm absolutely exhausted." That's what David brought out in me, the absolutely exhausted horseshit. He sipped the drink and continued to look out the window, a morose little boy.

"Stefanie and I met the revenue man, a Mr. Morton Katz. As of today he wants all the money. He acts as if we had cut off his allowance for a month. David, where will I find fifteen thousand dollars?"

"Your dress is dirty."

I looked down and saw a wet stain, probably a little rice pudding from the luncheonette. "David, my dress is dirty." I was wearing a cotton jersey print with an allover black-and-white splash design, Ohrbach's nine-ninety-five real cash. "Why are you acting this way?" I dropped my voice to little-girl conciliatory. I looked down on Eighth Avenue, we were two flights up, and saw a poodle's leg up against a hydrant. His lady in slacks looked like a St. Moritz whore. How do their men treat them, like poodles? How come she doesn't lift her leg and piss on the hydrant and go trotting back to the tyrant? Why do they always make us pay dues?

"I'm not acting any way. You are in a mood," David said.

"I'm not in a mood. I'm always in one mood when I see you."

"Bitchy."

This is what happens. You lean out to your man, ready to greet him at the end of a day, your feelings all mobilized, and sliding down your spine like a jellied snake comes the rebuff.

The countless hours, the numbers of men, the times I have felt the snake down my back, and he eventually reaches something at the base, the switch is touched and the entire body leaps into quick shock. Absolutely involuntary. The snake had hit the switch. My voice climbed up the pole without grease.

"David, I've really had a terrible day. Can we have some dinner? Mr. Newmark fired me." I would tell him next that my house was on fire and I had lost my possessions. I went on about the office incident, keeping an eye on the level of his glass. He may know more about Martin Buber than I do, but I knew my David. "I'm free again."

"I think the original line is right for the play."

"I didn't say it was wrong. Winnie doesn't have the concept right. Basically, she is without concept. Isn't that what the play is really about, being black today? Well, I'll tell you, mister, you get some colored fella in that audience and he hears Jim go on about Huck being the blackest white boy, that customer may feel good, but baby he knows it's a lie."

"She is so vulnerable, Jane."

Ah, Jane. He had inched it out at last. "And I'm a fortress. I had a crummy day and I walk in expecting to see you and I'm greeted by the sight of your collaborator. I like Winnie, who needs an enemy. But what about me? They're shooting bullets at me all the time."

"I'm pretty bloody myself."

"How was your day?" If there was a wound I would bind it, a weakness to wrap myself around. He could become my occupation. A late-day shadow from a standing lamp fell across the floor, like a Giacometti sculpture, long and stretched with pain.

"An absolute bitch of a day. I've got the most awful headache."

I went to the bathroom which he had recently redone in gold paper, gold fixtures, brass faucets, gold shag rug. In the medicine chest was a hypochondriac's arsenal. David was a specialist in head, the items on shelf one, but shelf two was loaded with stomach. On the top shelf he had joint and eye and skin. I reached for some pills and a glass of water. The glass was decorated in gold leaf. It all looked smashing.

I brought him the pills. "Not the Fiorinal, they're not for this head. Didn't you find the Percodan?"

I found the Percodan. "Take two." He took one. I took the other.

"Why did you do that?"

"Why not?"

"I have a vile head."

I stood behind the couch, drew his head back and worked the temples lightly with the tips of my fingers in a circular motion. A small face with clean lines, cheeks a little pouty, lips a little prissy, good bone throughout, the skin lying freshly on a tight, crafted frame. Light from the outside polished the cheekbone. Little blond hairs circled around the high place. I brushed my fingers against the hairs. "Do you want to talk about your day?" I was better than Arnold Seltz, mild, medicinal, maternal.

"A vile day. Before Winnie came up I had a squabble with Eddie Russell because he said Pam wasn't young enough for the part, the new show he's casting for, and I had a trial with Howard over some dumb bit in *Huck*, which could kill us all yet. A little higher, a bit more pressure, thanks, that's fine. A call from Ohio, the Wiggins sisters want to come back for another try. Mrs. W. is a driver. What possesses these women to push? Push, push. That's one thing I cannot stomach. They push. Pam's not that way at all. She is an absolute dear." He lifted his head and looked up at me. "She's separated from her husband, has the kids here. I found a place for them on the East Side. I told her to stay home with her Fletch but she's had it. She's forty and wants to start a new life. And she needs me, Jane. I don't know."

I increased the pressure. "She's in love with you. A forty-year-old lady."

"She is a dear. She doesn't try to cut anyone's balls."

"Like me."

"Keep doing that. I feel better. Jane, that is the one thing you have never done."

"Then I'm like Pam Haber."

"In many ways. I'm trying to get her settled and Howard off my back."

"You got Roger Voisin off your back."

"Roger is an idiot. A stupid, faggy, no-talent person."

"You want me to get in touch with Mrs. Wiggins. I'm free, David." It was seven years since the Weyer sisters, whom David and I sent back to the hills, the Weyer sisters, the Wiggins sisters, seven years, Pam Haber and Roger Voisin and now what, Percodan, Scotch and crazy shadows on the floor. I drank and continued rubbing. That's my baby. I'll outlast them all. I would get his little thing stiff as a stick and suck on it and feel the love draining through into my mouth.

"Not yet. Take a few days off and we'll talk."

"I can do it. For myself I couldn't. For you."

"I could bring you in on *Huck* and help pull the thing together."

Huck luck suck schmuck. I rubbed and bent down for a kiss on the rubbing spot. His temple hairs were aphrodisiac. "I could really help. I could be stage manager, David, let me be stage manager." I was the stage manager, like the first days at Civic Theater back home. Didn't I bring furniture from my own house for the *Junior Miss* production? I was the director, David was the producer, produced and directed by David and Jane Astor. We would sit over veal parmigiana and chianti, make delicious plans.

"I'm hungry." I took my hands away.

He let his lips part and he reached for my hand. I pressed his against my breast and gave him some tongue, a sweet little appetizer. I put my hand on the crotch. He stood up and we moved together. We were exactly the same height. My David, I could eat him up with my love. Don't wound me with your fags and your Pam Habers. We had the marvelous thing about equal height kissing, of laying shoulder against shoulder, where nose meets nose and chin meets chin, a plane of such sameness that you feel doubled on yourself, or maybe, a little more peculiarly but probably more accurately, that you are loving a physical projection of self, as if Narcissus literally faced a three-dimensional self when he looked into that clear pool. When I kissed David I kissed me and, always, a tremor of exquisite recognition went through me, my god was it possible that I loved me. In touching that athletic boy skin I reached through to bone and marrow. In giving me his petulances he gave me mine, sex dissolved. There would no longer be any excuses about what women go through and the fate of women. He was indisputably a man and he had my weaknesses. When I held David I held my life. He must know it. Of course he knew it. He comes back to me when he is on the edge. I was a last desperate act of survival. Instead of being sore about that I should cherish it. He loves me only when it counts.

We sat in a small Italian restaurant around the corner with the wine bottle between us and the lit candle stuck in another. Food was on the plate. I ate because I was hungry. They could have served me yesterday's dead salad. And me the sworn enemy of limp lettuce.

"Tell me how you feel." I crossed my arms on the table and leaned between the wine bottle and the wine bottle candle. "About everything."

"In the morning I wake up with a wooly mouth, and I don't smoke. I feel dreadful, burned out. Every morning I'm a shell. That's how I feel about mornings."

"How do you feel about Italian restaurants?"

"Italian restaurants make me want to sleep late in the

morning. Then I can get right up without feeling like a shell."

"Tell me how you feel about riding on the Honda."

"When I ride on the Honda I feel like a soundless hurrying fish who is flying to get back to water. On the bike I feel the destination receding before me. I chase wind and water. I am nothing."

"Tell me how you feel with me on the back of the Honda."

He held my hand and picked at my nails. I was very scared he would tell me everything. David and I, we tell each other everything, but what do we really tell each other. "Tell me everything."

"With you on the back of the Honda." He pinched the wick. The stinky smoke rose in a wisp. "Let's go and find out."

On Broadway and Eighty-Fourth Street a Puerto Rican kid chasing a ball ran in front of us. David hit the brake and we slithered around him. I held on and felt his abdomen draw tight as steel. The kid raced back to his stickball game. A Jewish man with a fishnet shopping bag stood on the corner shaking his head.

"Don't you just love it," David said.

"Tell me how it feels." We coasted up Broadway. I made no plans. He gave it full throttle and we flew down Riverside Drive. We stopped for a light. "Does it feel good?" He pressed his back against me and we clunked helmets. He revved the engine with the hand accelerator. Off, we dipped and swayed and curved, and back to his place. He parked the bike in front of the house not far from a hydrant. He counted steps.

"Ten and a half feet. I'm all right."

"How does the pasta sit?" We stood in the doorway breathing hard.

"Tell me how you feel," he said, and we laughed

Upstairs I made new drinks, put on a mush station and

sat at his feet by the sofa-bed-couch thing. With the cold hand from the iced glass he touched my cheek. A singer was telling us that he didn't know his right foot from his left, he was misty. We could have a hearth and a setter and look at the fire dance on the flaming logs, and on the big hearth rug he would fuck me and we would be fire. A police car wailed up Eighth Avenue.

"I could have hit that kid." He went to the window and looked out. I moved on to the couch.

"Come."

He sat down away from me and waved his glass. "Do me."

I put the glass on the table and moved closer. "I'll do you." A quick put-off kiss and the repeat order for the drink. In the kitchen whiskey splashed over cubes. On the calendar next to the cupboard a note under last Saturday's date: "PH drinks." I looked at other dates. No JC's. I would not "do him." Where was my resolve? How many times do I have to go up the trail and end up smelling skunk? Let him wait. I sipped my drink and looked at the names on the calendar. An army of initials, a life of activity, a world of power, competition, rivalry, pettiness, dish and wheel in a spider's web of intrigue. We respect success. David Astor, talent man.

We sat apart and talked. How were drinks with PH? One more drink and I would dare. Jane, Howard Milman is positively impaled on the deadly fingers of your Stefanie. If he doesn't get her off his back. You'll never get anything from a man who is afraid of his wife and sadistic to his mistress. David, he's not sadistic. Well, his selfishness is the same thing. You're not a prize package either, David Astor. Sadistic?

"Why did you hang that calendar in the kitchen?"

"It's near the phone."

"I see Pam Haber drinks and this one dinner and that one cocktails. I don't have to see it."

"Don't look."

"O.K."

We went on with who were the real sadists among our friends which meant the masochists were coming and then the s-m's, a lot of those, using their tongues as whips against themselves. We agreed that Howard Milman was a classic sadomasochist, Stefanie a perfect masochist, although I was a close second. But who was the sadist? You David, it comes down to you. How to inflict pain and love it. You read all the big philosophers, you know all about rebellion and revolution and suicide and *angst*.

"And the fear and trembling unto death."

"A lot of that. Boy, I need a drink." I brought the bottle in. We sat a little closer. The mood had changed again. Hysteria makes great bedfellows.

Night light from the signs fell into the window. The sofa was now bed and the light pinked the sheets. The drinks sat in thick old-fashioned glasses on the night table. The luminous clock face grinned down at us.

"There."

"There?"

"Right there. That's it. Oh."

He came up and sweet mouths touched. I sucked ear, finger, tongue around the eye, in the belly. He did nipple, tid-bit nips, then mouth. I pushed it all the way. Then the other. Then back. I got on top and trailed tongue from breastbone, slowly, down, into the hair, tongue at the base, up the underside, around, to the tip, lips on tip, sides, top, mouth, mouth, suck, up again.

"Good?"

"Unh."

"More?"

He went in. I helped. It was a small hot iron rod. My hands found his ass. Noises. Movement. Out again. He lay back. Too much booze. He is fucking his mother. He can't fuck his mother. I got on top, pushed it in, moved up and down, gently, bent over and found his mouth, tongues lashed, very furious, angry, dragon tongues. I shouldn't be on top. Too smothering. Too mothering. On our sides. More drink. Glasses on bellies, wet circles, back to action. Dog style. A try. Belly slaps against ass. He collapses against my back. All that booze. On top again he works. We find the rhythm. Animal whimpers from me encourage him. I throw it at him good and he fucks me. Come, come, my baby.

We lay on our backs side by side. "Was it a good come?"

"I'm drained."

"Tell me about it."

"Tell me everything."

"David, I don't want everything." He waited. "Just you."

"I have to do something about that."

We kissed and he told me the come was a true one, a surrender of the secret body inside the body. "Coming has always frightened me. Like I was getting lost. The surrender come is not like that. I'm not afraid of you."

"Don't ever be afraid of me."

"Sometimes I'm afraid."

I shuddered and he put his arm around me. I lay very still, feeling his arm. More than anything I wanted that arm. "Why is it so hard to love?" I asked Jerry Kay that question once, his long drooping cock nestled between his legs. He said he would like to but it was a luxury he couldn't afford, it got in the way of his pleasures. Love obliges you to give up something. He didn't know how to do that. I watched David's face as he composed an answer. Like an eagle swooping on an unsuspecting victim, I felt a down coming, descending like a black shroud. Answer me, David, please answer me.

"I'll try this. It's not hard to love. We do it all the time, from cradle to grave. Right now I feel it."

"Now?"

"Yes, right now. But it's hard to believe it can last. So you look for the lasting love, the one that is beyond belief. The rest of the time you make do."

Maybe a man would satisfy that ideal for him. "I can give you everything."

"You certainly would try."

"Then why not."

"I wish I knew the answer to that."

In the bathroom I found the bottle of Percodan, one a day, do not exceed the dosage. I took one. That would make two, one from before. In the bed David nestled his back against me and slept. I looked at the clock and at a painting on the wall near the bed, an abstract oil by a friend of David's. I tried to make a representation, a large red ear, cut, blood splattered over a white bull. David slept very quietly, his chest barely moving. The white bull was rushing to the frame intent on goring it. The light from the street threw pink on the white bull who looked now as if he were flying out of the sun. I let the Percodan find its way into the system and I picked at the maroon rope tassel and waited until morning.

Part III

Chapter 1

THE PROSPECT of being out of work for as long as six months sat like a good dessert on my stomach. I had been out of work before. When you bounce around as much as I have there are going to be frequent at-home periods. In the past I had been frantic, burning the wires or my friends, when I was able to overcome inertia, dead closed-door catatonia. I had never given myself a piece of time, a good solid hunk of it, to chew around the edges, taste its fragrance, live in its sweet indolence. I wanted to sit over crisp bacon and toast in the morning and plot a little. Wasn't it time to stop playing career girl and seriously apply myself to the business of finding a man? I was tired of work, tired of the foul moods of ambitious men and the petty sensitivities of inadequate women. If David Astor wanted me I would be well rested, with fresh underwear and a sparkling house. I thought of myself as clever, but profound I was not. I wanted nothing deeper than the length of penis in me of a man I loved.

I spent the next couple of weeks with a kerchief around my head and a dustcloth in my hand. I scrubbed and mopped and polished. The hamper was empty of soiled clothes, the kitchen porcelain shone, furniture glistened. I had a girl in one day, sent by Stefanie's mother from Brooklyn, and she vacuumed and did the windows (for a bribe), cleaned out the cupboards, washed down the refrigerator. I met Stefanie for lunch, Pat Seeley for lunch, went to a movie with Roger Voisin, had my old sleepmate Bernie Wasserman over for a friendly dinner, talked on the phone with Jess Olin who needed some emergency booking help, did I know anyone, no, but Richie Davis is in town I'll get him in touch with you, and another call from Ambrose Winter, an old agent friend, who needed help in the office, would I come down, and I did for one day, straightening out his books, eating an expense account lunch at The Brasserie with Ambrose. And a late night drunk call from Richard, no, not tonight, sorry I'm tired, no abuse from the other end. Betty Snow came over one night and we watched a late show, me with a bare foot diddling around her crotch for a minute, eyes were mutual, we weren't ready yet, and a little grass one night with Charles the writer next door, a pleasant smoke, I got dopey and he rapped on about his book. I even sat down with resolution one morning and started a journal, a record of thoughts while at leisure. I entered my weight, down eight pounds, no booze, clean life. I listed all the men I had slept with, I stopped at thirty-two, but there were more, a dozen one-night stands, I remembered the names but for posterity? So I closed the journal, a nice old-fashioned nickel notebook, now twenty-nine cents. I made another entry some days later after a visit to Dr. Seltz, an observation about self-esteem, whether you earn it or buy it or have it genetically transferred, but I started getting stomach cramps, stopped the entry, found that I was out of Tampax, bought a box at the store, discovered it was a false alarm, and realized I was a week late. Well, when you fuck around you pay the price, but the pill, which I was on, was supposed to take care of that kind of thinking. Evidently I had missed as I had missed once before with the diaphragm some years back.

Stefanie came over and we talked baby for a while, and we talked abortion. Stefanie said be realistic how are you going to support a kid. I'll get help from him I said, but who was him, and I told her it was easy, I hadn't touched anybody since John Ames and Jerry Kay and Richard Doyle and David Astor. I could hang it on any one or none.

"Jane, you have got to get a man to pay for this."

"You mean through the nose, Stef?"

"I mean cash, but if you're going to get rid of it you'll need help."

"I could have the baby."

I called Seltz and he thought no, the baby would be too much right now, I was still working through my own difficulties. But, Dr. Seltz, I'll always be doing that. Nevertheless, it was no, that was his advice. I was free of course to do what I wanted.

Stefanie thought Richard would make a nice father. "Although," I said, "John Ames has the hottest seed."

"How do you manage?"

"If I managed I wouldn't be here. You mean, how can I screw all those guys? I could ask you, 'How do you stick with Howard?' "

Stefanie was no help. Her doctor had gone out of business. There I was, my apartment looking like the deck of a Navy ship, my refrigerator filled with food, clean sheets on the bed, the terrace spotless, I was ready to open the door to new romance, rested and primed. And I had a baby in me, confirmed by my gynecologist, who knew somebody, not cheap, but very reliable, be sure to come back to him for post-op. I took the address with me, collected my check at the unemployment office ("Nothing for you this week, Miss Castle"), went home, locked the door, put myself on the bed, and considered the matter. The matter was that I was afraid and the matter was that I wanted to know who the father was and the matter was that I had no money and nobody to lean on. Could I run to Aunt Claire and tell her I got knocked up I need money and a place to stay and be taken care of. The

matter was that I was a thirty-six-year-old orphan getting by
on pills and thinned-out dreams of falling in love. I would
have the baby and it would love me. That's a laugh. What do
I want to clean baby's shit for when I needed to clean a
soiled interior. I could handle a baby, I really could. Haven't
I run out to Long Island and taken care of Helen's kids? I'm
a natural mother, warm, protective, spontaneous, generous. I
could take her kids and really do something with them. It
could be David's kid. Why not. He planted the last seed. Last
in, first out. He would give me money, support, come uptown
and take the kid to Central Park like the divorced daddies.
Or he could marry me. What if he came out a smiling Irishman like Richard or big, brown-eyed, dark-haired like Jerry
Kay. It could be another girl with the nose of Sam Castle,
and then where would I be. (In their room, through the
walls. "So she's got a nose . . . why did this happen to me . . .
it happened to both of us. . . .")

I sat up on the edge of the bed. Have the baby, have the
abortion, it made no difference. What mattered only was the
knowledge that I was the cast-out infant, Moses in the bushes,
ready to bring myself to the promised land, that my life at
this point was an act of self-discovery, a new identity, washed
clean of a half a lifetime of bad news, of tears and rejections
and frustrations and the clawing grip of self-pity. Didn't I
have to stop thinking, what is wrong with me, why won't
anybody love me, and say to myself, Jane C., you can be a
hero with possibilities. I had become without being aware of
it, like a killer in white sneakers, a person of taste, wit,
imagination, a ballsy chick. Oh, mother, I have paid my dues.
I'm not ready for a child yet. It's late but I have time. When
the man comes to me with plan, no accident, no sticky valves
in the engine, no by the way I'm pregnant it must have
slipped by, come with your blueprint, when you come it will
be our kid, and I won't give a shit if the nose is screwed on to
his ass, he will be mine.

I went downstairs and had a mayonnaise and green pepper sandwich on white toast and a glass of soda. I was very frightened. What if the man slips and I hemorrhage and my bloody life spills out. Just when I've discovered that if I play my cards right I can win. I was playing with a marked deck which said, cool it, stay within yourself, extend nothing, don't lay your *shtick* on them, be a Moses of Manhattan with ice water in your veins. Make the journey to the Red Sea and I'll bet dollars to doughnuts I can make those fucking waters part. The paternity issue was false. I had made my bed, blah, blah. I will manage my own fate. I called Gene Gordon in Waterbury and told him he had to come to the city, I needed help. Fortunately, he said, there was a builders' convention, and he was coming in.

Two days before Gene arrived I got a call from Randy Smith. He was between acting jobs and was selling mutual funds for a new black outfit, funded by the government as part of its venture in black capitalism. Randy was thinking of giving up the theater even though the breakthrough was here, Sidney Poitier and Ossie Davis weren't getting all the jobs, he was getting married soon to a nice chocolate chick who was going African but was still used to some bread, her father a big Harlem insurance man. I told Randy that David might start casting for *Huck* and the job was open, he could be Jim.

He brought a bottle of Courvoisier and we discussed the role. "I'm wearing Rogers Peet suits. I don't know if I'm up to a nigger role." Randy was wearing pinstriped blue, modified Continental cut, sideburns, small mustache. A light-blue shirt matched the suit. Tortoiseshell glasses, professorial.

"I think that's the whole point. It's a musical. You play against the nigger role, undercut it. It's a serious parody."

"Huck saves Jim a couple of times. Jane, you know where it's at. We want to do our own thing."

"But he saves him for the right reasons. Jim is a man, a father figure for Huck. Look at the father Huck had."

"We been motherin' and fatherin' you cats for a long time. Jim has to rely on Huck for his salvation."

"We all save each other. Don't you believe in the brother-hood of man?"

"You must be kidding. Who gave you that sauce?"

"I'm not kidding. I don't think black, white. I think people."

"Maybe you do, maybe you don't. I'll give you a demon-stration of what most people think."

We stood on the corner of Second Avenue looking for a cab.

"Okay, demonstration number one."

Randy stepped into the street away from the light and raised his hand. A cab came steaming down, stopped. Randy moved for it. It zoomed away screeching rubber. Another pressed the button after slowing down. Another stopped, and as I was about to get in the cabbie said he had to make the garage, his time was up. A colored guy was driving the next one.

We sat in Terry's Pub on Central Park West and Ninety-Seventh Street. "What do you think of the brotherhood of man?"

I was sympathetic, contrite. "It isn't easy." Why wasn't he bitter? "What about demonstration number two?"

"Later," he said, flashing black man's white teeth. As a kid I had a throwing game, the cover with the huge grinning teeth of a black boy. Come, hit the nigger.

"It's not so bad. We're riding a bull market. Look around."

It was a bustling middle-class Negro scene. They looked like young college graduates, a whole new generation, teach-ers, social workers, gorgeous girls in gorgeous clothes, the guys spiffy, preening with the sense of affluence you see in exclusive midtown clubs. It was a mixed scene, whites with whites, whites with blacks, very checkered, a wild scene, but very carefully watched over. They were not going to let anything happen. We sat at a table in the corner, something to eat and drink. No dancing. They would give away their background, which they did, a little.

"Hey, man," a slight, bespectacled, sweet-voiced guy said, coming to our table. "What's the news?" The accent probably represented the milieu at Terry's. A faint wisp of the old sod, but mainly pretty straight civil service American.

Randy got up. "Meet Miss Jane Castle. Bob Williams."

The guy bowed at the waist, deep. "A friend of Randy's. . . ."

"You got a nice place here. Rent-controlled?" I could fall in with this scene. It wasn't a chitterling crowd. What was wrong with a groovy middle-class black crowd?

"The man doesn't go for that jive." He winked at Randy. Randy winked back. He walked away and somebody else came up. "Randy dandy, long time no see." Very light, thin-lipped, Caucasian, but black. They all knew each other. The music was playing, the place was hubbubing, the air was solid with connection. Was I romanticizing? Mean or nice, there was community. I wondered what it was like uptown.

Coming home in the cab I asked him, "What do colored people think when they see white people with colored people?"

"The girls don't like it much. It cuts down the market. The last guy that came over, he married a white chick, and like they cut him off at home."

"Just like the rest of us, right?"

"The guys don't like it either when they see a black girl with a white guy."

"Big male ego threat. We're all alike, baby."

When we got home he tried to prove it. "You're like everyone else," I said, clinical.

"Yeah, but I'm darker."

"You look great against the blue sheets."

We fucked and he was very strong. The first time he got on top of me, the second time he rolled me over and fucked me from behind. When he took a shower I gave him a pink towel, and when he walked out of the bathroom the pink towel on his body, I couldn't stand it.

"I'm pregnant."

"The way to go."

"It could have been you, Randy. Listen, you're a theater person, you're not gay. You've got talent, you're human. Why couldn't it have been you?"

"We got to eat in them special places. That's like getting it from both sides. And if I'm your stud and I leave you with a tan number, what then?"

"I haven't thought about it. You make me feel good."

"I got my weaknesses."

"One of them is you like to fuck."

"Jane, you don't hide the truth."

"Well, then."

Off came the pink towel and the brown shaft came at me, not any longer or wider than that of the other race, but it was a courageous cock, gone through the race wars and other indignities. I loved the feeling of his black sensuality, boy was it true, but only because we wanted it to be true. We invented the black stud with the blazing dick, the white girl's erotic dream fantasy. It was like getting fucked by a dog. Randy was very dignified, almost restrained, royal. He went at me hard, but it was as if he was teaching me a lesson. All right, white girl, this is what it's like. You may think I'm a dog, but I know I'm a man, man.

He said he would like to contribute for the doctor, how much could he give me, but I told him he had given me enough already, a lesson in the brotherhood of man to begin with. "Be my friend, that's good payment."

"But don't look at the clock."
"Never look at the clock."

When Gene Gordon came I piled it on him. He was performing his function of problem-unloader. He took on the
world's dreck, flung his way, which he patiently let fly in his
face, two front teeth sticking out in that perennial toothy
grin of buckteethed people. At forty, suddenly successful as a
builder of prefab houses, he still maintained the old habits of
fidelity and propriety. In the year we went together it was
just those virtues that broke the back of the relationship. I
treated him with contempt. I had learned from the Jerry
Kays, abuse me, I love you, the oldest school in the world. I
told him the tax man was on my back and I needed money
for a lawyer who could find a loophole or make a deal. And I
told him I was a lady of leisure and the government checks
were small, I needed a loan to keep me going.

He put his fastidious, bachelory hand on mine, the comfortable touch of intimates who have opened all the closets
and let all the skeletons out. If he didn't make it by fifty, we
agreed, then we would marry.

"How much do you need?"
"When are you going to say no to me?"
"I've got lots of it. How much do you need?"
"I need two hundred for the lawyer and five hundred to
supplement the unemployment. Add that to what I owe you.
What does it make?"
"It makes me a pauper. What else? There is something
else."
"I need an abortion."
"Can't you get the guy?"
"I could get a guy."
"I paid for one. At least it was my own doing."
It might have been. I had had a one night with a guy

named Al, I forgot his last name, at fertility time. "I need seven hundred."

"It was five hundred the last time."

"And eggs were forty-five cents a dozen. Do you want to make love?"

"Will it cost me fourteen hundred dollars?"

"Ain't I worth it?"

His aunt is away and we have the lake cottage key. He brings a briefcase in from the trunk of the car, opens it and takes out books, *Money and Banking* and *Management*. "I have to do some studying." He is taking the summer business course at the Extension. With his seersucker suit and plain steel-rimmed glasses he looks the part already. It is a big adventure for both of us, alone in a borrowed cottage. It is very chilly, late August. He finds logs for the fire while I thumb through the books. I am sitting on the couch, an old by-the-fire vintage. "Cold as a witch's tit," he says, rubbing his hands in front of the fire. "It's warm on the couch," I say, hand draped over the back. I have been bringing him along, the fourth date and nothing more than tongue in the mouth until now. Gene is my first real innocent, practically a virgin at twenty-six. He sees me as the stylish demi-mondaine, a feeling I like, being the one who has been around. He sits next to me, puts his arm on the back of the couch, and stretches his feet on the coffee table and yawns.

"You shouldn't go out in the middle of the week," I say. I trace a finger along his arm.

"The management course is rough." He takes off his glasses and wipes them. I run a nail along his arm.

"How can you understand those graphs and things." My finger finds the ear and the curve of the metal frame. I make a path around the ear.

"I don't mind the graphs. It's the logarithms." A dark patch of sweat shows under the armpit.

"Why don't you take off your jacket. You won't be so warm."

He takes off his jacket and sits with a long-sleeved light-weight shirt and a summer rep tie. A small bead runs down the temple just past the earlobe. "I think I'll take off my tie."

"Why don't you do that." He also rolls up his sleeves. He leans his head back and breathes heavily.

"It's a rough course."

I let my finger slide down his shirt. I stop at the belt. "What have you got there?" Through the seersucker pants, a little rise.

He swallows. "I think I'm hard."

"Are you hot?"

"I think I said hard."

"That's terrible. Why are you hard?"

"I'm hot."

"That's awful." My finger goes below the belt and is a sleepy ant on a blue stripe of seersucker. It goes down the leg. He unbuckles his belt. "What are you doing?" I say.

"My belt is tight. It needs to be unbuckled."

"Should I help you?" I undo the belt and the button of his pants. The white boxer shorts peek out. "What is going on here?" My ant-finger runs around the top band of the boxer shorts, then a little lower, just above the bump. He opens his legs wide and slides down the couch. His head is pressed at an angle. I bend over and run my tongue around the edge of his mouth, then up around the nose and eyes. My finger has reached the bump and with the nail I make lines on the bump.

"Your bump is twitching violently. Why does it twitch so violently?"

"Suck me," he whispers in a gargly voice.

"But I hardly know you," I say as I unsnap the boxer shorts and release the bump, which springs out, a good medium-sized prick, head very full, very twitching. "Maybe a little kiss, but that's all." I bend down, keeping my finger moving gently down around the base and around his balls. A little, tiny kiss right on the tippy tip. I feel an iron hand clamped on my head. I push up.

"Gene, whatever are you doing?"

"Put your mouth down there, please."

"Pretty please."

"Pretty please. Put your mouth down there."

"Where?"

"On me."

"He's very big." I run my tongue on the underside from the top down to the base, then up again, and rim the head, a nice neat circle.

"Suck it," he commands, his voice gross with blood.

"Maybe just a little." My lips go over the head. I get my hand under and between his legs and my finger finds his asshole. He pushes his dick violently into my mouth. I come away. "You'll choke me if you do that. Maybe you'd better rest a bit." I keep my finger working in the hole. His prick is dancing.

"Suck my. . . . Suck me." His eyes are closed, sweat is streaming down his cheeks. He lifts up his ass and I help him slip his pants and shorts down to his ankles. They fall on top of *Money and Banking*. I cover his whole thing with my mouth and I start to suck. It is rock-hard and tastes good. I love the prick in my mouth. I tongue it and suck it and he starts to move in me. He shoves it in deep and I suck hard. My finger is way up in his asshole. He is furious now, jabbing it into me.

The sound of a car on the gravel path. He leaps up, flies to the window dick dancing in the air. "My aunt." The car comes up to the door, backs away, and goes down the road. "Somebody was turning in the driveway."

"Come here," I say.

"We'd better go, my aunt might come."

We stand in the doorway and embrace. He complains that he hurts. He holds me tight, moves against me rapidly, and comes. He shows wet through his pants. "I could have prevented that," I say. We go back to the cottage a week later and make love on his aunt's bed, a very soft mattress with very noisy springs. I let him go down on me but I worry about smells. His teeth press against my pussy. I suppress the urge to laugh. He tells me he loves me and we both go goopy. My eyes are filled and tender. We fuck a lot in the car on a secluded road near the cottage. It is very intense for a couple of months and then we settle into habit. We begin to needle each other. He says he treats me better than I deserve, stop being so superior who did I think I was, but I couldn't change, there was no style, he wasn't Jerry Kay, was he? He was a prissy man without even the virtue of fag stylishness, why did I sleep with you in the first place I felt sorry for you, you were so horny you looked sick and then you turn and start to take me for granted, which was the last straw. The lovemaking changed to an I-want-to-get-my-rocks-off thing, hard, flat, joyless comes for him, nothing for me, not that there was ever anything for me.

Chapter 2

I DIDN'T CALL John Ames or Jerry Kay or Richard or David.
I took Gene Gordon's $700 in hundreds, in an envelope and
walked the fifteen blocks to Seventy-eighth Street. It was
already late September and the smoggy summer air was making way for a fresh fall breeze, temperature in the sixties, and
I wore a sturdy denim skirt and white cotton blouse, like I
was off to work, passing my regulars on Second Avenue, an
extra big hello to the barber I didn't know leaning against
his pole reading the *Daily News,* consulting with the fruit
man on the races. Gene had gone back to New Haven, very
excited about a parcel of land he was buying, goodbye, good
luck, I could have been an aging aunt in California. I wasn't
terrified as I was the first time with Gene, but there was
something more ominous, something sweeping off the East
River with the new air and the fresh supply of clean soot that
peppered the streets and landed on the ten-cent Clark bar I
picked up on Eighty-sixth Street. It wasn't dying or pain or
the unknown doctor who sounded much less tacky than the
guy at the Peter Stuyvesant Hotel on the West Side. Pat
Seeley, who had gotten both names through the grapevine,
was waiting with tea for me, I wouldn't have her along,
spunky cool woman who didn't know from hysterics. The tea
was at the other end of the line, and it was probably that fact

that urged on me the new feeling, a sense of vacuum or wallessness, leaning against space and nobody with a rope to pull me back, not falling out into it, just pressing against nothing, a world without counterforce, you read the *New York Times* on Sunday, the most frightening thing alone people can do, the sheer bulk of it an illusion of weight and force and substance, a world of ballast as if the print itself cushioned you with its reality, its black-smudge certainty, how many times have I sat with that mass of the world's busyness on my lap, the theater page crawling with things. And it falls away into Sunday, absorbed into the vacuum of those dangerous late afternoon hours. Leaning against nothing, I made my way to the place. I had gone that morning for an interview for a job, part-time, recommended by Liz Neally, an RC friend who heard of this venture to orient dropout clergy to social action. It was called Crosscurrent, and the girl who interviewed me, Dee Tate, sounded great, a departure from what I had done. She had said something to me about love and suffering being helpless bedmates and I carried that in with me.

A nurse with dark hair greeted me, very efficient, locking the door behind me and asking me for the envelope like Bob Hope does on Academy Award night. She took me in to the doctor who introduced me to another man, older, they both spoke with accents, two guys with mustaches and gray hair, very professional. I thought, oh, these two guys they could rape me. The nurse had disappeared. I was scared. They laid me out on the table and put my feet in the stirrups. The younger gray hair who I assumed was my Dr. Sazac said, "Just a little local anesthetic. I'm going to punch you in the buttock. It will hurt a little. Dr. Visak is going to stand here and he is going to help me and he is going to comfort you." He gave me the shot. Then he said, "I'm putting this white cream on your vaginal area to keep the hair from getting in my way so that I don't have to shave you." Dr. Visak stood at the head of the table and Dr. Sazac sat on a stool at the foot. A big light was over my head and he had a dentist's swivel lamp beamed on my hole. My feet were up on these stirrups, my box painted white, my ass in the wind. I had done the scene before but it was strange, as if I had got my foot caught in the door of a subway car while carrying an armful of parcels. Once I dropped my purse on Sixth Avenue and Forty-eighth Street right on the road. Cars stopped, people bent to help me gather my spilled-out things. The embarrassment.

He began with his tools. An abortion is not a comfortable feeling. It is a raw, crusty, horrible, scooping feeling. You feel him scraping and scooping. I guess it's the scraping metal tool against the wall of the womb. Dr. Visak was holding my hands and he told me he came from Vienna, although he was really a Czech, and that he couldn't pass the medical boards, there was a foreign quota, he was head of a clinic in Vienna, while down below old plumber was fixing the pipes. I couldn't see him. My head was in a dentist's headrest. "It's only going to take a few minutes more," and more clink of instruments, very similar to the clicking of knitting needles, only not so fast.

In twenty minutes he had me off the table, over to a couch, brought a cigarette, lit it for me. Dr. Visak sat down on a stool near me and the two of them gave me a little birth control talk. They went out and I lay for an hour, not like the first time when the guy in Jersey got me right out still under the influence of the drug. Dr. Sazac came back, gave me two prescriptions for antibiotics, and told me to wear a Kotex and what hours of the day to call him every day for a week. I walked out of the office, thanking him profusely. This was no boiler room operation. For my seven hundred skins I was getting top-drawer stuff. I had given a man once again the privilege of being a garbage collector, cleaning out some dirty pieces of life, dumping them in the general stew of discarded membranes and entrails. Think of all these guys working away across the country, around the world, the thousands of legs in stirrups and the thousands of doctors poking around inside the cavern, all searching with their instruments for that last bit of offending life, awful offal. And the woman the vessel. One man puts it in, another man cleans it out. What the hell else can she be but the universal garbage can. I wasn't sore at those pricks for being pricks. It was just that at times you don't want to abide the humiliation. Ten thousand naked asses stuck in the air, ten thousand white creamed cunts opened for the inspector general. It was the collective image that sent me. Was it maybe a trick played by God. Reduce the whole pleasure-pain principle to absurdity. Take away the last dignity of joy and suffering. Shove cold steel up the snatch.

I left the place and walked slowly over to Pat Seeley's and we drank tea while I told her the saga, how scared I was, how really good these guys were, a great experience, you aren't a woman until you've tried one. Visit your Friendly Neighborhood Abortionist. Get your checkup once a year. Pat asked me to stay but I left and walked home, no cab, no nothing. When I got home I fell on the bed, exhausted, overtired.

I thought of the first abortion, with Gene Gordon, and the feeling I had then, a very quick, almost suffocating feeling of the exquisite perfection of having a baby and being happy with Gene. I could never be happy with him but at that moment sitting outside the doctor's office in his car I wanted to seize the chance. I said to him, "I'll never love you again as I do this minute." We went to this crazy guy who didn't even have a nurse, grabbed the envelope from Gene, stuffed it into his pocket, a fat guy, Lou Costello with a mustache, gave orders, "Come here Jenny, sit there Joe." And nonstop talking through the whole thing, Jenny and Joeing us to death while Gene wiped the sweat from my face. He was thorough, efficient, insisted on getting the last bit out, "O.K.

Jenny Joe, we're finished now, sit there for a few minutes I gotta have a cup of coffee it isn't worth it they're on my back I'm going to give it up you crazy kids better learn how to protect yourself are you all right now Jenny now remember," dramatically leaning over to us on the foyer bench, in a stage whisper, "they're out to get me. I tell you because I trust you. They will get the best surgeon on the East Coast." When we left he was sitting on the examining table with a mug of coffee and a cigarette with a long ash hanging from it.

I wore the Kotex for a few days, lying around in bed taking it easy, watching the boob tube for hours, quiz shows and forties movies, called in to Dr. Sazac who cautioned me, no relations for another week or so, and certainly it was time to take vows, a little celibacy if not poverty. Resolved, I would be celibate, put a halt to the superficial cocks, the pussy-hungry men who can so easily send you down the trail from Librium to Demerol, depression merchants, the best of them. I lay in my bed with a single pillow watching Ronald Reagan with his legs cut off turning his face to the wall when Robert Cummings, the famous Dr. Parris Mitchell of *King's Row* returns from Europe to press his cheek to his old buddy; Ann Sheridan with a wet face at the foot of the bed, and I say to myself, what is the matter with those creeps, all of them, can't they come into my house with a new pillow once instead of a bouncing penis. "Janie, I see you have only one pillow." If you can't cultivate a two-pillow philosophy what good are you. Everybody wants to jump into bed and nobody thinks of bringing another pillow. At least Ronald Reagan and Ann Sheridan looked too poor to have two pillows and what could he do anyway, poor guy, in shock, no legs. But he got out of that bed to become the governor of California, the creep, which is a lot more than Richard Doyle has done. There really was only one thing to do with my life, to capture David Astor. A letter came from Katz the tax man reminding me of my obligations. I tore it up. I had another obligation to myself. I've paid my taxes. Let him chase me. Everybody wanted something from me but myself. The truth of that fell like a drop of clear water, the way the drop forms itself into pear-shaped perfection before it falls away. I had to make David want me more. He loved me, but it was once a month or two, the rest of the time who knows he had his dick up some guy's ass. If I could understand the double nature, if I could feel what he felt when he was turned off me, that would be a source of power, new knowledge to shore me up against disaster.

I kept busy getting myself set for the new task, putting my psychic house in order, so to speak, a good visit to Seltz to purge the postpartum *triste* and other sundries, trying to raise money for my debts, going to the beauty parlor to have my chin waxed, collecting my check, shopping for some things on Grand Street, some great Pucci print bath towels, five years without new towels, took a trip to see my Aunt Claire, thinking all the time David Astor, the time is ripe, but frozen-handed with the phone, call, don't call, do this do that, got Stefanie's bad advice to stop torturing myself, he is a confirmed homosexual, which maybe he was but he has given me love, baby. I bought him a gold corkscrew and bottle opener and kept it in the drawer for the right moment.

Then a small miracle happened. Somebody fell in love with me. I was going one night a week up to the Crosscurrent office on Seventy-second Street to help Dee Tate work up some brochures for a fund-raising mailing. Dee was a thin, tallish girl out of the straight hair and sandals school with great legs and small breasts, a blanket-in-Central-Park girl from Radcliffe, who collected Portuguese folk songs, majored in math in college, and played the recorder with a group of doctors from New York Hospital, one of whom, doing research in genetics, she married and divorced inside of three years when they discovered their passion was spent in the chamber music group and not in bed. A very bright girl from a class light years from mine, with crazy interests in yoga and archaeology. Organized, with a friendly Wasp even-tempered, sensible grasp of things. The Crosscurrent job fed that strain of social-work-public-service dedication that was so very alien to the jittery, ego-starved, publicity-hungry theater world. Right away I saw that she was smarter than I but dumb about such practicalities as how to hook dough from a potential source, how to connive with agencies and foundations, how to stick your chin in the next guy's soup without embarrassment. We worked alone in the office every Tuesday night while I rapped on about the tricks of promotion, taking over pretty much, and she sat at the table, opposite me, with black coffee and cigarettes, filling me in on the coming revolution in the church, the Episcopalian girl from Rockport, Maine, and the Jewish girl from Connecticut, plotting the fate of disenchanted Irish Roman Catholic boys. And the talk rolled on to comparative ethnic habits and the problem of faith, with Dee filling me in on her dippings into things Oriental, Krishna, and western Gnosticism and the quest for order and harmony, the home church a complete bust, wiped out by a genteel materialism which understated viciously its ownership of everything, from the country club to the soul, top pew to top dollar.

We had a late snack one night and Dee suggested a nightcap at her place which turned out to be what I expected, wall hangings from Peru and carved African heads and bamboo curtains and Polynesian weavings and a mosaic table from India, an apartment fertilized by an imagination that hunts for symbolic extensions in the clutter of objects from exotic cultures. In the Elm Street house my mother had a jade bird from China and a Kerman rug from a W & J Sloane sale in New York. Dee poured Benedictine into A&P shrimp cocktail glasses, a rare native design, I remarked, and we shared a joint of marijuana from the small supply of grass I kept in my bag. Passing it back and forth I asked her about her marriage. She talked through the pot in that slow, sleepy way that grass works, the great legs crossed, the skirt careless and high, finger smoothing the side of the glass. There was never anything wrong, she said, talking down into the mosaic table. We did everything right but love each other. She didn't know if she could explain the feeling of appropriateness in the relationship.

"I think the best word is decorum. Deron probably left the passion with the chromosomes in the lab."

"What is Deron Tate?"

"An old Albany family. His grandfather was in chemicals. Deron grew up like so many of us. We make virtues of our limitations."

"I think that is an excellent concept." Under a little grass I like to move directly to concepts.

"But you're not like that at all. Do you get what I mean?"

"I'm digging you."

"We have rings of iron around us, and we call that jail a palace."

"Up tight."

"That is the truth. This is a good smoke."

"What else about Deron?" My urging was gentle. I was bringing this strange chick out and I didn't want to kill her before the shell opened. I felt a little wet between the legs.

"You mean the sex?"

"Isn't that where it's at?"

"Love is a funny thing. In the chamber group we were transported. What I like about this stuff is the music in it. That's what drugs are about, great music."

The curtain falls away with good stuff. The mind is very clear. The message reaches the lips without interference. "I get a good feeling down here." We drank a little more. Dee got up and put a record on her machine, an Egyptian group, tinny and slow, like Sydney Greenstreet waiting for the vic-

tim to come into the back of the store. The room was beginning to swell with the odor of the marijuana and the reedy
tones of the music, plus an unmeasurable quality of anticipation, which seemed to float up from us and mingle with the
pungent air and turn the African masks on the wall into
satyrs. There was nothing in Dee's slender arms and narrow
hips that even faintly suggested eroticism. I had taken her for
what she looked like, the somewhat dehydrated gentile who
had been brought up in an atmosphere of watercress and
wheat germ, without a trace of opulence that puts a round-
ness on the angularities, without the quality of being that
seeds the air with fertility. She stretched herself on the Mexican rug and let her hair fan out behind her. She closed her
eyes and hooked her thumbs into the chain belt around her
waist.

"When we had sex we acted as if it were a necessary dis-
turbance. We wanted to be decent about the contract. When
we got aroused it was as if a stranger had possessed our bodies
for that moment. Deron wasn't making love to Dee. We were
both looking at two strangers. We were voyeurs toward our
own act." Her voice came up above the music, high and
pinched. I found myself staring at her legs again and the
thighs, which were well exposed below the short skirt. With
my other life of small town and Jews and theater and college
and jobs I lived on a knife edge of doubt about my looks and
my personality. Even when I was very skinny, throughout my
childhood, the fact of skinniness did not alienate me. I was
merely rejected, but it was a rejection from within my frame
of reference. My world was painful, but whole. Sitting in
Dee's apartment I felt something entirely new, the thrilling
discomfort of an unknown sensibility. I felt my body gross
and cloddy, spread through with tiny pits of revulsion. They
were surface sensations so different from what I had known
that I thought I was hallucinating. Maybe it was the grass.

I was sure she wanted me to do something. I would have to

take the lead, but I was without strategy, too newly into my feelings.

"Did you ever make it with a woman?" I asked. The sensual air was irresistible.

"No," The "o" came out like a cigarette puff. Brave girl.

"I haven't either." I wouldn't tell her about the Betty Snow byplay and my feelings of the summer about going down on a woman. Very fragile, the whole thing could crash down right into the silky web of air.

"I have never been free," Dee said. "The young men, the guys who come out of the Jesuits, I'm trying to help them. They tell me they want to be free, to act out the word of God in the world."

"They're babies."

"I'm a baby. I don't know anything." She sat up, brushed her hair back, and the look was not beseeching. "Teach me." It was an appeal that had the force of a command. Under the influence of generations of Maine rocks she knew only the craggy way. Sometimes she was more boy than girl, and then the beautiful sweep of calf and thigh, all woman, an androgynous breed which stumbled around in search of its singular self. If that was the case I was Earth Mother again, and I was in comfortable territory.

A letter came a few days later on a soft powder-blue paper with an aroma of fresh purchase. I let it sit on my dining table, propped up against a pewter fruit dish. I had let the matter drop from my mind when David called to discuss a new idea for the *Huck* show, the introduction of a love element. He wanted to make Jim younger and instead of being separated from a wife and kids it would be a girl friend, a young sweetheart around whom he could write some good songs. It would make a good subplot and shift the major interest to Jim, which David was really after. We made a date to go over the idea with Howard Milman and Winnie Worth. Why didn't I come over earlier to talk about it over a cocktail? Throughout the call David's manner was cautiously warm and I felt what I had always felt, that he was coming back to me after something else, a worn edge of waste in his voice. I opened Dee's letter with a thought of evening advantages somehow. Waste not, want not, buddy.

Dee wrote that she had been "up and down the last few days, random thoughts tumble-washing over and around the Everyday—amazed delight and when again? So sad a world to be almost 30 and only rarely knowing gusto . . . so glad a world where thirty is not the end of Finding Out. . . ."

I went up to the Crosscurrent office the same night, waited for Dee to finish up, we had a bite together and went directly to her place. When we got inside the door without hesitation I put my arms around her and kissed her. She put her head on my chest and began to cry. I stroked her back with long smooth maternal strokes and we moved over to the couch and I held her close and stroked her and she wept against my breast, years of water coming out from among the rocks, and I lifted her face and kissed the tears and I kissed her eyes and then with a sense of burning urgency, almost like a flash diarrhea attack, went at her mouth and we stood up and lashed tongues, now her hands and mine moving, moving, hers lifting my dress and slipping under my pantyhose, mine snapping open her jeans and plunging under her pants and clamping around that tight, sweet small ass. We held each other's asses and we pressed frontal parts together. I couldn't wait for the bedroom. We got on the floor and I pulled off her jeans and unbuttoned her shirt and started my tongue on top around the tight little breasts and sucked there a little, my hand working, brushing against her crotch and she slid her hand in mine, inadvertently, a blind hand feeling through darkness. Not a single word since we had entered the house. We were busy with the business of love, two virgins in hot exploration of the forbidden fruit. Back to the mouth again and the incredible sensation of kissing a girl, sweet lips and tongue, and to the breast and to the navel, the tongue around and just above the hairline of the pussy, then up again to the mouth licking the neck and the armpit, the side of the breast, tongue grooving under and around the breast, down the side and over to the navel and slipping down, as if by error, to the thigh-crotch joint, tongue in the crease of leg, up once more, this time the last, the tongue straight down the middle between the breasts, trailing over navel, brushing over the crotch hair, and the tongue tip dancing into the cunt crack, a light quick dip in the ocean, a bird of a tongue, and Dee screamed, a short, moaning, dying animal thing. I was concentrating too hard even to ask her the necessary redundant question, "Do you like it?" so that I could hear the "Yes, yes, do more, I love it" reply and feel the transfer of ecstasy. She had by this time forgotten me and was lying back, hands flung out over her head, legs spread wide, knees up and I got down below and went at her. At the moment my tongue went in I felt the dropping away of all aversion. I was lost in a sea of hair and flesh and ambrosial flow, burying my face in with the thirst of forty days in the desert. Our sweat-glistened bodies clung and I caught out of the steamy air the knowledge of Narcissus. I was making love to my alter ego, I was performing an act of self-love born of all the acts of self-hatred, my skinny fourteen-year-old despised body before me, the lousy crow body, ignored and vilified and despised. It was an act of transcendence, and transcending all was the fact that she loved me.

We showered and dressed and we drank orange juice in the kitchen standing next to the open refrigerator, gulping the drinks like ballplayers between halves. I walked out of the house on watery legs and took a cab home. We had not said one word to each other. No jockeying, no recrimination, no cocktails and chatter and feelings-out and testing of egos. No rejections. I was bathed in a delirious air of sensuality without a single pulsing prick rearing its selfish head, spitting its conceit into my face. It was a miracle of total acceptance. The first time in my life. And I was in control. I had the power over another life.

In a week's time I was certain that Dee had fallen in love with me. A phone call and another letter preceded my day at the office, both of which were not hysterical, quite the opposite. The call was serene, almost distant, the letter with the tone of a state dinner invitation, noble, gilt-edged. They were saying, there is little that can alter the force of history, we were inevitable, and as all things are inevitable, one need only take one's sweet and regal time. If she were younger, she was twenty-eight, or if she were Jewish, I would have caught full in the kisser a guilt-dependency thing, not a what-have-I-done, we're all too much into the twentieth century for that, lick a cunt, dildo up the ass, big deal, but a neurotic relationship, with all the blurry edges and soft breakdowns and sweaty phone calls and nerve-end, head-filling analysis. Not my *shikse*. This one, and it was my first, was going for the full boat. In a single night my whole life readjusted itself. Under the initial heave of intense feeling other business seemed bland, without danger or threat or complication. Only David lurked, and it was hardly David but what I was conceiving as David to match the miss from Maine. I would have to beef him up on pills or maybe bring in one of his drag queens, make a brew of a stew. I was not cocky, but I could only revert to form under pressure. Talk fast, kid, Sam C. says out of the side of his mouth, with the George Burns cigar jutting from his fingers, keep 'em laughing.

When I saw her at the Crosscurrent office the following Tuesday we agreed by a tacit eye signal not to allude to anything that had taken place. We busied ourselves with a mailing list and talked about the implications of the widespread publicity given to a priest who had left a teaching position, given up his order, and married. Was it the beginning of a trend? Would it help the Crosscurrent movement?

Was it the end of Vatican rule? It was another area about which I had limited knowledge, and under the normal circumstances, in a social gathering, I would feel compelled to contribute, offering my scant information with a great deal of assurance, resting on *Time* or *Life* as my source without mentioning them. I was scornful of *Reader's Digest* experts, who seemed to me several cuts below my intellectual dignity. It had never particularly bothered me that my interests did not include the contents of the front page of the *New York Times* and that whole areas of national concern were handled with glances at the headlines or summaries in *Time*. As for the affairs of Protestant, Catholic, and Jew, I couldn't have picked a more remote interest. I bought Christmas presents and lit a *yahrzeit* candle for my mother, the first year of her death. Worship, prayer, theology, ecumenism—what could they mean to the girl in the secular city? Dee was the opposite, the first bona-fide female intellectual I had met. I had read a Mary McCarthy essay on Vietnam. Dee had the same kind of mind, full of easy allusions and hard elliptical thinking. She never dealt in small change, didn't know Ann Landers or Earl Wilson, gossip to her consisted of reading about the backbiting feuds among the Socialists of *Dissent* magazine, a copy of which she had on her desk.

So our conversation skimmed along on these fragile lines, Dee with gentle and subdued superiority showing her wares, and I, with an honesty that refreshed rather than undermined my ego, played the role of student. Far from being threatened by her better mind, I felt an increase in power. It was clear to both of us that we were playing a game of delicate balance. With such a new and volatile relationship facing us we approached it with the caution of a cat stalking a frightened and trapped bird. (If he pounced too soon the bird would fly.) If we weren't careful, that first night of love might be the last. As we talked about the marrying priests there settled in the room an air of innuendo. For every word spoken there was a word behind it, so that the word behind the word became the true dialogue, and we carried on this nerve-stretching activity, seeking to find new thoughts to keep it going, the more prowess Dee showed, as she did when she trotted out her encyclopedic knowledge of Vatican II and the Dutch catechism, gibberish to me, the more I knew she was asking for reciprocation later. But later had taken on a feeling of apprehension. What would we do? How would it go? So we delayed and got thickly into the church thing. My questions were asked lazily, but very specifically, and she answered as if she were at a lectern, the more naïve I was the greater urge she had to be master teacher, until at one point I put a few things together and had an insight, the equality suddenly and dramatically restored, and a mild mutual beam of smile exchanged. Her master role was at last too burdensome. I *was* the older woman, she had come under my spell, and the usurpation of power might thrust her into a directionless void.

This time we took a cab up to my place and I poured brandy and played Jacques Brel records. Whatever the exchange in the office had done it had not weakened my position. I felt invulnerable. There was nothing this chick could do to wound me. I kept that fact snugly in a corner of my head. Imagine, what kind of new strength came from my not caring if I appeared dumb. I put the record on with firmness, poured the brandy with the snap of a good waiter, and sat down beside her with the casual comfort of a veteran personnel manager. Now see here miss, what can I do for you. And I was hot as a pistol.

We sat alongside each other, knees a shade apart, hands reaching for brandy glasses without touching. Knowing what was in store was enough, and what we both wanted was the body-filling buildup, to make this event the opposite of the previous one. Now it was proximity. Now it was anticipation and delay. Now it was the challenge to us to find talk so banal that the very heat of our excitement would furnish it with portent. I was in the exquisitely joyous condition of not having to calculate actions to satisfy or hold off a man, of not having to wonder about his need and his helpless vessel-filling rage. Was there ever a time when I was with a man that I did not doubt the motive? Motive's need and need's motive, two conditions slave to each other enslaving the man, making him the victim of guile and strategy, manipulating whatever was valuable and free in him and brushing over him the false honey to get his real honey.

I would have to be first. The game was to say something else. "If I can get some money together I'm going to redo the terrace."

"You've got some nice things out there."

"It's hard keeping this place up. I could really fix up a terrace."

"We have a big garden back home. I could help you."

"Is there anything I can do in the fall? I've planted my tulip bulbs."

"That's good. Some crocuses for early color."

"That's a good idea."

"I love gardens, even city ones. It's like buying a survival kit."

"Yes, that's true."

"Keeping a flower alive is more than an act of charity."

"It represents something."

"Everything represents something." We leaned together, lifted and drank, absorbing that last remark. I decided to wait and see if she would make the first move. We were a bit embarrassed. The memory of last week was dreamlike. "In the Koran," she continued, "it says that as the fruit grows so the spirit grows in man. Spirit is the fruit of man. Maybe it was Confucius."

"You read a lot of that."

"Just enough to remind me that there are other ways of being in the world."

"I've thought of that too."

"You know how to live in this world." She drew away and lit a cigarette. Something had shifted. I knew nothing about this girl. What could there be but some deep terror? Why else would she come to me? What was flattering was also confusing. She had really turned me on, but she had cast me as mother. I wanted to do both jobs, but I wasn't sure what her need was reaching to. I knew how to live in this world. Either that was a joke or Dee saw me in a vital way that I needed to see myself. But who could trust her? She loved me. That was suspect enough.

"Meet Miss Success."

"You're a woman, Jane."

"You can bet for sure I'm not a man."

We turned heads and kissed gently. Slipping up from nowhere a feeling-thought intruded. I wanted a man to love me. I wanted David. I was without resources. There was a sandy bottom to this embrace. We would sink without a trace. Panic bit me in the heart. "Why don't we go to my room," I said. Did she catch my watery self-esteem, this girl, sprung from nowhere, like a detour sign on a dark road, driving me on to a rutty bypath, making my wheels spin in the soft, uncertain surface? I was beginning to understand, finally, the meaning of the most celebrated phrase since the invention of central heating. It was never, my love, let us be true to one another, or, I can't live without you. Into the bed, that was what they knew, those hard-on bastards. No detours for them. Drive it right up to the service station and pump it full of gas. I really didn't give a shit about this person, so bright, so perceptive, so vulnerable and human. I had the advantage and I was in the driver's seat. Carrying our drinks, and watching that good movement of cloth, muscle and bone, I saw the meaning of role reversal. I could be Jerry

Kay taking Jane Castle for a bang. All he wants to do is fuck me. Some songs and witty sayings, some whiskey, but it was a piper's tune. Get them down to the river and drop them in. Could I ever bother with her sick need? That would mean becoming involved morally in somebody else's life. I see where Richard Doyle hurries to my side, where John Ames calls to hear my voice, where Bill and Ron and Al and Lennie and Bernie and, and, and, I see where all of them gave me something of themselves, freely. The only gratuity was the tip of the prick. I had something special, a gift to make them more powerful. Surely, the mythologies invented a goddess of my sort. The All-Purpose Sacrificial Queen.

"Love me, love me," she whispered, her voice and eyes gelatinous with need, as I worked every side of the street, obsoleting the sex manuals with wall-to-wall coverage, my tender tongue and miracle mouth responding to every barometric pressure of the instrument at my side. A golden tongue in a golden cunt was a mere exercise, a kind of Lenny Bernstein podium coattail flourish to the perfectly orchestrated music of my love-making. Now that I understood that I *was* Jerry Kay, I knew what it meant to get my rocks off. It was a figure of speech, a metaphor, unleash the burden. I wasn't going to be some stupid, fucking Sisyphus rolling that job up the hill all day. Think of all the lonely delicatessen chicken I have eaten when I could have been mistress of a wall-to-floor oven. I can drive a station wagon full of kids with the best of them. I got my rocks off. Yes, I loved her up, my tongue crawling between the toes, up around the instep, inside the back hollow of knee, around and into the crack of ass, back, neck, ears, eyes, breasts, navel, and pussy, pussy, the clitoral lick and come, what more can a woman do, unless it's an artificial cock, and in ungoverned heat she pulled me away and tore at my cunt, not afraid of mama any more, moaning, she, not me, oh my god, I love you, right through it all, could you believe it, I love you, while I stroked her sandy goyish hair and looked down at her like a triumphant Roman general.

In the morning she slipped out of the house while I watched with half a sleep-closed eye. Nice, she was nice, with some style in her, the way she opened the latch, a six A.M. firecracker thrown into the hall, didn't fuss, opened the door without rush, and went out without looking back, easy, like it was her place. Her back told me that she had come away good from the adventure. I found a note on the night table next to a sticky ring left by the brandy glass:

> It's not possible to write unforgettable prose after an unforgettable celebration. There are some things I'd like to say, but the words sag, ridiculous, outwitted entirely by events. Consequently, I'll confine my remarks to—wow! Love you.

I think I got a note from Jerry Kay once—wash my underwear and save it for the next visit. Yes, Bernie Wasserman in the first months left good notes—there's ten dollars behind the clock, or, roast beef is in the refrigerator. Gene Gordon tried once, but all that remains is something like "luminous orbs." Dee was a Radcliffe magna. I boiled up two eggs, three minutes, couple of slices of buttered toast, tea, and gazed through the steamy things at my own *bakakte* past.

I could have been a theater cum laude at Wisconsin if I applied myself to it. In the 90th percentile in high school, top ten in the graduating class, pick my spot, the doors wide open, the nose straight, what would it be: Cornell, Barnard, Swarthmore, William and Mary, University of Pennsylvania. I wanted Cornell but Barnard would be nice, I had a cousin going there, Swarthmore of course would satisfy my parents' snobby pretensions, working all the time to deck me out in their status hunger, my father the big shoe salesman from New Haven, push, push, the logic was, good clothes from

Lord and Taylor, new face, best school, right guy, ordinary ambitions I guess, but with them it was a way to salvage a leaking marriage and a disaster childhood of their daughter. We waited, the three of us, especially my mother, sitting home extra days, not going down to the office, playing her fifteen solitaire variations, cigarette smoke staining her teeth, the mail, anything today, whispered voices in the kitchen, my father's stage voice husky with the effort, elbows on the table, the attitude of their perennial secrets, the teeth-gritting conferences. Nothing today, but Helen got Smith and Rita, the *shtilenke*, Cornell, but so did Rose Rosario, below me at school, now the mailman a carrier of the plague each day, the world suspended as I hovered in my room again, yet again feeling that plumb-bob weight of despair, the personal interview at Cornell, eager to please, giving pablum answers trying not to wring my hands, it was probably the Jewish quota, Marilyn, they couldn't take more than one from Waterbury, but Sam, look at the college boards, and the silent mailman, and then no, no, no, every single one of them. But Mother, *everybody* in the honors group was accepted. And then Big Sam got to work, calling alumni, direct calls to deans, letters, a call to a congressman, now mother in desperation calling an old friend turned enemy, what it must have cost her, yes Marilyn, I'll talk to somebody. They knocked their brains out—nothing worked, turned down, cold. Over at the drugstore I said my mother wanted a new prescription for the sleeping pills and I kept them in the drawer, I won't go to college, I'll kill myself, and my mother found them, I made sure she did, her tone miraculously softened, wouldn't I reconsider, the University of Connecticut (nobody went there), she never went to college, all right, I'll go to Katherine Gibbs, I'll be a secretary, hairdressing school if you'd like. The other girls were shopping, new wardrobes, summer turning to fall. My father sat down with Bernice in the office, he was angry by this time, his ego threatened now,

letters to every school under the sun. The house was unbear-
able, shrill voices in curtain-darkened rooms, thousands of
dollars for the nose, could there be a better guarantee, out
the window.

The acceptance came from Wisconsin. A fine school, next
best thing to the good private schools. What they didn't
know, the people in the east, was that the big universities in
1949 were crying for out-of-state money. They would take
anybody, you could be a moron. We had a big nervous relief
discussion, lots of sound parental advice laced with the exhaustion of near-failure. The governor sends the reprieve
and the family of the condemned man bubbles its gratitude.
Jane, are you responsible enough to go twelve hundred miles
from home? Yes, daddy, it's time you trusted me, haven't you
brought me up to be self-sufficient? What do you think, Marilyn, as if there were a question, they would have carried me
there in a box, yes of course, clothing, we emptied the stores,
a wardrobe beyond belief, that will take care of everything,
nobody is rejecting us.

The trunk of the car loaded, off we went, the scenic route,
four days to Wisconsin via Niagara Falls, across Lake Erie in
a boat overnight to Detroit to Muskegan, Michigan, where
there were Indians, another boat to Milwaukee. We fought
the whole trip, right from the driveway on Elm Street to
Madison, wearing off quickly the skimpy edges of our truce.
They had never been able to do anything with me and we
weren't able to bring off, at this moment of separation, the
lie of a lifetime. I wanted love and tenderness from my
father and a shared mother-daughter femininity from my
mother. They could not give it, but who can believe that
parents can almost literally reject their child? So it took the
form of petty arguments about money and manners. What
was it that they saw in me that mirrored, even compounded,
their own weaknesses? Every time they looked at me or lis-
tened to me did they turn away from their own fatality?

"Daddy, I have to go to the bathroom."

"You just went at the last stop."

"Hold it in," from my mother.

"I have a weak bladder."

My father: "Hold it in. It will get stronger."

"Daddy, I have to pee."

My mother: "Jane, you must learn to control yourself."

My father: "Are you going to walk out in the middle of class? 'Teacher, I have to pee?' "

"I didn't ask for a weak bladder."

My father: "It's time you learned a little self-discipline. You can hold it in if you want to. You just don't want to."

My mother: "She'll have to learn it fast if she wants to stay."

My father: "There's only one way to make it. Stick to your guns. Be a fighter."

"I just want to go to the bathroom, not solve the problems of the world. Can't I make a simple request?"

My mother: "If you get hysterical it will get worse. Sam, when is the next stop?"

My father pulled over to the side of the highway. "Right here."

"Here?"

"Just go in the goddamned bushes and drop your pants."

In Madison they stayed at the fancy Edgewater Beach Hotel and got me set up in a little room. They stayed for a few days until everything looked right and off they went. They got back home in less than twenty-four hours. They must have been happy to get home. I remember squatting in the bushes, not scared. I think it was disgust. Right there I resolved I would show them, I would be self-sufficient, restore my shattered academic honors. One of the things I had clung to in school, through all the misery, was my brightness. You don't live in a middle-class Jewish community and pre-

tend to be anything unless you can prove it through the edu-
cational process, and money. Piss on them. I wanted to prove
it.

In the white room the curtains were open and the tray was
white, the glass with the bent straw untouched, flowers too,
very red in the white room. I had come and gone back the
first time, when Aunt Claire called me at Barnett, "Your
father is very sick," not telling me yet what it was, I had not
made any attempt to get in touch with him, he made none
with me, and I was terrified, was his Bernice going to throw
me out of the hospital room? Dr. Slazenger got through to
me, saying, "You haven't been emotionally involved with
your father for years. You've been running the train around
and the track has been gone." The guideline was, if she tried
to throw me out, I say, "He's my father and I have a right to
be here." She wasn't there and he was conscious, and he did
recognize me, trying to say something, his hands over the
covers perfectly still, the flesh flimsy on the bone, and I
couldn't get it, finally the message croaked, "I am not a
meshugah, I am not a meshugah." It had moved from the
lungs to the brain and he had these blackouts, she kept the
business going and a hospital bed in the house. But it got to
the brain and she couldn't handle it. I put my hand on his, I
wanted to, and I was able to do what Slazenger said. I said,
"Daddy, you know how much I love you." Whether it was
true or not didn't matter. "And you know how happy I've
been that you've been happy the last few years. I'm glad you
had the chance to be happy with Bernice. And don't worry
about me, I have a job and a boyfriend." And I could see he
was happy to hear that, and then he tried to say something
which I couldn't get, and I said, "And I love you very much,"
and he started to cry.
She came and I said I was able to tell him these things and
she said, "Well, he ate his carrots today." We went out in the

hall and I said, "Bernice, I know you don't have any use for me but I want to tell you I really sympathize with you, I really feel for what you are going through." She was incapable of bending.

I went away and another call came. I came right back on the weekend, three days later. The hands were still over the covers, he hadn't moved. Alone in the white room his head barely denting the pillow, the skin around his throat hanging loose as a rooster's, and he couldn't talk, not even a wheezed-out, "Hello my daughter" or "I'm not meshugah." Still, still in the bed with my eyes old fishface with the big fish eyes, staring, white-and-blue glass balls not rolling around, but intelligence in them, blue staring fish eyes that had to talk for the stilled mouth, still for the first time, Sam Castle a man of mouth. And she came in with some of her family and he kept looking at me, trying to say, "Be nice to them, be nice to them," and I knew that he was proud of me, that I was his daughter in spite of her, she was sixteen when she came to work at the office, a stocky kid from the other side of the tracks, went to the commercial high, with a family of short stubby people, short Poles with meaty red hands. And he kept following me with his eyes around the room, and I felt like a piece of shit, the frozen smiles to the short Poles, vying to be in charge of this dying man, edging closer to the bed, Bernice and me each claiming a piece of turf, she at the head me at the foot, my hand patting the starched shroud of a sheet. I couldn't take it and I went back to the city and the very next day the call came from Aunt Claire, it's over. I wore my best which was nothing, I was broke, I didn't really have a winter coat, just a royal blue raincoat with a laminated foam rubber lining, and she came in a very nice mink stole he had given her. I couldn't wear my mother's mink, it was old-fashioned now and had to be remodeled.

At the funeral parlor Aunt Claire sat between Bernice and me. It was my fifth trip, my mother, my grandmother, my grandfather, my Uncle Ed, but this time I was a stranger. My own father's funeral. They all sat away from me, Sylvia Dubinsky and Leila Frucht and all the shrew-type ladies who had known me all my life, silent purse-mouthed blame, as if I had caused the cancer of the brain, as if I had married him off so quickly to Bernice after my mother's death. And later, while I waited in deathly isolation at Aunt Claire's house, they all went to Bernice's. I couldn't go there. I was *persona non grata*. Even Claire visited Bernice. Talk about the prodigal son. And it was my father, lying there with fresh new dirt on his face, who had spread the stories about his rotten daughter. What could it have been but to ease his own guilt? One friend, Andy Raskin, came, and he held my hand and we sat absolutely alone in Claire's dark living room with Russell Stover candy. Bernie Wasserman sent flowers from New York. I carried them back on the train and left them lying on the East Side IRT. They had rejected me and accepted her, the whole Jewish community. It was more upsetting than my father's death—the terrific sense of aloneness. Later on I got a condolence card from old Benny Groman, a wholesale butcher who couldn't make the funeral, he was blind and living in a nursing home outside Hartford.

Chapter 3

I GOT TO DAVID'S an hour earlier than the others, including Randy Smith, who we agreed might give us a black angle on *Huck*. Years of being in the business had steeled me to the cordialities of the day-after sequel to the night in the sack. I had been around too many theater people who cultivated a survival technique for the separate lives of business and pleasure. Unfortunately, I had not learned my lessons well in the past. It seemed to me the most logical thing in the world to carry the joys of love from the boudoir to the office. The payoff was in the assumed intimacies under the public guise of business politeness—an eye, a gesture, a phrase, little air reverberations that thrilled the skin and quickened the blood. I sat alone with David Astor and the unwritten law was, it never happened, so don't refer to it, not on company time. Conversations of this sort usually go: I've had an exhausting day, so-and-so called, what do you think of, has X been around, the latest word on Y is, busy make-do talk, David in a terror of chattiness, with the first act this and the second act that, not really afraid of me, the scene had been rehearsed too many times, but always protecting what had to remain inviolate, that other self that my womanhood threatened to invade. There was that about him that showed during the business hours most, a cruel efficiency that hid an even crueler deficiency, and I didn't have the guts to get past the German in him, that willed masculinity, to the sweetness at the bone, not in itself a deficiency, only the cruelty lurked in his inability to exploit that sweetness, except for those moments when the guard was down and there rose out of him the real manhood that was denied to me in my father, in Jerry Kay, in Jonathan, in Gene Gordon, in David Vogel, in every man I've known, perhaps Bernie Wasserman excepted, denied to me in David himself.

"We bring in the girl for the female lead, we shift Huck's role slightly to narrator-participant, we bring in some new songs, we change the focus to a black liberation thing." He sat down at the piano, threw off a few bars and sang about "the big Muddy being bloody with the sweat and blood of the black man's body, and there ain't nobody goin' to deny it." Something like that for Jim, with the girl coming in for a duet, but did she ever get to the raft with Huck and Jim, in fact the whole problem of the raft on the set was a big one.

"The raft can be the set," I said. "What color do you make the girl, high yellow or African black?"

"That's no problem." He stood in the center of the room, blue-striped shirt, sleeves rolled up, pencil in his ear. "What if we keep them on Jackson's Island and never let them go down the river? But that won't do, will it?"

I told him I didn't think any of it would do. Why not leave the old idea, forget the girl. "There could be a wedding scene on the raft," he said, "with the King or the Duke performing the ceremony, a bogus wedding scene. We could play off the natural beauty of Jim and Ruby, the girl, against the degeneracy of the white institution as parodied in King and Duke."

"Did you want some opinion from me?"

"If you like." He sat at his desk writing something. I knew that back. It wasn't possible to find a place between the ribs for the knife to go through.

"I don't think that is necessary."

He continued writing, then looked up. "What do you think of the wedding scene idea?"

"I think it's just great."

"Why are you taking on that tone?"

"I'm not taking on any tone. Why do you say I'm taking on a tone? I think it's great. What else do you want to know?"

"Would you put up fresh coffee. They'll be here in a few minutes."

I went into the kitchen and banged pots around. He came in and watched me as I measured out the coffee with brisk movements, dipping in the plastic measuring spoon, tapping the inside of the can to level off, then into the pot, eight times, two bracelets clacking against each other with every move. I was wearing my special reject-occasion look, sang-froid-injured. David wasn't strong enough to withstand that. It was too close to mother's silent treatment. I knew what I was doing but could I stop it? Could I prevent the pain of slight that I identified as a pain of slight the second it occurred, almost seizing it in mid-passage as it slithered down my gut and choking it but instead, caressing it, because I knew it was the weapon of victory. But what price would I pay for this pawnshop full of sulks and simmers, instantly negotiable gewgaws of my secondhand personality.

"Don't forget one for the pot," he said.

I offered him the measuring spoon. "You want to do it. Do it."

"You do it."

I finished and brushed past him to get to the refrigerator. "Excuse me, please." He moved an inch. I pulled open the refrigerator door, looked inside, and closed it. I went to the sink and washed a few dishes and silverware. "I don't have to take this shit from you." I went into the bathroom, closed the toilet lid and sat down. Out came tissues from the decorator box on top of the toilet tank, blue fleur-de-lis on a white-ground designer box, with gold tissues. Above the shower on the ledge bottles of cologne, powders, shampoos, deodorants. I wiped my runny nose with a gold tissue. I would come up early, have a little cocktail, sit on the couch away from him and talk shop, nice and cool, the way he liked it, his game, but since I knew it my game too, rewarded by the late afternoon glow of shared attitudes. My advice would be keen but deferential, tempered by his knowledge of my awareness of the necessary nicety of mood that assured him I asked nothing from him in return for being in his presence. Talk that skimmed on the surface of that water like a bird, wings still, gliding just above a serene lake in patient quest for food. Instead I sat in his faggy john shot down by a stray bullet of a careless hunter. The outside door opened and shut and sounds drifted in from the living room. What was he saying to them, she is in there having one of her fits? (Jane, come out of the bathroom this instant. Sam, she won't come out. I won't go to the dance with Sheldon Fisher, I won't, scream, sob, scream. Jane, daddy's voice like thunder against the door, and then the fist, and the fist again, terrified the tears stop, paralyzed, I hear the fist against the door, come out, unlock that door, nothing, my voice stops in my throat as the fist goes boom, boom, and the splintering of wood as the fist comes through the door. Daddy, I scream, Sam, mommy screams, come out you little bitch, the thunder roars with choking rage.)

They were all out there now, voices matching body types, Winnie's Betty Boop piping over the rumbly baritone of sour Howard which matched like glove in fist Stefanie's thick-lipped man voice which more properly belonged to Randy Smith's ironed-out no-accent creamy alto, and least audible, David's soft boy-voice, the ten-years-younger sound that always surprised with its assertiveness giving away only that bitchy edge that ran like a seismographic fault down the length of him. They rang against each other with the coffee-in-the-living-room ease of British society, and how, I wondered, would I ever govern the sense of social claustrophobia that would free me to be human in groups? At my first party when I was twelve I found myself in the corner of the finished basement in the shadows near the fireplace. I managed to enhance that image of the skinny long-nosed outcast, hiding in corners, hysterical behind locked bathroom doors, crying on beds in guest rooms on top of piles of coats with the solicitous friend rescuing me from my smothering self-pity. Who would come after me today?

But they talked on with a silent code no doubt that she can sit in there and stew, we have had enough of that. Howard, the big politics *maven* and periodicals radical, had taken center stage, because it wasn't often that he had the opportunity, a Bronx Amalgamated Housing Project Jew, to be sharing an experience with a Negro. Howard loved the Negroes, but in the path from the co-op to Carnegie Hall he had not met one. Now with the Negro fast disappearing into history, and with him Howard's lost strand of idealism, he saw the opportunity to rescue his integrationist beliefs before they fell forever before the charge of the blacks. That's what excited him about the play, to be able to write a score that would have the feel of a Paul Robeson musical, which is what Jim should be, a tragic figure with the stature of an Othello. Howard's theatrical imagination was very much like his musical imagination, cautious, joyless, which he tried to break up with a heavy cynicism that tried to make ironic humor out of all subjects. "Listen, black is beautiful was a slogan of Adam Clayton Powell's twenty years ago. What did Father Divine preach, man." I could see him nodding at Randy, asking for a free ticket to the Apollo with that word. "You don't buy all that jazz? This play is about the new social order rising out of the stench of the corrupt capitalist society. Huck is a working-class figure."

"Huck?" Randy gave it the black man's special voice of incredulity. You're putting me on. I don't want to be fooled again. Look at the Indians. Fooled too often, they lost everything except desert dignity. So the black man went the other way. In bed Randy simply could not wipe off that sly fox grin, come on now, baby, stop jiving me.

"He wears overalls," Howard said. "You join the working-class youth with the deprived Negro and you send them down a commercial waterway, I'm not kidding, and every place they touch is a sign of a degenerate system. I think some of David's lyrics catch that quality. I don't want the girl in there. What we want is a today thing. We want demonstration theater."

"That's not exactly what I had in mind," David said.

"We're in this together," Howard said. "I want to make money too. Look at the raft scene in the book, the chapter where they escape from those hillybilly aristocrats. They take off their clothes. Huck and Jim sit on the stage naked and sing a song."

"I have lyrics for that scene," Winnie said. "I call it 'It's Lovely to Live on a Raft.' " I moaned through the door. *She* "called" it. It's in the book that way.

"You could rig a production number with everybody in the raw, Huck and Jim and the King and Duke and the girl," Stefanie said.

I got off the john and on my knees I looked through the keyhole. I caught the bottom part of the piano bench with Winnie's feet reaching for the pedal. She sang in that lilty, slightly jazzy voice that caught me by surprise the first time I heard it.

> Look at the sky all speckled with stars
> There goes a steamboat coughing along. . . .

"I see the play as a waterborne pastoral romance, Huck and Jim shepherds of the river, a play full of song." Winnie was the house sentimentalist, trying to satisfy her own boozy yearnings for romance.

"That makes three concepts of the play," David said. I waited for him to ask Randy for his version. Randy was supposed to tell it like it was, the resident black of the company, the word from headquarters. Then mount the big play, a rousing musical comedy of our time, repair in one stroke all the patchy attempts to fashion successful careers, all of us, limping into our late thirties with dozens of fly-by-night dreams yellowing in bottom drawers. Get the black man to salvage the operation with a dive to the bottom, but the ship wasn't sunk, leaking a little bit maybe, and here comes Randy Smith, bail-out man, who is nothing but an actor, plain and simple, suddenly elevated to the role of demigod. If you were a black buff you did believe, now, if you hadn't before, that he was unique, that he did run faster, fuck harder, laugh longer, music better, suffer more. Tell me, Randy, what kind of perceptions do we have. Never mind what happened in Twain's novel, what we're after is some dry land for ourselves, some open territory where we can throw off all the shit of this civilization. Huck and Jim together in any kind of weather. Why was that picture so winning, so beautiful? The truth is, between the sheets you're like the next guy, but when you sit in a room with a nice attentive face and hold up a white palmed hand with the black back and you say something like listen man, we listen and hold our breaths, ready for some major claim to be staked in our hearts.

"I see Jim as daddy to Huck," Randy said. "He knows Huck's father is dead. So a father-son play, but the big switch is that the father is an outcast too. Instead of the typical contest between father and son in a struggle for power you get a loving, a joining. The real dream of love is father and son."

"The bourgeois myth," Howard said. "The world's ills will be cured if we keep the family together. But what about the economic realities? It was the slave society created by the need for cheap labor that brought Jim into being."

"You could do both," Randy said. "Huck is a product of the same class structure that made Jim a slave, right? So they run to freedom out of a double need, to restore the family and deny the corrupt society."

"But flight is not revolution," Howard said.

I had enjoyed my private booth long enough. I came out and sat at the piano bench next to Winnie. They gave me entry quips which I dismissed. I was going to save the ship, I mean the raft. I was Miss Production Boss. "Howard, we're trying to put a show together, not a revolution. You would put a gun in their hands and make a Western out of it."

"We could call it a Southern," David said.

"With the niggers as the bad guys," Randy said. Then he drawled, "The only good nigger is a dead nigger."

"I hate that word," Stefanie said. She couldn't undo her Flatbush orientation.

"Twain calls him that," I said. "We could call him Colored Jim if you like."

"I have an idea," David said. "Twain loved disguises and mistaken identities. Jim could mask himself in whiteface in order to escape; he meets Ruby, slave girl, and then on the raft, under a full moon, he peels off the mask, and then he sings a recognition song. Move over." He squeezed in between Winnie and me and started to fiddle on the keys.

"You thought I was white, but I'm as black as I can be."

Winnie shoved up next to him, ran a few chords on the bass and falsettoed deep:

"Black is the color of the soul and black you are to me."

"I thought it was Huck's story," Stefanie said.

"It is," I said, "Huck is a double agent. As Jim and Ruby are about to escape to Illinois and free country, Huck springs up and guns them down."

"The criminals are apprehended and the social order is restored," Randy said. "There's a comment for you."

"So you buy the girl thing," Howard said to Randy.

"I buy what sells."

"That's selling out."

"I'm buying in."

Howard looked around in appeal. It was the look of a man who has been denied something valuable but who has not yet been able to accept the imminent loss. Behind his bile, he wanted a life without it, like the man who has lost his faith and has adopted indifference as a new faith waiting only to lapse back into faith again. "I'm for fun and games too," he said. Howard saw Randy as a poster figure for NAACP. David didn't bother to categorize since the black man had no emotional or moral dimension to him. In David's Ohio there were no cleaning ladies around, so he couldn't fight the great liberating battle of undoing the *shvartze* label pinned on the colored help by our parents. I wasn't even rid of it myself. With Randy in bed I was fucking colored help. Underneath, David probably wanted to make a fag musical but didn't have the guts, so he found the proper vehicle to match his intentions. He wasn't bold enough to bring out the show of our time—a white-black homosexual rock musical, and so he settled for the "innocent homoeroticism" he had read about in an article by Fiedler the critic. And it hadn't been written yet, the gay musical with a grand anal-oral finale. So we sat around with our conceptions and convictions, at least *they* did, trying to reconcile Howard's revolution musical with Winnie's lyric-romantic musical with Randy's father-son musical with David's all-purpose musical, each pursuing his own version of the dream, while Stefanie sat next to her man keeping her usually big mouth shut, with a confident careless hand in Howard's lap. And I sat next to my man and waited for signals in this strange semaphoric relationship that thrived on signals, blinker lights and buzzes and flag wavings, the two A.M. blinker, the I'm-busy-with-a-client buzz, the I-called-you-first-last-time-why-don't-you-call-me-first-now flag. Worst of all was the you're-rejecting-me signal which

came after an intimacy signal, when I said, sitting on
the piano bench, my buttock pressing lightly against his, "We
were working this out the other night, David and I and we
thought that——" David cutting in with "Is the coffee
ready," shunting me off to the kitchen where I busied myself
with plans for new signals to rectify the slight, and coming
back with the tray I chipped in with "We feel that the black
freedom thing is the main theme," everything I said a testing
signal, not a single remark not designed for his ear, who
cared about the black freedom it was the "we feel" that I
threw out for acknowledgment, and if the others accepted it
why not David? And pouring the coffee, the others doing
their own while I gave him his, one teaspoon of sugar, a little
milk. He reached for the pitcher and poured more milk, a
sheer act of defiance, another signal, you see, people, she
really doesn't know anything about me, and I, "I didn't
know you liked café au lait," and he, "It was too dark," and
from under the brow the irritable eye as if I were a cinder
that fell in there.

"We have to play everything against Huck's innocence," he
said stirring the coffee too much, another signal, since he
usually gave one perfunctory stir before sipping. I took a seat
in the corner. If he didn't want me to contribute it was his
problem. If I waited long enough that would be the offended
female signal. It would draw some blood. "Yes," he would
say later, "as Jane pointed out," probably directing his remark to Stefanie who knew me best. "I'm really a considerate
guy but she is so difficult to deal with," and turn the whole
thing around on me, when we all knew that the feline in
David was bound to come out under any pressure, that is,
faultless behavior was the only thing to be tolerated. Since
when was a stirred cup of coffee so overbearing it shoots you
up. And it didn't seem to make any difference whether we
were in company, except that in company the signals were
dimmer, shaded by the need to cover up. What I got was a

lot of littles, eyebrow a touch raised, voice a decibel dropped, hand a fraction moved, leg adjusted an inch. David was a symphony of small movements, known only to the aficionado of small movements, in this case me.

"What did I do that was so terrible?" We were alone, the others gone, to play out noncompany signals, the bolder game, where the nuances harden into assertions and intonations swell into declarations. David was capable of arranging his moods to fit the needs of the occasion. Since the meeting hadn't come off too badly and his vanity wasn't wounded, the situation called for less irritation than he would show at other times, particularly when he went for a trying audition with an important client or received a cancellation of a voice lesson from one of the people he was bringing along; and sensing an up mood I felt freer to let myself go with a direct appeal when I might normally remain in a sulky silence and wait for him to come around to me. We had also established a tit-for-tat arrangement based on who owed the other an indulgence. One late night drunken call which brings me in a cab to his house to solace and fuck him for whatever unstated hangup from his other secret life earned me at least one tantrum or one more appeal to establish the relationship on a more permanent basis. I wouldn't think of saying to him, "David, I love you and I want to marry you," unless he had overdrawn considerably from the joint emotional bank we had long understood was mutually invested in.

So I didn't expect his sharp, flouncy, warp-voiced "everything" which scalded my ears. There was some real anger there, enough to make him momentarily fall into what I was sure was his manner with his gay partners, whoever they were.

"What is bugging you?"

"You asked me a question. I gave you an answer."

"You didn't like my sitting in the john?" He shrugged. "You didn't like the way I talked to Howard? I don't see what he's going to contribute to the show. I don't see how you stand him."

"I wish you wouldn't sit in a chair with your legs spread wide open."

"Do I do that?"

"You do that."

"David, what is bothering you? I'm sorry if I bother you. I didn't know that my presence bothered you."

"It's unimportant. Let's drop it."

"I don't want to drop it."

"I prefer to drop it."

"But I don't know what I've done wrong. If I've done something wrong tell so that I can correct it." He was silent. "Will you please tell me? Do I act badly? I thought everything went well. If you don't talk how will I know?" He refused to answer, so I started to gather my things.

"Where are you going?"

"I'm going home."

"Sit down." I sat down with my handbag in my lap. I kept my legs together. Very deliberately, he went into the kitchen and came back with a bottle of Scotch and two glasses with ice. He poured and handed me one. "Put your bag away." I set my bag down on the floor. "Put your coat down." I folded my raincoat and placed it on the floor next to my bag. He turned on his stereo and came back and sat on the piano bench near my chair and sipped his drink, looking over the glass at me. "Cheers."

I drank. "You are not going to get away with it, David Astor." He put his glass down, came to me, leaned over, kissed me, and went back to his seat. "You are a son of a bitch." That was a musical phrase announcing that the truce had been accepted. I had slipped into my wenchy voice. There was nothing I could do, but I tried once more. "Am I so terrible?" Shopping among the remnants of my feelings I pulled out from the bottom of the pile a handful of silk, a soothing cloth of security to stroke away the pain.

"You're awful," he said.

"You're a sadist." It was true. He had to bring me down, reduce me to fright, scrape out of me with his abortionist's tool the last bit of offending ego, work me over with his hostility. Is that what I loved in him, his need to make me suffer before he could come to me? Bring me to the brink of despair over and over again, then rescue me with the sudden phone call and the quailing note of a seventeen-year-old, spreading his pimply adolescent anxieties over me with buttery hunger? What continued to astonish me was my lack of will, the body without resistance to the disease. They could hang a quarantine sign on the door forever. Worst of all was my fear of offending him. Someday I would say the wrong word and everything would stop. I lived in terror of the fatal word, like the guy climbing Everest and missing that one step. Because suddenly you are out there in space, falling, dropping away, into what? The game was to provide against the fall, to manipulate your fate, calculate and plan and scheme and use the sharpest tool to cut the best toehold into the side of the mountain. Just the way Sam and Marilyn Castle did, wasn't that right? Oh, brother.

Why did I feel the constriction, the beating of the thickened chest cavity up into the throat? Wasn't it all the same to me when you get down to it, the same pants dropped, the same hard tool bursting the drawers, the same powerless fetching look mingled with a sly gleam of the score because the minute you lift a willing hand you are victor and victim, and that is exactly where they are alike, in that moment of poise, they too are victor and victim, all advantages leveled, before the touch, just before the hand reaches out to throw the balance off, and whatever their disposition or character, no matter whether they came empty-handed or with a fifth of booze, regardless of their tactics, hard and direct, soft and circuitous, honest, cunning, abusive, tender, they stand before you waiting for triumph but not yet, and ah, it was the not yet that mattered, the breathtaking sweet-juiced air of power that rushes through you, Moses reaching to touch the hand of God, not yet, give me my god-moment, paralyze them with my awesome energy, Jane, Jane, now here yes please do, hand urgent, veins lacing up through skin, helpless they are before the holy touch, Jesus, I could make them pay.

But he frightened me, riding through the magic moment of delay, lips practically curled with disdain, give me what I want, just a skinny kid, wiry yes, a rod of steel he was, and I, these days of bologna and mayonnaise, ballooning, up to one-thirty-five, an inch taller, outweighing him, outreaching him, casting caution to the wind, the defenses gone once more, the strategies defeated again, the pledges unpledged, the resolution to hold my own evaporated like cotton candy in the mouth, turned to him with all the openhearted girl-voiced liquid yearning, here a lady in her thirties, coying up to him with the tiny bugs of love crawling through me in a feast, abject teenager screaming for Frankie or Ringo or whatever, I can't stand it, I can't stand it, I faint for you. And looking up from his spent gun, my face shining with love, I saw that thin shadow of contempt, not that he really meant it, more reflex than design, who knows, curled around that flag of victory there might even be a border of self-contempt or guilt or hatred, it was hard to say, he was fast asleep on the couch, three-drink Charlie. I covered him with an afghan his mother had knitted for him and I sat on the couch with a glass of diet soda wondering why I felt tears slowly descending, as if somebody had tapped a well source and the involuntary water surges up from the dark below. It was eight o'clock. Soon I would wake him and go to dinner at the Italian restaurant across the street, negotiating that river of Eighth Avenue traffic like Huck and Jim on the raft. If he was Huck then I was Jim. The question was: Was I slave nigger Jim or colored help Jim or free black Jim, or Jane, as the case may be? Was he going to take me to freedom or go

past the turnoff point down, down, dragging my helpless
floating self to the terrible waters where the ego smashes up
against the barely submerged rocks of indifference.

Living with that constricted feeling, the kind you experience after hastily swallowed food lodges in your chest, as if
everything in that area forces itself against an overworked
heart, I went through the week, the visit to Dr. Seltz without
relief, leaving my mail piled up on the wicker tray near my
bed, all the official stationery of all my pursuers—the quarterly bill from Blue Cross, the now regular letter from my
Mr. Katz of income tax, past due bills from Saks and Ply-
mouth Shops, a bank loan note due—a nightmare of paper,
plus a note from my cousin Toby confiding in "Aunt" Jane
about the sexual advances of her boyfriend, how the sticky
stuff got over her dress, at eighteen, shouldn't she know better
how to handle this, please don't tell mother, letting that sit
too while I came up to Monday and dinner with Dee, waiting
for the call from David, seeing myself at the other end of the
telephoto lens, the lady in the flat with a quilted housecoat,
the sharply drawn-in breath, let it ring twice, it was Stefanie,
a fight with Howard, Pat Seeley for a movie, no I feel rotten,
a friendly call from Jerry Kay from his office hinting at estab-
lishing a regular thing but not pressing, almost charming,
and from out of town, an old friend of Gene Gordon's, Buzzy
Rizzo, a little dinner maybe, I'm not going to go to bed with
you, Buzzy, that's all right, but he remembered he might
have to fly back, ring, ring, the nervous lady in the housecoat
waits, what was it like at that end of the camera, can you
arrange it to look nice because who knows maybe mother is
watching me, at least wash your stockings and brush your
teeth every night if you don't want to shower. Mother, don't
watch me, I can take care of myself.

Dinner was at my place and Dee arrived promptly at seven,
hair pulled back ballerina style, cheekbones shining, fresh

athletic walk. The way she entered and the way she sat down showed a gain in assurance. We had moved to a third-date stage of familiarity. She knew where to look for the whiskey for cocktails, where the glasses were, how to handle the ice cube tray, sliding past me without saying anything in the confined kitchen space, settling herself on a high stool near the cutting board where I worked on the salad, Dee taking short *noshes* from the bowl as I dumped stuff in, leaning her forearms on her knees, glass in hand, cigarette between fingers, neither of us thinking past the nice moment of pre-dinner drink and chat, Dee telling me about some work she was doing for a science periodical and the call from her ex-husband to go to a concert, talking in that even-tempered, laconic way that guarantees you the world is turning correctly on its axis. With Stefanie it was a contest, who could raise the temperature higher in a match of feverish neuroses, score a point for her big problem, score one for mine, each of us paying with the familiar change of our anxieties, exchanging laughs at the expense of each other. Dee was a comforting apprentice to the school of intrigue and dissection and when she opened up the husband talk amid the smells of onions and beaten eggs and breadcrumbs it was with the hope of being initiated into the club. She had to learn how to be confessional in that clubby way that was second nature to me. She imagined she had great secrets but by the time they were aired they became nothing more than Schrafft's luncheon revelations, the semiwhispered gossip of ladies whose jewelry ringing against good china told more about them than their weak tea tales.

"I think he is seeing somebody and wants to tell me."

"He still feels obliged to tell you."

"From what he hinted at on the phone it's not just anyone. He wants me to know how far he has come along in discovering who he is. I'm certain it's a man."

I stopped my busying around, picked up my drink, and clinked glasses with Dee. "May they live happily ever after."

"I'm terrified."

"It's mix and match. You see it in the stores all the time. What's so terrifying?"

"I may discover something about myself. Deron married me. He must have seen something. He knows something."

"You don't trust your own responses."

"Jane, that's what terrifies me. I feel guilty about nothing, but there is something in the interior soul, good doesn't dwell there, evil is excluded; in that dark center lies the truth of feeling, the secret of identity. I can't reach it. I don't know who I am."

"Join the team."

"Oh, that's not true. You know who you are." She dropped her voice and looked right at me. "You proved that to me."

"I may not like what I know."

"But you do trust your responses. I won't let myself believe that I may love you." She stood up and walked away. "That wasn't so hard, was it."

"It was easy." I would make love to her to satisfy her uncertainty about her love for me. My sexuality is opened up because the risks, the dangers of emotional terror, are on the other side. I was learning more about the nature of power. Was I a sadist too in getting pleasure from her fears? So pleasure stands on one side and love on the other, and love gets dumped, every time. Three cheers for pleasure.

We were into our second drink when David called. I didn't give him much of a chance to signal me, friendly call, drinking call, rocks-off call, I was greedy to have him here, come over, come over. I put up three bottles of wine to chill and checked the remaining liquor, about a full bottle of gin, and hummed around the kitchen, not thinking too much about his last bit of information, he was going to Europe later in the week, my mind turning on the single absurd fact that he had called me, that I hadn't been forced to pick up the phone. "I'm having dinner with a friend," I had said, getting a nod of approval from Dee, who had brought with her instead of knitting a queer assortment of plastic shapes that she began to busy herself with at the coffee table, the atmosphere spiced with a tangy domestic flavor.

"You don't mind," I said, beginning what I later saw was the first in a series of tests, because nothing would do but that I should arrange events to satisfy a cancerous need to engineer disaster.

"I don't mind," she said. Strong finger worked away at the colored plastic parts. I could see the hands from my worktable, not supple, forcing the shapes to their will.

"I mind a little. There has been something bothering me in our relationship. Of course I regret nothing. It's just that I want to be available to him first."

"You mean you don't want me to think you're dumping me."

"Let's say I don't want to be accused of being opportunistic."

She left her toy, came into the kitchen, and put her hand on mine. "How often does one have the chance to be opportunistic?"

"I just don't want to take advantage of you."

"Maybe I'm taking advantage of you." The hand was firm on mine, pressing. "Please don't concern yourself. Give me a sign and I'll leave."

"Like it's a disease. Always preparing myself against rejection. You play with the dice loaded against you, but you keep playing."

"An infirmity of the heart. There is no known cure. Does he know anything about us?"

"No, but he's very bright."

"Why don't I leave now?"

"I want him to meet you."

"You want an advantage. He will know you're being loved."

"That's a tremendous thing to hear. I wish he could say it. I would believe it."

"What we've done is not believable." She let her hand off mine and returned to the coffee table.

"You've made me feel very good. I don't know if I can trust that feeling." Creeping around the edge of my consciousness, the intruder, on padded feet, worked his way. I didn't care for her, only that she cared for me. Stranger, intelligent woman, how could she make me believe in her? She should love a man. I was middle-class enough to suspect her weakness, for what else could it be? Eating another woman wasn't a weakness, but loving her was.

"You don't trust the feeling because you aren't able to trust me. Why should you trust me?" Dee said.

"Any fly-by-night shrink could tell you it's me I don't trust. Maybe you shouldn't trust me?"

"You've already told me what you want." Her tone had shifted into a higher register. She didn't like what I wanted. "I'll tell you what I want," she said. "I want life to bounce around. I want it to burn away, not leak out."

"And I want to bring a man his slippers. Love and human respect and a body with a shape I recognize. I'm tired of fucking my way through the Western world." I should give her a catalog of waste, of burned-out nights and empty whiskey bottles and cold ravioli on the plate.

David arrived an hour late bearing nothing except his lateness and right away got a cold, cranky introduction from me, exactly the kind of thing you do when you want to show someone off. Later in Dr. Seltz's office I was to see that opening setting a pattern for the evening, what better way to league them against me, Dee working her plastic model indifferent to time, David a cavalier about it; only I with my fingers dripping in batter and shredded lettuce and whatnot, checking the chilling wine, Macon Vivé 1966, inexpensive but a best buy, the Port du Salut the right temperature with Euphrates crackers circling the cheese on a lovely lusterware plate, only I was edgy, practically cracking my knuckles and walking around Bette Davis-nervous, the shrew leaping on the victim, the very thing she loves, a minute's worth of pique, no more, a glancing blow in honor of domestic punctilio and punctuality; in fact, the kind of thing I abhorred and would normally accuse David of, his prissy time-sense and fussy domesticity. But I poured him a fat gin and tonic, the weather in early fall still good for that, another ill-fated event, temperature degrees above normal, the door to the terrace open; and drinking, we all steered our way through my crazy annoyance, with me taking the lead, shopping for the right subject to get them going while I could subside into my role as Mother Superior, striving for that exact balance of control and license that would make it seem to them that I was indeed what I imagined they wanted me to be. Dee finally provided an out when she held up her finished product, a model of a moon rocket.

From the kitchen I heard them go on about space voyage and interstellar galaxies, Dee confessing that she had built telescopes as a kid, the news offered to David in her cool, horsey-set manner, which David picked up and returned, he had considerable interest in these matters, being himself a student of the Eddington-Hoyle controversy, did Dee subscribe to the steady-state or big-bang theory of the universe, David not at all sure that either mattered much except as it thrilled the imagination.

"I'm a big-banger myself," he said, which set us all laughing, and to my credit I resisted announcing what proof I had of the statement, but I couldn't resist an extra ho-ho, just to establish priorities.

David was easy in the armchair, inviting the casual reply, but Dee came back with something about quasars and velocities and frequencies, the use of big instruments, the possibilities of intelligent beings out there, and the two of them were into a dialogue about space and origins of the universe and a whole business of first causes, exclusive and absorbed, at which point I piped, "Listen, you got to believe in God or it makes no sense," leaning over both of them, pouring the first of the white wine, which right on top of the gin would set us up nicely for dinner. What I got for my trouble was a distracted nod from Dee and a look from David as if I were a wisp of stray hair that had fallen across his eyes.

"I think the cutlets are burning," he said.

"I know how to take care of my kitchen. I'm not an astronomy maven or anything like that, but how can you talk about beginnings if you don't bring in the concept of God." I flung this over my shoulder and marched back to the kitchen, the injured theologian. But they were thick into their talk and I decided to relax and see it the way a sane person would: my two lovers having a chat, feeling each other out. What could he, closet queen, or had he really come out, do with a dyke in the making? That he fucked me and she had had a husband was no particular big deal. At the moment they had agreed to the amenities, displaying for effect of course, how drunk I was not to see it until later, the intellectuality they shared. Let's show Janie what we can do. I mean it was obvious with the leg-crossings and the glass-raisings and the voice-meetings and eye-sparklings, that they had diverted their interest in me to each other. But I have to blame it on something. That white wine for sure, because it wasn't until after the fact, lying exhausted a day later, in absolute hysterics on Dr. Seltz's couch, that I saw it all, or rather he saw it all for me. Was Seltz trying to help me or was I being treated to another one of those elaborate support operations, which turned everything around and made me the heroine instead of the victim? Because anyway Seltz sliced it I should have come out a winner. What I could not account for was the depth and subtlety of Dee's jealousy. Seltz argued that I had misread the situation, taking Dee's action as a positive heterosexual act when in fact she was most likely a clinical homosexual, already beginning to act out latencies, and even the buried hostilities to men now surfacing in her using David to get at me. Unless, and I must give myself credit because I asked this from the couch, I was out of the chair, my nose bubbling mucous, the familiar windup whine of petulance and desperation, that it may as well have been my daddy sitting there—unless of course for my sake she didn't want to seem to be rejecting David. A truth lurked there.

Because what could you make of it, the food devoured, the salad demolished, the gin gone, and into the second bottle of Macon Vivé 1966, not a bad year, good bouquet, blah, blah, all very loose by this time, unbuttoned you might say, which in fact we started to be, I was pissed, mind you, having had quite enough of their mutual admiration society, going on with that kind of conversation pitched slightly beyond me but not enough to appear disdainful, Dee flailing her arms a bit, David stirring the wine with his finger and giving her a little suck of wine-finger; so I got a little pushy and said, "I don't think that is very nice." David, a glassy-eyed fish by this time, these low-threshold guys, sticks the finger of the other hand in. "Here, try this one." And I can swear it sneaked out, the *faigele* had flown the coop. I was greedy so I sucked, but managed to let some teeth go in there. He said what I expected, "You bitch," and he offered the bit finger to Dee. At this point a thread of air hung floating. A little look she gave me, an arc of pain, a short-circuit job. She was sending out the S.O.S. but I wasn't plugged in. Why should I be? I didn't give two shits for her machinations. She sucked the bit finger and I slopped down on the couch with a "This is too much" and Dee said, "This is not enough." It was in desperation, but did I know it? Sitting on Seltz's couch, kleenexes strewn around, I saw it with the delicious sense of hindsight power, that hard-won knowledge that still tastes sweet after the fact, wasn't there power in that? Couldn't your blindness make you see? "Let's get under the hose on the terrace," and she didn't wait, zip zap, dropping it all off and out she went. "Chicken, chicken," so I followed suit, got out there, turned on the hose and along came little David to meet his two Goliaths, with his little slingshot hanging between his legs. "I'm going to give it to you, you bitches," Dee flapping around like a bird and I, "Let's grab his thing," chasing around, dizzy with drink all of us, descending on him on top of my bed of myrtle, David screeching and reaching, his hand going a shade faster for Dee's small nippled boob, and I grabbed the hose and shoved the stream into his face, and that was it, played out, we stumbled into the house and dried off, the wine out again, the glasses filled, the clothes piled on the couch. We knew that if the terrace business was a climax there would have to be a denouement, and anybody who knows the drama knows that climaxes are nothing, denouements everything, the primitive need to bring things to an end urging us on. So the scene was set, the action I had set in motion moving toward an inexorable end, structured by me, so why should Arnold Seltz, comfort salesman, think he has to pacify me with the following interpretation: When David put himself in the red wing chair and you two girls perched yourselves on either arm David was hoping to place himself in the middle, *between* Jane and Dee. He would do anything to avoid putting *Jane* in the middle, because putting Jane in the *middle* would be too threatening, a recognition that there was a relationship between the two women. David's struggle to achieve bourgeoisification would be defeated. David does not want a reinforcement of his homosexuality. He comes to Jane to prove his manhood. He will do what is necessary to defend that manhood.

Now that was a lovely formulation and I was ready to fold up the kleenex box and go. Of course he was right, I was a fool not to see it. But that was asking too much of me, Dr. Seltz. How could I tell that the two of us, sitting completely bare-assed, practically on top of him, were not vying for his attention, that he was not at the moment making a conscious choice between us. Which he did. He picked her, on the left side, his body leaning, his left hand quicker than his right, his eye cast up to her, her leg sliding down to brush his thigh. What do I do, me, the original hysteric, so full of smashing self-confidence, that I can witness the spectacle of my man choosing another woman? I don't blame Dee, she didn't steal him. He went for her. How can I forgive him? I don't know her motives. I don't think she was really interested. Could it be that this chick would ball him to destroy the thing for David and me? I did my leaning in this armchair competition, the more he moved toward her the more I moved toward him, until we looked like a sinking ship listing badly to port. The wine was coming out of the bottle fast, so it was easier to perform all the twists and nudges and fingerings and strokings, David still without an erection, too concerned with steering the boat. And I couldn't take it, dashing off to the bathroom, in the end it will be the razor blade in the bathroom, to pee out the wine and cry drunken tears. Not five minutes in there and out I came to find them in the bedroom in bed.

"Nobody's going to fuck in my bed but me," and a fresh supply of tears. They made a place for me, David wedged between, lying stiffly, not touching, Dee lying way over at the edge, hands clasped over her head, unshaven armpits showing hair, the good small boobs lying free and high just over the top of the sheet.

I was up now, off Seltz's couch, in the leather chair, facing his desk. He said, "You were saying that you structured this out of greed."

"What I did was manufacture a small tragedy. I brought my own house down on myself. I found out that David never cared for me."

"Do you think he cared for her?"

"He cares for nothing but himself. I can't buy the line that he wants to fuck her to prove that Dee and I were not having a relationship. I told him, finally, after she had popped out of the bed and was taking herself to the couch in the living room, after she had come out with, "David, don't just let her lie there," I said to him, "I know you. All you want to do is fuck me." I mean I said this after we had screwed and the booze had worn off, morning light coming in, "I want to give you some love, what do you want, what do you want, what do you want?" and a new wave of tears, I'll die from drowning, and there was no answer, I had fallen asleep from exhaustion, and the next thing I knew, there was an empty space beside me. I threw on a robe, the naked night was over, and I ran into the living room. They were on the couch, him on top of her, ready to shove his rod in. "Stop it, stop it." I think they both sat up and shrugged, like, what's she getting excited about. You ask, did he care for her. The answer is that they were trying to get some sort of revenge, or maybe I'm beginning to understand that she is an animal, with a boundless appetite for novelty. I have contempt for her, David has contempt for me, and she has a mountain of self-contempt which she is ready to act out. I saw her face, a quick glimpse in the gray light, he was about to *shtup* her, but there was no ecstasy, a little curl on the lip, the eyes demonic, the *meshugenah's* amusement at the absurdity of everything. "Get out," I screamed at them. Dee said, "I'm sorry." David said nothing. They dressed and left. I sit here and see it now, I make it so that I have to be rejected. I come here and pay you and talk and watch the smile behind the mask and the glasses being folded back and forth and all that swivel-chaired wisdom, and you'd better believe it, you're with them. Listen. I would reject me too."

"Do you want to wash your face?"

"You see what I mean. You're as crazy as the rest of them."

I waited three days by the phone, going out only for some deli and soda across the street. My little lady with the cardigan said, "What's the matter, girlie, you don't look so good," and for her I managed a smile, but in the apartment I waited. I had the golden corkscrew, gift-wrapped and ready. There had been silence since the night of the hose. I was not yet at the end of my obsession. Would I ever be? If I didn't have David, what was there. The unemployment was running out, my creditors were at me again, Stefanie was making a good adjustment with Howard, and I had just discovered a run in my last good pair of pantyhose. Hang in there, Seltz had said. I'll hang up there, I said.

So I called him. "Why didn't you call me?"

"I tried to call you. I tried to call you on Monday night. And Wednesday night I woke up at three o'clock in the morning. I couldn't sleep because I was worried about talking to you."

"Why didn't you call me? It didn't bother you to call me at two o'clock in the morning?"

"I called you at two o'clock in the morning when I called you earlier in the evening and you hadn't been home."

"Why is seeing me such a big problem?"

"I'm not giving excuses. I'm telling you what I've been through getting ready for Europe. I did try to call you all evening long Tuesday night."

"I was out Tuesday night." A big pause. What was I supposed to do, not go out? He knows I'm not going to sit around waiting for him. "What you're saying doesn't make any sense to me. Do you think that I am such an ogre that you can't tell me that you don't want to see me? What would have been so terrible for you to call me and say that it's absolutely impossible to see me next week?"

"You would have made waves."

"That's rotten of you. I really resent that. Now I'm talking about seeing you for a few minutes. Yes or no."

"I want to see you. What time can you get here?"

"I will make it my business to be there at one-thirty."

"I can be here at one-thirty."

"Are you sure it's all right?"

"I want to see you. Don't say any more."

When I got there he was on the phone. I sat on the couch and when he got off he came over and jumped on top of me, straddled me. "I don't want any part of you," I said, trying to be funny about it. He got off and I threw the present at him. "Here, go and have a good time, see if I care." He opened the present and said he was thrilled. He always wanted to buy one for himself.

"Is there anything you want me to do?" I asked.

"Yes, I want you to call Cynthia, my secretary, a couple of times. You are to be the person to call if she needs advice. I want you to be in charge of her."

I said let's open the present and we got down like two kids in a sandbox and tried out the corkscrew. Kneeling next to him I felt completely exhilarated. He kept trying to hug and kiss me, and when he put his arms around me, the comfort, the familiarity that has grown up between us, the physical familiarity, the sense of well-being. I got very weepy.

"I really want you to have a good time." It was hard for me to sound like I meant it because I was so busy trying to keep from crying.

"You don't mean that."

"I wished you hadn't said that."

"I was only kidding."

I got teary and he hugged me. "I really want you to be happy," I said.

"I know you do."

What I wanted to say was, if you get somebody else good luck, I don't begrudge you any happiness. As long as he gets what he wants, fine. And I walked out and he came out and hung over the banister and said he hoped everything would be all right when he came back.

"I don't know, I may not even be in New York."

"Maybe it's time for you to make a change," he said.

I went out into the street thinking how these guys have to get their rocks off, how they can't stand their own vulnerability. Better to send me into the street in hysterics than live with his own duplicity. Kisses me and sends me out of town.

While I was waiting for the crosstown bus Louis Pfeffer came along. He was stage-managing for an APA play, and looked a little fatter than the early days at the P-town Playhouse. I let the bus go by and went with Louis in a cab up to his West Ninety-third Street apartment. After he fucked me he gave me money for a cab, but I pocketed it and took the long walk across town, picked up a pint of Louis Sherry coffee ice cream and a bottle of Bosco chocolate syrup. I would sit up with the late show. Maybe it would be Jimmy Stewart and Margaret Sullavan in a whisper romance. When David comes back I would have to act out the fact that I don't like just being a receptacle. He could not any longer get away with calling me in the middle of the night. If he wants to fuck me he's got to take me out for a good dinner. That happens to be the price at the moment. We would see. It was his move now.

Part IV

Chapter 1

TORREMOLINOS, SPAIN. Well, Phil, you can write the bottom line now. I thought that when I left the first time, The Book was in the can. Stop with David and break open the surprise package in Part IV, the struggle to get me to say what you wanted, the other hassles. But you let it sit because maybe there would be another ending, The Life and Loves of Jane Castle not complete without the Europe bit, and the little irony you had working all along, having me set myself up as the girl who will absolutely not become the leather-faced chick with the desperate first-class luggage, Katy Hepburn chasing after some technicolor guinea in Venice, I said I'm not going that route. So off to Portugal I go and I can hear you cackling in the wings, "I'll have an ending, heh, heh." The weary young spinster finally going to burn out the center of her life on the hot Mediterranean sands with a vague, rancid Latin, cut loose from all the smoggy *dreck* of Sin City, all ties broken, all deals canceled, all debts dissolved, free for romance and terror, meeting that Nazi in Lisbon with the Mercedes coupe, zooming from town to town, checking at the mail drop for David to magic me back. Then my letter to you about Miguel with the automobile agency and all the middle-class tastes I've grown to love and despise. A Spanish lover, his apartment, a seacoast town, fucking in the morning, fucking at siesta, fucking at night. He sells cars and fucks me and bosses me as men expect to do down here. Likes to philander, even when he's got an American lady.

When I got back after four months of it I had this terrific down, the European caper over, the apartment in shambles. And they were back on the phone, my faithful crew, except Dee Tate, the end of that affair, a drunken call from David and a drunken appearance from Richard and a drunken call from Jerry Kay and an out-of-town visit from Lenny Kaplow, a ghost from Waterbury Civic Theater days, with his screw-and-sob story in the high floors of the St. Moritz, Lenny, a bald and nervous producer from Television City, tells me "Come West, Jane, there is a spot for you in the office, LA, a new life, work you into a production setup." There we go again, Jane Castle, human furniture. I sat on that one and waited for a decision to surface. I was afraid at this point to sum up my life, what could I discover about me that would undo the knowledge that I was a commodity, a usable thing, wash cleanly and return for deposit. I mean I didn't give a shit about Lenny Kaplow, another premature ejaculator, but I've been to the Coast. I needed support. I wanted The Book to give me the big insight, the green light for the future. How I've been counting on it. I got ready to close up the apartment and head for California. I wrote Miguel and threw in a friendly note about longing for him. I got the call in the middle of the night, buy a one-way ticket, come and we will work something out. I told the Kaplow office I was getting married, find yourself another girl, sold the stuff in the apartment, got a thousand bucks for the key, the lease transferred, and flew Iberia. Jane, make a new life for yourself, I said. Before I left I went to David's for a fond farewell. How I hate him for making love such a real possibility. A gourmet meal and gourmet lovemaking. We have such a buoyant thing together. Unbelievable. He did not tear up the ticket and I went in the airport limousine by myself. I had time in the night air over the Atlantic to think about Miguel, but I found my thoughts fixed on your duplicity.

The fact is that in your own interest you betrayed me, manipulated me at every turn to get your "essential air of verisimilitude." The fact is that you doctored the tapes, suppressed the real relationship and victimized me with the fake clinical manner and the fake scenes and the fake concern for my welfare. It would be better for me if we cut through to the truth you say, so you give me your knify questions, cutting away at the real flesh to lay bare those "truths" your greed demanded. You never believed I loved David, that we have something that transcends your art. What you want is a theme and you turn the whole thing into a fag operation. I know I'm drawn to men like that, but you pushed it beyond reason. You went with a friend of yours cruising the gay bars for material, and you bought books on the gay world to discover the truth of David Astor and you badgered me with your clinical itch, Jane, how does he fuck you, what is the size of his prick, does he go down on you, for how long, behind the questions a hostility so apparent I could laugh, you never once believing he could do anything. A fag is a fag, right? Wrong.

I sit at the lunch table and break off the stem of the wineglass. I've saved three broken wineglass stems this way. I haven't told Miguel, who is very busy selling cars and ministering to his erections. When I break the wineglass I do it with one hand, gripping the stem with the three fingers and snapping off the bowl with my thumb and forefinger.

Remember the coffee-pouring scene at the last Huck session, after I came out of the bathroom. You try to show my attempt to be possessive of David. Here comes Miss Full

Charge again, clutzing her way into another insecurity situation. You think you have me pegged: "He reached for the pitcher and poured more milk, another signal, see, she really doesn't know anything about me, and I, 'I didn't know you liked café au lait,' and he, 'It was too dark,' and from under the brow the irritable eye as if I were a cinder that fell in there." Clever, but wrong. If you knew anything about us, David, with his natural grace and good manners, would never tip his hand that he was party to such domestic intimacy. Because whatever we do, wherever we go, it is established that he is the man who orders the drinks and the food, he rides the bike, he is the aggressor in bed. We live by that code, that is where we are at and have been for years and it's better all the time, giving confidence to his virility and esteem to my femininity. The coffee scene is more than an author's misconception, it is an outright distortion born of your own hostility to my being attracted to supposedly faggy men, and if I may be permitted a moment of analysis, isn't it your own manhood that is in question? It doesn't take a lot of logic to prove that if Jane Castle has successful affairs with guys who are working out their manhood thing, then maybe you're like David and that leaves you nowhere except to retreat behind the barrier of The Book and shoot your word bullets from behind the fortress.

If you consult the tape you did on me and Richard,* and see the remarks of Phil, you get a character which you entirely suppressed. Instead you chose to write the scene of Richard and me at Rigby's. The real tape reveals too much of you pushing all that exact detail in the interest of science, but it is really suburban Phil getting in his vicarious licks. What could you want but a piece of the action, having your book and eating it too. Isn't that the story, not the desperate loneliness horseshit of the single girl, because I have a busy life, lots of friends, faithful lovers, a life I've carved out for

* See Excerpts from *The Tapes*, "Richard Doyle."

myself. I cry a little for a man now and then, but I have my men. Isn't it Pirandelloish, you said, the art and life thing slipping in and out of each other, and as you move closer into my orbit you start to manipulate the men, making them contemptuous of me, so that you can save the day with your compassion. And then in your power hunger you turn it around and become contemptuous of my life. Jealous of my sexual adventures, you diminish them, when it is self-comtempt that is the story. It is your story, bringing yourself to the well and afraid to drink, with the mountain of rationalizations—not good for The Book, damage the marriage, you might not be good enough. So you attack me. I don't lick assholes, big deal, make a federal case of it. Hound me, distort my relationships, because you're afraid it might be too good and expose the whole thing at home. I love you and Judy, you're my family. You want the truth, but to write yourself into it would be too much pain, loss of power, the writer with the Olympian detachment would go down the drain.

Here on weekdays it's a family scene, and I can hear them rattling on about me, shooing the kids away from the American lady in the flowered bikini, a little heavy in the haunches, indeterminately and determinedly youthful. Here and there a stray buck preening for a score, Miguel safely off at the store. I make an overture to a dumpy, friendly looking mother, who gives me a slow, cautious smile and very fast Spanish. The buck slides past my blanket, and I watch the kids at the water's edge shouting in kid Spanish. I feel dumb under the sun, my face in a fried grin, and everything is moviesque, soon they will find my body washed up on the rocky shore, with the local *polizei* gibbering about the mess, bad for tourisme. At home in the backyard on hot summer days the hired hand, bare to the sweating waist, ladled cold water onto his body from the outside tap. The broken wineglass stem flashes against the sun in the sand. If I break three more I'll have a set.

Once I brought a nickel bag of grass out to the suburbs to share with my friends. C'mon Philly, let's turn on, a family smoke before the tape session, a little *entre nous* thing. We can all face the music together. So we smoke but Judy can't bring herself to it, sits and watches us, her swinging single chum who has tried one of everything, so why not one husband of close friend. She turns her fear into superiority, pitying me my childless life the way she raps on about the kids. The kids are great but who needs that scene. I'm pushing freedom, catching out of the corner of my eye a pursy-mouthed look from her and from you the look from Mission Control, freedom is a big word in the uptight world. I'm a threat with my pad in the city and a ready bed, the three of us trying to be terribly good in the interest of The Book. How else could she tolerate the Captain's Paradise, you running into the city in your car with the black briefcase under one arm and the tape machine under the other, come in, a fresh roll and coffee, plug in the machine and play shrink. It's not so bad, if you could both loosen up we could have a *ménage à trois* right here in sunny Spain.

Instead you manipulate me with your contempt, and now that I look at it you've got all my men wrong, John Ames and Richard and David and even Jerry Kay, who you understand best, and you drop Jonathan, four years at Wisconsin, and Bernie W., living with him, the only man I can claim as husband, really they are all out of it. You paint a grim picture despite your effort to show me as tough. You started with a premise that you wouldn't let go, the lonely chick who fucks her way through the western world, without roots, a thin-skinned hysteric just this side of the razor slash. There she is, ladies and gentlemen, a product of twentieth-century civilization, with the straightened nose and the twisted psyche. If that is a premise you buy, then where am I. What piece of this world's beauty is left to me if you start with compassion and end with contempt and do the one thing I believed you incapable of doing and that is betray the trust, sacrifice me for some creature you call Jane Castle who wanders through the debt-ridden streets of New York with a soul the size of a bug and an imagination the length of the abortionist's tool? That is the conclusion I come to. How can I escape it?

And that is where it's at for me. Now I am living with Miguel who doesn't even know why he asked me to come. I am a complete raving maniac, although managing to have outward control. I feel trapped because of the terrific change in my life style and in the quality of life around me. I have visions of being here the rest of my life, hating every minute of it, and never leaving. I don't have enough faith in my ability to structure the situation to fall apart, if that's what I want. I'm not sure I'd know what I want if it hit me in the face, but then maybe it hasn't hit me in the face. However, with my bottle of Librium tucked in my purse I shall persevere for a while. Perhaps some *deus ex machina* will straighten everything out for me. I go through the days in a daze. Miguel is starting a new business and he is worried and frustrated. He doesn't know what he wants any more than I do. And he is still very interested in other girls. This will always be a big problem, but I do have to learn how to deal with it, or if it's worth dealing with. And I wonder if I haven't just changed Peter for Paul and that is my lot, to be the universal all-purpose douche-pot. The very hot weather here slows down everything, so even my anxiety is sluggish. I feel like I'm trapped in a vat of slowly melting butter and that sooner or later, it doesn't matter in the soft swill, I'll be swimming without care to something better, the better butter. Meanwhile I save the stems of the wineglasses and count them. By the way, the bikini underwear Judy gave me is really wonderful. Miguel loves it and I wear it all the time. It's just perfect for here and makes me feel supersexy.

Chapter 2

Notes on Jane Castle

THE BOTTOM LINE has not been written. Jane is still living in the Mediterranean resort town with her Spanish automobile salesman, a balding, mediocre man of thirty who brings his career-hardened frown to the bed, a man who rescues an occasional piece of generosity from the sea of cautions and resentments that mark his type. Smiling when it costs him nothing, laughing when he smells a sale, Miguel moves between office and flat taking his pleasure with his American mistress, both worrying how long the bloom will last. Janie sits brown and bored with her pills and her wineglass stems, hoarding her treasure against despair. Waiting with despair has been the leitmotif of her life. We wait for the scene, Jane and I, that will justify the closing of the book.

The major problem came early in the tape sessions when Jane began to mistrust my motives for writing the book. She interpreted my examination of her sexual life as prurient interest, a voyeurism that had no purpose beyond its own gratification. In my denials, sometimes cool, sometimes furious, I couldn't tell her that my problem was not my sexual excitement but her lack of imagination. The tapes revealed a thinly furnished mind, and my badgerings were attempts to irritate her into revelation. Frequently she lashed out at me when I pushed hard to get past the daily summary and the incessant round of self-analysis that her Dr. Seltz had to bear. When I cut her off she argued that she would get to things in her own way, and I fell into the mollifying yes-dear, afraid to ruffle her feathers, adopting a clinical cunning, circling around her sensitivities and making quick thrusts into the interior. With each session I became cagier, feeding her lines, waiting for the click, the line that lives, the telling anecdote, the sharply observed detail, and then pressing the advantage home. We usually ran a one-hour or a two-hour tape, the session starting off at her house or at my office with a pouring off of the day's travails, "I want this on the machine, it's important," and we went through the Richard trauma and the David crisis. "O.K.," I say, "very good, we have it all down, very good stuff, real self-penetration." Then I ask what was her difficulty in the summer of '58, the period we have been working on, and she comes up with the "fuck-and-pay" routine.* She is sharp, tough, funny. What makes a woman like Jane interesting is the faith and confidence that her body will carry her through, atoning for the head weaknesses. Whenever we fought, it was always about a matter of intellectual judgment. Jane would get defensive and shrill, forcing her banalities as given truths, and I would fall into my indulgent-smug posture, which was not unjustified. What I felt the book was all about was the celebration of her virtue, the claim her body makes on the world, that it demands its share of the life process, that in her sensual determinism she is heroic in the way that blind, desperate belief in a single source of energy can be heroic as well as vulnerable and foolish. The sessions from time to time became saturated with her peculiar power, so that the machine would be

* See Excerpts from *The Tapes*, "Fuck-and-Pay."

running uninterruptedly as I dropped my therapy-cool and fell under the sway of her narrative, and the roles were reversed. I had become another of her men succumbing to the sensual heat, trying very hard not to louse up the credibility of my role by falling into pleading need, exactly the circumstance the virile psychoanalyst encounters when his patient tries to reverse the power structure, who is ready to risk loss of power, authority, privilege, the whole show, in order to plunge the erected member into the wanton creature.

So we alternated between her power plays and mine and a field of energy was established, which became the driving force of our sessions. We moved between poles of power, sometimes striking the center of the source. I would arrive at her house, set up my machine, have coffee and start with the warmup stage, Jane's previous day, then into the specified period of her life, the district-attorney-type questions, reactions, resentment, push, push, push, then the clicking detail and the shift of power, she is off and I listen to the self-absorbed voice, out of herself, thick into the felt experience, then exhaustion, emptiness, dismay, self-recrimination, tears. Or else the following. In my constant pursuit of that essential air of verisimilitude that seemed to me the lifeline of the book, one day I let myself into her apartment with my key, looking for significant filler, the kind of detail out of crappers and pubs and cemeteries that Joyce fashioned to shape Bloom's imagination in *Ulysses*. I started with an inventory of her refrigerator:

BOTTOM SHELF
Vegetable and fruit bin empty

SECOND SHELF
One pound chopped meat, wrapping paper open, meat discolored
One brown paper bag with stale onion roll

THIRD SHELF

Three bottles French white wine, Macon Vivé 1966

TOP SHELF

Large pitcher for orange juice with drop of juice
One Birds Eye Cool N' Creamy Pudding
One can Danish bacon, opened
Three moldy peaches
One box plum tomatoes in carton, overripe

She arrived from work around six with a half pound of bologna, a large Spanish onion, a small jar of mayonnaise, and a bottle of Pepsi-Cola, purchased at the little grocery store across the street. The onion roll was too hard to cut, so I went across the street for rolls. Over two Dagwood specials and the Pepsi poured into a blue-tinted mead-hall glass she talked about her day

JANE: The debt thing is murder.

PHIL: Murder.

JANE: That's one of the things that's been bugging me the last couple of days when I sat down and wrote what I should pay back, fifty to Jack, seventy-five to the trustee in bankruptcy. He's getting a postdated check. And the money I owe you. I've got to get some bread. The snowball is going down the hill.

PHIL: Do you know the myth of Sisyphus?

JANE: No.

PHIL: The man who rolled the stone up the hill and it rolls down, and he rolls it up again and again. Camus made it popular.

JANE: No.

PHIL: Sisyphus was a mythical character.

JANE: Jason was always talking about rolling the stone up the hill. That's the way he operates. I can't buy it with him because I don't have any sense of value about it being worth the sisyphean effort. I think that any sisyphean effort to become a mature human being who can have a good human relationship is worth it. Success in business is not going to contribute to my mature individualism to be worth this effort where I ignore my personal life. The grass smells like cement.

PHIL: What?

JANE: The grass smells like cement.

PHIL: Why don't you. . . .

JANE: You want me to just ramble?

PHIL: Ramble a little.

JANE: I think I'll have to sit David out this time so that I have the ammunition if I have to. I said, "If I didn't ask you, I wouldn't see you, right?" I need as much ammunition as possible.

PHIL: What were you saying about the pot? Talk about the pot.

JANE: Oh, the pot.

PHIL: The past.

JANE: The past or the pot?

PHIL: I said the past and then you said the pot. Maybe you should talk about it.

JANE: You said the pot.

PHIL: No, the past.

JANE: The past.

PHIL: Jaystar and the past. You were borrowing to get the show on the road.

JANE: I don't want to talk about it. It is making me anxiety-ridden.

PHIL: Do you attribute this to the—

JANE: Grass. Absolutely.

PHIL: Grass works like some other drugs which do something to the psychic mechanism.

JANE: Yes, I've got an anxiety attack right now.

PHIL: Did you in the past?

JANE: I don't remember.

PHIL: Is your heart beating faster?

JANE: I have butterflies in my stomach.
PHIL: That's the way it goes with the—
JANE: The anxiety.

Anxiety rules her life. Jane is frequently on the edge, coming often from a casual slight which she converts into a major rebuff, which leads to a refrain that runs through the tapes, "When do I get mine?" To get hers she plays a long running game of solitaire: "If I play my cards right I can get him to come around." Then she is on the phone telling me she pulled the wrong card from the deck, she spoke too soon, she spoke too loud, she spoke too often, she was too pushy or too timid, what is the right strategy, Phil, some magic key to unlock the secrets of her character. The tapes become an endless reel of catalogs of denials of worth, accompanied by a barrage of self-erasing rhetorical questions: Am I too fat, am I too old? am I too weak, am I too aggressive? do I walk into a room wrong? do I talk too fast? am I blind, dumb, foolish, sick, sick?

The force of anxiety is so great that antidotes must be superficial, quickly assuaging. Anxiety's bedfellow is sentimentality, and the result is the "Cole Porter" tape.* Terrified by reality she seeks cause and purpose in romantic evasion. "It was just one of those things" becomes a soothing directive, a lyric balm washed over the terror. I get angry with her and order her to stop being the fool, she weeps out her helplessness and I comfort her into one of our moments of understanding. But it never goes too deep. I am touched, but it is for the sake of the book. Is my compassion really pity and is the pity really contempt? I have pages of notes devoted exclusively to the shaping process, start a chapter this way, break up a chronology here, include this character or that, strike for tone here, concerned only with putting it together. I never ask myself who Jane really is. I never ask myself, do I

* See Excerpts from *The Tapes*, "Cole Porter."

really care? All I want to do is structure a life on paper, be the objective writer, the cool vampire, who feeds on the blood of the world. Or, to change the image, why do literary people always refer to Joyce's Stephen Dedalus, sitting on top of the cliff, paring his fingernails, dropping his droppings on the quotidian? It is the master image of contempt. What is important is technique, science, the tape machine, God *in* the machine. It is old Yahweh, the god of wrath, cloaked in a smile and offering a willing ear. Listen to this truth I discovered from E.M. Cioran, the Roumanian philosopher:

> When angry we feel alive, since it is, unfortunately, only a passing mood, we must be content with its by-products, ranging from backbiting to contumely. . . . We discover, to our delight, what keen pleasure besmirching others can bring. At last we are on equal terms with them, we are struggling, we are no longer *alone*. . . . Perhaps we should mind our own business: it is abasing, ignoble, to pass judgment on others. That, however, is what everyone does; by refraining, we ostracize ourselves. Man, splenetic animal that he is, never offers a commentary on his fellow men without disparaging them. Not that he is unable to speak well of them; but speaking ill of them gives him a far bolder sensation of pleasure and strength. If he humbles and executes them, however, it is not to do them harm as to save the remnants of his anger, the remnants of his vitality. . . .

The author, god-hungry, wants his power both ways. Jane Castle, I want to treat your life with tenderness, compassion, understanding. Jane Castle, I want to do you in. I offer besmirchment under the guise of compassion. I ask myself, how dare you adopt the voice of a woman unless it is to perform a subversive activity? In her person I can sequester my contempt. There I can heap upon her all the ignobleness that leeches upon oneself. When she tells a vivid· sex tale I feel the blood drain away, the power sapped, my body a trap. I am absolutely helpless. I sit with caked mouth and plot my own place in the next adventure. I arrive at the knowledge that Jane Castle has me in her power any time she wants.

But she does not want to own that power. She wants a different kind. The crucial idea she has about her life, it amounts to an obsession, is the desire to will her own fate, to "structure the situation" and be accepted as normal. What can she do to be like any other nice middle-class girl? She wants to know where she has gone wrong. Will she ever stop mortgaging her body for the dream of a permanent lease on a decent life? The noble banality of such a hope, born of the despise of her parents, should be measured against the meaning of Jane for the men, who are not so ready to consign her to the kitchen when she belongs in the bed. For the man, in his dream of freedom and license, in his quest for gratification without retribution, Jane Castle looms as the carrier of the achieved thing, the corporeal object, released by her fate to fulfill the wish of sexual rage. But who can stand such vulnerability, such a kind of woman who screams at the world, I am a receptacle. He heaps upon her his contempt. How dare you act this way, displaying your weaknesses so effectively as to make us powerless in our need to exact the last bit of waning power remaining to the species. What is the lesson of Jerry Kay and Richard Doyle and the rest of us who come parading into her place with our vanity and our seeking, drawn to her through the years, what is it but the lesson of self-contempt, the graceless burning away of ego fevers, hopeless victims of the sensate, looking to convert it all to fuck and release and a marching away with the easy smile and the dropped note of the patronizer: All is well again, you poor, useless woman. Purged, we leave. She remains, affirming again in her used flesh her instrumental function. Denying nobody, she says yes to her scavenged life, and to that sacrifice we bring our sniffiness, edging ourselves around her rank and beautiful body, pecking at the carrion with our dull and useless pricks.

Excerpts from the tapes

"Richard Doyle"

JANE: You want to know the specifics about the sex?

PHIL: Eroticism is a feature of the book. It has to be juxtaposed against the desperate loneliness.

JANE: My psychiatrist asked me about writing poetry. We have this corny book by Rod McKuen, *Stanyan Street*. It is rather *au courant* in the way he expresses it. I attempted to write a poem in a *Stanyan Street* manner, in a rather direct everyday language approach and it's not coming badly. I was working on that a little bit. Around midnight he arrives. He doesn't call. He just uses his key. That is the ab—so—lute end for me. He was a little high and I fixed him a good one. He had a Glenn Yarborough record, most of it Rod McKuen. Mushy romantic folk songs, wonderful. We are sitting mooning at each other, and of course very quickly he gets excited. He turned off the light and we proceeded to have sex on the couch. I was going to be open and free. We did every position and the last position was the conventional one. He was not as active as I was. Of course this is always the case with me with men. I also find that when I want something I don't even have to ask for it. I just sort of put my body in an

235

open position and he responds beautifully. He tends to be a rather passive man.

PHIL: He will reciprocate too.

JANE: Right. I think there is a tendency in men to do this. Anyway, I started and he responded, and the wonderful thing about him is that when he is not needing the sex so much he can last forever without coming, and that is very important to me. I've gotten to the point that I can honestly say that I've had an orgasm with him. I don't think it's a huge wild orgasm, but I do let go. He had me lying on the couch here with my back to him and he came into me from the back, and that wasn't quite good, so he stood me up on my knees. I just followed along. He added an extra fillip which surprised me.

PHIL: Dog fashion.

JANE: It was great. I don't particularly groove it but it was great that way.

PHIL: While he was in you?

JANE: Yes. It was very exciting.

PHIL: What was it that was extra or special about it?

JANE: It was just something he did. And we rolled over again to the front. This goes on forever.

PHIL: After he came.

JANE: Yes.

PHIL: What happened in the play beforehand?

JANE: There was all kinds of play. And again I didn't respond freely.

PHIL: You mean he went down on you.

JANE: He would have.

PHIL: Did he lick you—your breasts?

JANE: No, no, no. He was licking me all over. I still have that inhibition. I could have gone with it. I got up to change the record and that stopped it.

PHIL: So you never let him really let him go into you with his tongue.

JANE: I will now. I'm not so afraid of its being unpleasant.

PHIL: Did he try the tongue elsewhere?

JANE: Everywhere. He likes it when I get on top of him. I really move a lot.

PHIL: When you lick him prior to all this does he strip?

JANE: Oh, sure. Sometimes, very often, he undresses me. He rarely will let me undress him. But Saturday night he let me.

PHIL: And when you started playing with him did you lick him all over?

JANE: Oh, yes.

PHIL: What is all over?

JANE: All over his body.

PHIL: His balls, his ass, everything?

JANE: Everything.

PHIL: His asshole?

JANE: No, I haven't done that.

PHIL: Not everything then.

JANE: O.K., O.K. Not everything. When we are in the throes he often kisses my feet and my ankles. I cannot tell you what that does to me. Nobody has ever done that to me.

PHIL: When you suck him aren't you afraid he is going to come, in the pre-play?

JANE: I can tell. For instance, this business of getting up and doing the records was a very good thing. I'm really getting proficient at sex because I'm learning how to delay, which I never knew how to do. It used to be, one, two, three, on again, off again, finnegan. Now I allow myself to wallow in the excitement while I change the record. And so, as I said, it was a kind of around the world. I started on top of him, he got behind me, I ended up on the bottom with him on me.

PHIL: Did you do a sixty-nine?

JANE: No, we didn't do a sixty-nine kind of thing. We still have inhibitions about that. Around the world was the expression that occurred to me because we went full circle in positions. We ended up in the normal intercourse pattern.

PHIL: Didn't he come into you in the dog fashion, from the rear?

JANE: Yes, yes.

PHIL: The rear isn't the normal fashion.

JANE: You mean as far as coming. He came but then he stayed in me.

PHIL: Let me get this clear. You say he entered you from the rear.

JANE: Yes. When we were finished he rolled me over with him still inside me.

PHIL: But he had already come.

JANE: Right, but there was still more lovemaking.

PHIL: Postcoital lovemaking. Did he stay hard in you?

JANE: No, that runs out but he stayed in for twenty minutes more.

PHIL: Do the various positions give you greater freedom with each other?

JANE: Definitely. We were very together.

PHIL: How long did it all last?

JANE: It must have been an hour and a half.

PHIL: An hour and a half before he came?

JANE: It must have been. It goes on forever.

PHIL: How could he stand it. It must have been the liquor.

JANE: It must have been the liquor. It was a groove.

"Fuck-and-Pay"

JANE: A great deal of my relationship with men has been to let them know how sad I am about something so they have something to talk to me about and commiserate with me. Like Richard, at the end, he was always saying, "How's the situation with the job?" I would say, "Well, I don't want to talk about my troubles with you." But I had set up that pattern. I lean on men emotionally for the wrong things. I like to cry on their shoulders.

PHIL: How do you lean on them emotionally for the right things?

JANE: How would I? I don't know. If I knew how, I would probably be married, wouldn't I?

PHIL: What do you mean by leaning on them for the wrong things?

JANE: Well, crying on their shoulders for all my problems, like with my father.

PHIL: Always bringing up your father.

JANE: Always. My troubles with my father . . . all the men. Telling everybody what was going on in my mind.

PHIL: That's not such a terrible thing to do.

JANE: When that's the whole basis of your relationship? You don't say, "My name is Jane Castle, and let me tell you about my troubles." Which is what I did. Richard Doyle said to me, "Hello, my name is Richard Doyle and I've got a bad marriage, and I want to have fun and no demands." We were two of a kind. And I said, "That's nice. My name is Jane Castle. I'm a single, thirty-six-year-old gal who has never been able to make it with her guy, and I want to have fun with no demands. Let's make each other miserable for eight months." Which is exactly what happened.

PHIL: What were you in trouble about in the summer of 1958?

JANE: The job, everything. I traded on my troubles. I thought I couldn't be interesting unless I had some interesting troubles to tell. Poor Janie. She's got so much to offer, but she's got so many troubles, instead of offering what I had to offer and take a chance. I don't talk about the good things. I feel everything very strongly. I experience everything very deeply, very intensely. But I trade on the trouble thing, like getting the attention because I'm paining.

PHIL: Always paining.

JANE: I'm afraid I won't get it otherwise.

PHIL: The attention. What about getting it through objective means?

JANE: What?

PHIL: Talking about things outside yourself. Not so self-involving.

JANE: Yes, but the point is that I do that but on a minimal basis. I was not aware of a lot of my self-involved conversation. But that was how I got a guy emotionally hung on me. You see, it was the old fuck-and-pay routine.

PHIL: What's the fuck-and-pay routine?

JANE: Like cash-and-carry. I let you fuck me but you've got to let me cry on your shoulder.

PHIL: That's the deal, the pact you make.

JANE: I made it with myself. And he's so guilty, he doesn't really want to listen to my troubles about my father. He doesn't really want to listen to buh, buh, buh, but he's guilty because he knows that he fucked me when he shouldn't have, and I didn't have enough sense not to let him.

PHIL: Him being anybody?

JANE: Him being anybody. As we get into the Richard Doyle era, it takes on a slightly different tone. I've changed. I have matured somewhat, but the base of self-involvement is still there and the whole basic thing about buh, buh, buh. You know, I just may be a very nice girl with not a great deal to offer every single conversation that there exists in the world.

"Cole Porter"

PHIL: You were pointing to a generalization about your behavior in the world, and your attitudes, which are always local and personal, and you prefer human social encounter.

JANE: That's what I'm interested in.

PHIL: And the larger, abstract issues.

JANE: Are overwhelming to me. I don't concern myself with them. Like, for instance, I am bugged about this black thing right now, and I want to do something. I read about all these things being done and they all look terribly complicated. How do I get into them? How do I get involved? And then I say to myself, "Well, just walk up past Ninety-Sixth Street someday and see what happens." And I have a big dream that if I were to marry a guy from New York, we'd buy a house up in that area, and we'd move there.

On the other side of my fantasy is, "They're being given too much. It's coming too fast, too easy. Why can't people treat them like human beings instead of spoiled, special kids who have had rheumatic fever." So that's more appealing than the actual doing something. I'm trying to find a way to act out. I was thinking coming out on the subway today, there was a groovy subway attendant, and he was married, I checked for the ring. I did what I would do with any normal white man, check to see if he is married. If people would begin to accept this, the sphere of the market gets bigger. I'm not just limited to marrying a white guy now and there are more chances to get married.

PHIL: You personalize it. The same for Vietnam?

JANE: I don't feel strongly about Vietnam. I have a strong feeling about colored people. It's all very superficial. I know a little bit about a lot of things, but I don't know a lot about love.

PHIL: "I know a little bit about a lot of things. . . ."

JANE: "But I don't know *enough* about love."

PHIL: Your whole life has been marked by songs.

JANE: Absolutely. I was listening to PAT, song lyrics, for all they are put down, they really do grasp what people feel at heightened moments, they really do.

PHIL: You identify the song by the heightened moment.

JANE: The song, the lyrics. A Cole Porter lyric. All the nights

I have lain in my house dying for Richard, dying for David, and then the Cole Porter lyric, "If we'd thought a bit, at the end of it, when we started painting the town, we'd have been aware that our love affair was too hot not to cool down." That happens.

PHIL: It's a very romantic thing.

JANE: It actually happens.

PHIL: "So goodbye dear, and then. . . ."

JANE: "Goodbye dear, and *amen*, here's hoping we meet now and then. It was great fun, but it was just one of those things." True. True. True. It happens a zillion times a day.

PHIL: That's a good song.

JANE: I'm saying good song lyrics really do talk real things. They talk about real feelings.

PHIL: The use of songs. . . .

JANE: I could tell you this whole story in song lyrics.

THIS BOOK WAS SET IN BASKERVILLE TYPE BY

MARYLAND LINOTYPE COMPOSITION CO.

IT WAS PRINTED AND BOUND BY

THE HADDON CRAFTSMEN, INC.

DESIGN IS BY

LARRY KAMP AND BARBARA COHEN